THE HAUNTING OF
LINDY PENNYWORTH

THE HAUNTING OF LINDY PENNYWORTH

S.M. POPE

uclanpublishing

The Haunting of Lindy Pennyworth is a uclanpublishing book

First published in Great Britain in 2021 by
uclanpublishing
University of Central Lancashire
Preston, PR1 2HE, UK

978-1-9129-7957-8

1 3 5 7 9 10 8 6 4 2

Set in 10/16pt Kingfisher

Designed and edited by Katie Dandridge, Sunshine Tucker and Megan Pressler.

A CIP catalogue record for this book is available from the British Library.

Printed and bound in Great Britain by Clays Ltd, Elcograf S.p.A.

This book is dedicated to my family.
Thanks for accompanying me to all the graveyards,
past and present, even though you thought
I was weird!

NOVEMBER 2020

I'm writing this in an old, blank notebook that I found in the common room. I keep it hidden inside my pillowcase and move it on laundry day, tucking it under the waistband of my jeans and covering any bulges with a loose jumper. I don't want anyone seeing it. They'll either take it away or use it as proof against me, to keep me here even longer.

Everyone here thinks I've gone temporarily insane. 'Psychosis', they're calling it. They say that grief has warped my mind, made me unstable, a danger to myself . . . That's how they persuaded my mother to leave me in this hospital when, at first, she fought to take me home. They even threatened to put me under the temporary care of social services if she didn't agree to me being sectioned.

That's because they can't accept the reality of what I told them happened to me. Their minds are too narrow, their outlook purely clinical. What they can't see or touch or hear doesn't exist.

Tomorrow they're starting me on medication to make me 'normal' again, so I'm rushing to write this down before the pills make me forget everything. Even if it takes me all night, I will ensure that I have a record of the last couple of weeks so I don't start believing their patronising insistence that I've imagined everything because I've gone crazy with grief over my father's death.

I've *not* hurt myself to give my grief a physical outlet; the injuries are real and not self-inflicted.

Every word of this account is true. I *am* sane. I *can* speak to the dead.

And they can speak to me.

1.
RUMOUR MILL

It was lunchtime and, as usual, I was sitting in a smelly toilet cubicle, pulling out my hair. I was trying hard not to choke on the fug of stale cigarettes mixed with cheap body spray, when Zoe and Chloe – or 'The Rhyming Couplets' as I called them – came in. Everyone knew that the best way to keep up with the school gossip was to visit the girls' toilets.

When I heard that day's subject, I froze – the talk was all about me.

"You know Lindy Pennyworth?"

"The girl whose father died?"

"Yeah."

"He drove his car into a tree, didn't he?"

"Yeah, I think he was drunk or something."

I wanted to burst out of the cubicle and scream at them that my father wasn't a drunk driver – it was my fault he crashed into that tree.

Instead, I yanked out a clump of hair.

An explosion of body spray. I held my nose and stifled a cough.

"People are saying there's something wrong with her."

"'Course there is. Her dad's dead."

"No, I don't mean that. Can I borrow some lipstick?"

"Here. So? What's wrong with her?"

"Haven't you noticed that she's always asking to go to the toilet?"

"I just assumed she was going out to cry or something."

"She's skinnier and her hair's looking different too. Patchy, like it's falling out."

"What, do you think she's having chemo or something?"

"It'd explain why she's always running out of classes. Probably throwing up – it's one of the side effects."

"You don't know that for sure, though, do you?"

"All right, no need to be all preachy. I'm just saying what other people are saying. Maybe she's got bulimia."

"Bulimics don't rush out of lessons to throw up. They do it after eating, don't they?"

"I don't know, do I? Can I borrow your eyeliner?"

"God, don't you have any make-up?"

"'Course, just left it at home today."

"Well, don't blunt the end."

"Would I?"

"Yeah."

They stopped talking. My heart was thumping so loudly I was sure they'd hear it in the silence. How had they noticed? I'd been so careful to try to pull my hair out in different places so I wouldn't get any obvious bald patches. Either I hadn't done a good enough job, or I was pulling too much out. I looked down at the strands in my hand and dropped them into the toilet bowl.

"So, has anyone asked her?"

"You're joking, right? No one's going to risk that. You know what Mr Hardcastle said about not upsetting her."

"Well, what about Immy? She's her best friend – she'll know."

"Immy's even scarier. She guards Lindy like a Rottweiler." Zoe growled and they both laughed.

"How about Jake? They had a thing, didn't they?"

"Not really. He got off with her at that party at the start of term, but he said it was just because she was practically throwing herself at him. Now he won't go near her – doesn't want her to get all clingy now she's got issues."

I cringed.

Is that what people are saying?

"Can't blame him, I s'pose. Still, he's a bit of a loser."

"Yeah. Totally up himself."

"You finished? I need to speak to Sarah before next lesson."

The door slammed behind them, leaving the stench of their body spray and their rumours ringing in my ears. I knew that people felt uncomfortable around me – that's what death did. It didn't just rob you of the person you loved, it also took away others because they didn't know how to handle you.

I had to find another way to cope, so I pulled out my hair: my lovely, long chestnut mane – the envy of many of the girls in college.

It began by accident when I caught a few strands in my watch strap while tying my hair into a ponytail. The brief sting distracted me from the unbearable pressure in my stomach every time I thought about Dad, which was pretty much all the time. It was so easy and effective, I wished I'd thought of it earlier. All I had to do was escape to the girls' toilets during breaks and pull while pretending to pee.

3

I used to love holding the fine, wavy hairs up to the light, looking at the tones of gold among the brown. Little silken trophies waving in the air – proof that I was master of my emotions. Then I flushed away the evidence and got on with the rest of the day.

Those few strands held down the threat for a while, but the tension in my stomach became more demanding. I tried to ignore it, but it grew bigger, crawling up my throat, forcing me to excuse myself from lessons so I could pull four, five, six times a day. The teachers never asked why I needed to go so often – they knew to cut me some slack – but it was obvious my classmates were looking at each other with a *"WTF?"* expression every time I slipped out, mid-lesson. More hair had to come out each time, too, to get the same sense of relief. The hairs now looked less like trophies and more like tentacles, reaching out to claim my sanity.

At least at home, Mum was oblivious to what I was doing. She was walking around in a daze, gulping down cups of coffee to counteract the hangover she'd given herself from the night before. However, the morning after that particular episode in the toilets, she was obviously more on the ball because she realised I was running half an hour late for college and came into my room, unannounced, catching me in the act.

"What are you doing?" She frowned. "Why's all that hair in your hand?"

I stammered the first excuse that came to mind. "I, uh, caught it in my brush. I couldn't get it out, so I had to pull really hard."

"But it's in your hand, not your brush."

"I've just pulled it out of my brush to put in the bin." I looked around for my bin and dropped the hairs in it.

"You've been up here for ages."

4

"I'm having a bad hair day. I can't do anything with it."

She rolled her eyes. "So? Don't be so vain; you're going to college, not a beauty pageant. Just shove it into a ponytail."

"It won't go."

"Don't be daft. Your hair's halfway down your back. Here, let me—"

I backed away. Her eyes narrowed. "What are you hiding from me?"

"Nothing."

"Come here a minute."

"No."

"Lindy – show me your head."

The game was up. I took a couple of steps forward and bent my head.

"Good God," she whispered. "What have you done to yourself?"

2.
I KNOW YOU ARE LYING

The doctor signed me off college for the rest of the month, saying we should meet then to review the situation and consider if I was ready to go back. I think he knew what was behind my hair loss but told my mother that it was stress-induced alopecia, rather than worry her with the fact that I was pulling it out, which was good of him. But then he referred me to Dr Greenwood, which was not good of him.

Dr Greenwood was supposed to be one of Oxford's top consultant psychiatrists, specialising in teenage mental health. All I can say is he was Oxford's top irritating jerk. On the several occasions when I visited him, he just sat in his chair with a professional expression of kindness plastered on his face, raising his bushy eyebrows at ten-second intervals – I counted – and steepling his fingers every five minutes or so.

Our first hour-long session was all about "getting to know Lindy", but I didn't want to tell him anything about me, so it only lasted ten minutes. He called my mother into the room.

6

"Lindy seems reluctant to talk right now, Mrs Pennyworth, so I'll just cut to the chase and tell you what I think is wrong," he said.

"Our GP already said it's stress-induced alopecia—"

"Not alopecia, I'm afraid." He shook his head. "Trichotillomania."

We both looked at him in confusion.

"Alopecia normally means your hair falls out on its own," he explained. "Trichotillomania is when you pull it out yourself. It's a form of anxiety-driven self-harm."

Mum looked like she was going to faint.

"Can we stop talking about this, please? You're upsetting my mother," I said.

He held up a hand. "There's no point in avoiding it, Lindy. Let's call it what it is. *That's* the first step to recovery. Your mother needs to know because she can support you while you're getting better."

"I just don't think you should be worrying her—"

"She's already worried. *That's* why you're here. The next thing we need to do," he said, as he produced a pen and started writing, "is to give you something to help calm down the compulsion to pull. We have an antidepressant that has a very good track record of helping teenagers with anxiety and obsessive behaviour."

"You're putting her on antidepressants?" Mum asked. "Isn't that premature? Maybe we could try counselling first."

"By the look of things, Lindy has been engaging in this behaviour for quite a while now, Mrs Pennyworth, which is why the antidepressants are strongly indicated as a necessary course of action. But the great thing about these pills is that they help calm down the mind so that it is ready to reap the benefits of counselling. I've pencilled in a session with Lindy next week, in fact."

Lucky me.

He smiled as he handed me the prescription.

"Start taking them tomorrow, with your breakfast. They may make you feel drowsy or sick initially, but if this happens you should start feeling better in a week or so. If you have any ... er ... *distressing* thoughts, call us immediately." He gave my mother a knowing look. "It's all in the contraindications."

I went to stand up, but he raised his hand again.

"One second, Lindy. Before you go, I'd still like to hear *something* from you. For example, what kind of things do you like?"

What planet was this guy on?

"Er ... I don't know."

"Come on, Lindy – don't be rude," Mum scolded me, like I was a naughty toddler.

"It's all right, Mrs Pennyworth. Talking about ourselves can be a difficult thing. Why don't I get the ball rolling, Lindy, and tell you what I like?"

I shrugged, ignoring the darts of anger Mum was shooting my way.

He cleared his throat. "Well, let me see. I love wearing cartoon ties to work because they make my patients laugh. Isn't this one great?" He held it out towards me. "I chose it because I think the Mr Men characters encapsulate human emotions really well. If you could pick one of these on my tie today, which would you be?"

"Are you joking?" I snorted.

"Lindy!" Mum hissed.

"It's all right, Mrs Pennyworth, let her speak – I want to hear her reasoning. What makes you think that I'm joking, Lindy?"

"Well, firstly, they're all male and I'm female. Secondly, Mr Greedy, Mr Noisy, Mr Nobody, Mr Bump and Mr Worry are all *bald*."

He looked less sure of himself. "Well, yes, but I fail to see why this is so important—"

"Do they have Trichotillomania too, Dr Greenwood?"

He wore Kung Fu Panda the next week.

The sessions were not going well. I wasn't trying to be deliberately nasty or anything, I just knew that the guy was patronising me and I despised him for it.

Just before we left for my third session with him, Immy called. I hesitated – I didn't want to answer, but I also felt guilty because I hadn't replied to any of her messages since I'd been signed off college.

"Hi, Immy."

"So you *do* still exist."

I smiled. Her humour had kept me sane – relatively speaking – since Dad's death.

"I've been so worried!" she continued. "Why aren't you at college?"

"Ask Zoe or Chloe. According to them, I've either got an eating disorder or cancer."

"Idiots. If they don't know something, they make it up." She paused, then said more carefully, "But you were going to the toilet a lot. Are you sick?"

"No, course not."

"So what *were* you doing in there? You weren't . . . you know . . . "

"What?"

"Throwing up? You *have* got really skinny."

"I'm not bulimic!"

Mum yelled up the stairs for me. "Sorry, Immy, I've got to go."

"Where?"

I sighed. "To see a psychiatrist."

A pause. "Oh. I'm so sorry, Lindy. Are you OK? I mean, of course, after what happened—"

Mum shouted again, louder, and Immy heard it this time. "You'd better go. But make sure you call me later, OK? Have fun . . . "

There was that sense of humour again.

Mum and I were mainly silent on the way to the clinic, apart from a brief discussion about what to have for dinner. I fiddled with my beanie, something I'd started wearing out in public since the bald patches were obvious now. I didn't want Dr Greenwood staring at them, though I reasoned I could always point out his if he got too personal.

Mum dropped me off outside the clinic and carried on to the supermarket. I considered skiving from the session, but I knew they'd call her and I'd have to come back another time. It was best to get it over and done with.

Dr Greenwood was sitting, as usual, behind his massive wooden desk, pushing his podgy fingertips together as if in prayer. "How are we today, Lindy?"

"I don't know how *you* are, but I'm fine, thanks."

He chuckled. "Impressive way to deal with the royal 'we'. It's good to see that you have the courage to challenge my way of speaking. May *we* assume this is partly thanks to the medication kicking in?"

Smug bastard. "It's still making me feel tired."

He nodded. "That's a fairly normal reaction because they work by calming down your nervous system. It should improve soon. I see you're still wearing your hat. How many times a day have you pulled your hair since the last time I saw you?"

"Excuse me?"

"Have the urges to pull decreased?"

"Yes. I'm down to one or two times a day now."

The eyebrows rose. "That's ... better than I would have expected."

In other words, you know I'm lying.

He picked up a piece of paper and handed it to me, along with a few colouring pens.

"From our previous two sessions, I know that you find talking about your emotions difficult, Lindy. I think that this might be what drives your Trichotillomania. So, today, I'd like you to draw me what you're feeling instead. Many people find this an easier path into therapy than talking. I'll leave you alone for a minute or two while I have a word with my secretary."

He shut the door as he left the room. I wanted to scream that I didn't need a psychiatrist to make me feel better. If I needed help from anyone it would be in the form of a psychic, but if I admitted that to him then he would use that as proof that I *definitely* needed psychiatric help.

The more I thought about it, the more I could see sense in talking to a psychic. The one thing that I wanted more than anything was to talk to Dad and take back the horrible last words I'd said to him before he died. I needed to tell him that it was the anger talking, not how I really felt. I needed to hear him say that he understood and that everything was OK.

11

I needed his forgiveness.

I'd tried tarot cards, I'd bought a Ouija board on eBay and I'd sat by myself in a church hoping that he'd whisper something in my ear, like you sometimes see in films. None of that worked, so I'd started working my way through *Talking to the Dead – Your Guide to Spiritual Conversation*, which I'd picked up at a second-hand book stall in the market for five pounds. It was a huge book, filled with lurid illustrations that screamed the 1970s. When I found it, I felt as if fate – or rather, Dad – had thrown us together.

Imagine if I told Dr Greenwood this. He'd have me committed. I wished Dad could have met Dr Greenwood. He'd have had a great time imitating his nasal voice, daring me to draw a caricature of the hairy doctor as one humungous eyebrow.

My phone vibrated with a text from Immy.

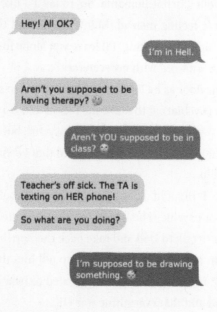

Hey! All OK?

I'm in Hell.

Aren't you supposed to be having therapy? 😶

Aren't YOU supposed to be in class? 💀

Teacher's off sick. The TA is texting on HER phone!

So what are you doing?

I'm supposed to be drawing something. 😁

Why?

Because this guy's insane.

You'll never guess what he's wearing.

False beard and moustache?

Ha. No. Socks and sandals. 😑

IT'S OCTOBER.

LOL. 😂

He's coming back. Gotta go.

As he opened the door, I picked up a pink pen and stabbed a dot in the middle of the page before replacing the lid.

Dr Greenwood sat down and looked at it for a minute. "Interesting. Is the tiny dot you and the white expanse of paper the overwhelming grief you battle every day?"

"No."

He looked surprised. "Oh. All right. You've given me a challenge, Lindy. I'm considered quite the expert in this field!" He laughed. "Why don't you tell me in your own words what this does mean to you?"

"Uh . . . it means I can't draw?"

"Is that because you're too afraid of what might come out?"

"No. It means I'm bad at drawing."

He sighed. "Lindy, it doesn't matter if you're not an accomplished artist. The aim is to help you release emotions that you might otherwise find unspeakable. It's extremely therapeutic."

He gave me a fresh piece of paper, which I thought was wasteful considering what deforestation does to the planet. I decided that this drawing should count, to make the dead tree's life matter.

A few seconds later, I pushed my drawing across the table to him.

"Much better, Lindy," he nodded. "Right, here goes . . . This stickman is your dad. And the strange fish clinging on to his neck is you, desperately trying to stop yourself from drowning in a sea of grief. Your penmanship shows pain; anger. And the speed with which you drew this shows me that, despite the barriers you always erect in my company, you're desperate to tell me about it all."

He leant back expectantly.

I grabbed my bag and stood up.

"You have *way* too much faith in my artistic ability, Dr Greenwood. Here's what the drawing means: the stickman is you and that thing you think is a fish is one of your ridiculous ties. But thanks. I do feel a lot better now I've got that off my chest."

I smiled at the receptionist as I walked out, and she gave me a surprised nod. Maybe I was cured after all.

3.
AMATEUR PSYCHIC

I wasn't.

I texted Mum to say I'd left the appointment early and skipped home, happier than I'd been in a long time. But, as predicted, she'd heard about my behaviour and as soon as I shut the front door, she started yelling at me for walking out of my session. I ran upstairs and locked myself in the bathroom, wrapped strands of hair around my fingers and pulled, while she yelled outside the door that I was deliberately trying to make our lives difficult.

"You don't get it, Mum," I said, trying to block out her ranting. "He was awful! He was smug and patronising – you saw that – and he treated me like a five-year-old—"

"So you decided to behave like one and throw a strop and walk out, did you? I don't understand you, Lindy. You've got a problem – don't argue with me, you *know* you do – and people are trying to help you overcome it, and all you do is throw it back in their faces."

"He made me want to pull my hair even more. How is that helpful?"

A pause.

"I admit he's not got the best manner, but we need him."

"Why?"

"Because I can't do this on my own! Look, I can't keep talking to a door. Please come out."

I didn't want to see her. I didn't want to look at her strained, pinched face. I knew she shared my guilt. She could have stopped me that day. She could have stopped me from yelling, "I *hate* you!" as I ran out of the house – the last words I ever spoke to Dad. But she just stood and watched.

"I just need time," I mumbled.

She walked away and I pulled some hairs from my crown. The relief was instantaneous.

"I'll be back at seven. There's a ready-made risotto in the fridge – can you heat it up in the oven for then, please?"

"Sure," I said, as Mum grabbed her yoga mat and headed out the door. She was calmer than earlier but still needed to find her "Zen", apparently.

I headed upstairs and grabbed *Talking to the Dead – Your Guide to Spiritual Conversation* from under my bed. Since things hadn't worked out with Dr Greenwood, I figured I might as well try this again.

The book instructed me to sit in a dark, candlelit room, so I drew the blinds and clicked on some battery-operated fake candles, hoping that spirits can't tell the difference between real flames and LED ones.

I breathed deeply, holding Dad's watch as a spiritual conduit – apparently, an important tool for the amateur psychic. I closed my eyes and focused on his face – his scratchy beard that tickled my cheeks when he leant in to give me a goodnight kiss, even when I was old enough to tell him that it was gross.

"Where are you, Dad? I need to talk to you – tell you that I'm sorry. I didn't mean what I said."

All I could hear – and feel – was the ticking of his watch in my hand. I gripped it harder, remembering when I gave it to him.

"Happy Birthday, Dad!"

He grins as I hand over the parcel, wrapped in silver paper, then gives it a playful shake.

"Interesting. It's making some sort of whirring noise."

I want to shake him for drawing this out, but settle on tapping my foot with impatience and excitement. I'd saved up my pocket money for weeks to help Mum pay for this.

"I think I'll just have another coffee—"

"Dad! Stop kidding around."

"Sorry. OK, here goes."

He pulls the bow on top and puts the ribbon in my hair before opening the box and revealing the silver watch nestling inside.

"Wow!" He whistles. "This is amazing."

"It's a kinetic watch. It charges itself through your body movement whenever you wear it."

He holds it up to his ear and tilts it backwards and forwards. "What a clever idea. I can hear the mechanism inside it."

"And you'll never need to buy a battery – it will keep going as long as you do!"

He stands up and envelopes me in a huge hug. "I love it. I'll always wear it."

When he died, I asked Mum if I could keep it – I couldn't bear the thought of it dying with him. I wore it halfway up my forearm on the tightest setting – by keeping it running, I could still keep a part of him alive.

A slight disturbance rippled through the air. My heart quickened.

The temperature hadn't dropped – a common sign that a spirit is near – but the air felt different; charged. My skin prickled and I held the watch up to my lips.

"Dad? Is that you?"

Something brushed against my right arm. Something hairy, soft and familiar.

Bofur.

One of my cats meowed as he climbed into my lap, nudging his head against the hand holding the watch.

I laid the watch down and gathered him in my arms, inhaling the strange scent of pears that always perfumed his fur. He headbutted his face against my chin and purred loudly, placing his front paws on my shoulders.

"Silly boy. What sort of witch's cat would you make? There's no way we'll make contact with him now."

Bofur pushed a whiskery face against my cheek and darted a sandpaper tongue against my earlobe.

I giggled, then buried my face in his fur. "Where is he, Bofur?"

He squirmed to be let free, so I put him down on the carpet and tried to stand up, cursing my right foot, which had gone to sleep. I wiggled my toes as Bofur watched me, sitting on top of the psychic guidebook.

"Keeping my place, huh?"

I got up and hobbled to turn on the light switch. "Or are you telling me that book is just another waste of money, like the Ouija board and tarot cards?"

Bofur yawned, lifted his hind leg and started cleaning his rear end.

"Thanks for your honesty."

If I couldn't contact Dad myself, it was time to find someone who could.

4
A NEW PAGE

We sat at the dining table, picking our way through a vegetarian risotto that was both burnt and undercooked.

"Did you get any college work done while I was out?" Mum asked.

"I did some reading."

"What about that French vocabulary?"

"I couldn't concentrate on it. I'll look at it later."

"You always say that." She set her wine glass down on the table. I noticed that she'd started drinking more each night. "Even though you're not at college, you still have to do your work."

"I know. It's just these pills—"

"Are making you tired. So you've told me. Perhaps we need to ask the GP to review your medication if you won't go back to Dr Greenwood. Maybe he can put you on something different or take you off the pills altogether. They don't seem to have made much of a difference."

I shrugged and she sighed.

"You've got to make more of an effort, Lindy. I know you're hurting, but life goes on and you must too. You're in your final A-level year and you can't afford to fall behind."

"I'm NOT falling behind!"

"Yes, you are." She took another sip of wine. "People recover from bereavement. They survive. *You'll* survive. You just need to get back to college; back to your old routine."

I pointed to my head. "How can I go back to college looking like *this*? Everyone thinks I'm having chemo, which is bad enough; if they find out what's really going on, they'll think I'm crazy. Besides, they all just ignore me because apparently I'm a freak since Dad died. They don't know what to say to me, so they just say nothing. It sucks."

"I know, but we've still got to get you better as soon as possible. You need to go back to the real world. Being shut away in this house all the time is unhealthy."

"You do it," I spat back.

"That's different – I work from home."

"You don't have to."

She pursed her lips. "You're right. But I went freelance when I had you so I could be here for you when you needed me. Who always picked you up from school and was around for you in the holidays, so you didn't have to go to after-school or holiday clubs?"

"Well, I'm older now and I don't need you to babysit me any more."

"That's not true though, is it? Because right now you *do* need me here. Until you get better and get back out into the real world with all your friends, and stop punishing yourself for what happened . . ."

I blocked the rest out. I reached up and wound a strand of hair around my forefinger, getting ready to pull, but Mum leant across the table and grabbed my hand.

"Don't. You'll have to cut it all off soon if you don't stop this."

"It helps—"

"Do you think your dad would want to see you like this?" I loosened my fingers and let the hair fall back.

Mum poured another glass of wine.

"All this . . . sadness . . . won't bring him back, Lindy. Neither will sitting in a silent house with all his things around."

"Just because you want to pretend he never existed!"

"It's more complicated than that."

She looked away. I'd gone too far. She was probably grieving too but, apart from the drinking, there were no signs that she was sad. If anything, she seemed angry. While I clung to anything that reminded me of Dad, Mum started going through his wardrobe and drawers before the funeral, stuffing underwear and socks into rubbish bags and putting the rest of his clothes into bags for charity. It was like she was determined to remove all trace of him from our lives.

One night, I went downstairs for a glass of milk and found her filling the boot of the car with all his stuff. I ran down the path, shrieking, swearing, feral. Mum stood aside, aghast, while the neighbours' curtains twitched and curious eyes watched me dragging the bags back up the path and into the house. I put the bags into my wardrobe and checked them every morning to ensure that she hadn't sneaked one out or replaced them behind my back.

"His clothes still smell like him," I whispered. "It's like he's still here, not . . ."

"Dead," Mum said. "You've got to say it, Lindy. Ignoring it doesn't make it less real. Dr Greenwood said—"

"Don't talk about that moron—"

"—that you won't get better till you accept his death and move on."

"I know he's dead. That's why I've been trying to . . ."

Damn.

"Trying to what?" She frowned, sitting more upright in her chair.

Don't tell her about the psychic stuff.

"I've found a teenage mental-health website with tips and chat rooms."

She exhaled and the tension in her face relaxed a little. "That sounds good. Is it helping?"

I shrugged, amazed at how easy it was to lie. "It's too early to know yet, but it's nice to know there are others out there like me – going through the same stuff."

She paused. "It will get easier with time. I know that you blame yourself for the argument you had the day he died, but that didn't cause the car accident."

She took my silence for agreement.

"So, we've got to get you out and about again," she persisted. "I popped in to see your college counsellor today and she said that there are various social events coming up in the next few weeks – concerts, parties, etc. These would be a good way to build up your confidence and get you used to being around your friends again."

They weren't exactly banging down the door to see me.

"In the meantime, she suggested using social media to start breaking the ice. You don't even have to speak to people in person. You could use Instagram or Snapchat or whatever else you all use to communicate nowadays. Why don't you get the ball rolling tonight?"

This was so typical. Just a couple of months ago, she and Dad were always nagging me for being on a screen too much. Now she was begging me to get online.

"I've been chatting to Immy already," I said.

"That's great. I like Immy – she's such a sensible girl."

"Sure." I got up and scraped most of the risotto into the bin, before putting my plate in the dishwasher. "I'll give her a call now."

"Good!" Mum beamed, downing her third glass of wine and standing up."I'll head up to my office now and get some writing done. Let me know how you get on. I have a feeling that this will be the new start you need."

5.
THE PARTY

Curled up on my bed, I turned on my phone and stared at the screensaver of me and Immy hugging and laughing at Jake's party. I'd downed at least four bottles of beer and some seriously strong tequila by that point.

Everything is buzzing, happy, good. Jake's taken me by the hand into the garden, where we lay on the lawn, looking up at the stars. I think that life can't get any better, and then he kisses me and my whole body tingles. His hands are getting a little busy under my shirt but I'm so relaxed by the beer, I don't mind.

Then Immy puts a stop to it.

"Come on, Lindy – it's time to leave."

"Chill out, Immy," Jake murmurs, as he nips my ear with his teeth. I giggle.

She grabs my hand and practically drags me along the lawn, out of Jake's reach. I squawk with outrage as she yanks me to my feet and shoves me through the house and out the front door.

"What the hell were you doing, Lindy? Everyone knows what Jake's like. Do you want to be just another number on his list?"

"Maybe."

"For God's sake – have some self-respect!" She sniffs the air. "Ugh – you stink of alcohol. You can't go home smelling like that."

She makes me walk the couple of miles home to sober me up. Immy, of course, only had Diet Coke all night. She hates alcohol because she doesn't like feeling out of control, and her mum and dad wouldn't approve.

We arrive at my house and I fumble in my rucksack for my keys. The porch light is on, but my fingers feel like sausages – pawing at stuff but unable to pick anything up.

"Let me," Immy sighs, grabbing the bag and tipping it upside down. Suddenly, the front door opens and Dad is filling the doorway, watching me and Immy shove make-up, tampons and hairspray back into my bag.

At first, I think I've struck it lucky. Dad will see the humour in the situation and usher me in quietly so Mum won't find out. We'll wink at each other at breakfast in the morning over our shared secret, and that will be it.

"What the hell is going on?"

"Sorry to disturb you, Mr Pennyworth," Immy says, looking up. "Lindy's lost her keys and I'm helping her find them."

"It's OK, Immy. You go home now – Lindy and I will sort this out."

"It's no problem, Mr Pennyworth—"

"I said, go home."

Dad never gets angry. Immy freezes, and then slowly stands up.

"Sure . . . Sorry, Mr Pennyworth. Uh . . . bye, then. See you later, Lindy."

She turns and scurries down the path. I wait for Dad to say she shouldn't be roaming the streets on her own at this time and offer to drive her home. Or maybe say that she could stay with us. Instead, he bends down, shoves the stuff from my rucksack back into the bag and pulls me indoors.

"You lied to me, Lindy."

I burp and the sour taste of alcohol burns my throat. "Dunno what you mean."

"You told me you were going to the cinema with Immy, but it's midnight and you smell like a bar. Where have you been?"

"Jake's house. He was having a party."

"I assume his parents are away?"

"You assume correct, sir," I giggle, with a mock salute to try to lighten the mood. It doesn't work.

"Stop being stupid, Lindy. There's nothing funny about telling lies and rolling in drunk."

"What's the big deal? You always give me a small glass of wine with dinner."

"That's different."

"How?"

"Because you're at home and I can keep an eye on you."

I laugh. "Oh, come on, Dad! What's up with you? Why are you so serious all of a sudden?"

"That's enough, Lindy."

I should have heard the warning tone in his voice, but the booze makes me brave – or stupid.

"Come on, Dad! We always have a laugh together but you're

behaving just like Mum. I'm not a little girl any more, so what's the fucking problem?"

He slaps me across the face.

I hold a hand to my stinging cheek and stare at him. His face is white, his arms are shaking and he looks nothing like the adoring father I know and love so much.

I vomit.

"Shit," he exhales and jumps back as I heave again, all over Dad's brown suitcase which, inexplicably, is sitting in the hallway.

"What's going on down there?"

Mum is standing at the top of the stairs.

"Oh no," I groan. This is all I need.

"She lied to me about where she was going tonight. She's been drinking. God knows what else she's been doing in this state."

"And that's a good reason to hit her?"

Mum runs down the stairs and takes my hand. "Let's get you some water and put you to bed, Lindy."

"No! She's got to clean her mess up first!"

She glares at Dad. "I think you'll find that's your mess, Ben."

She leads me upstairs, as I try to understand what's just happened.

I gripped the hair above my forehead, ready to pull, before running my hands to the back where it's less visible. The sting helped briefly. Before long, I noticed a pile had grown around me. I dumped it all in the bin and tied the tops of the bag so Mum wouldn't see it.

I turned on my phone and opened up Instagram to see what was happening in the world of non-hair-pulling people. Not much, it seemed. There was the usual stuff – posts about make- up and selfies of girls I vaguely knew trying on clothes and posing in changing rooms; pouting at the screen.

I chucked the phone on to the bed and walked over to my desk, where Bofur was busy cleaning himself – again. I sat down, scratched Bofur behind his ear and then googled, 'spirit mediums in Oxford'. A list of names and links popped up: psychic websites and organisations. Some were based outside of Oxford so I ruled them out – a session could take at least half an hour and if I had to add travel on to that time, I wouldn't be able to explain my absence to Mum. Some offered Skype sessions but only if I paid by credit or debit card, which was out of the question. Mum kept a close eye on my bank account.

Towards the bottom of the page, I clicked on a Facebook discussion forum link for Oxford-based psychics, where a woman had asked for recommendations for local mediums to give her a reading. There were the usual cynical answers:

"I predict that you're going to get ripped off", but also some genuine replies. One person linked to the Facebook page of a spiritualist church that was only a ten-minute walk from my house. I clicked on it.

Welcome to the Freeda Madill Spiritualist Church! Situated in the historic neighbourhood of Jericho, we owe our church and group's existence to the family and friends of Victorian medium, Freeda Madill, who died tragically from tuberculosis in 1850. The church was established to honour her memory and, to this day, we hold bi-weekly meetings to sing and pray and listen to visiting speakers. Our clairvoyancy and healing sessions form a

vital part of our meetings and we are keen to welcome newcomers
to our friendly community.

Perfect. Not only was it near, it was also free.

"Looks like I have a date for tomorrow night," I told Bofur, jotting down the address on a scrap of paper. He looked up in surprise.

"Unfortunately, not that sort of date," I said. "But this is OK, too. All I need is an excuse to get out of the house."

Immy.

6.
TRICHOTILOMANIAC

She answered after only two rings.

"So, tell me, Lindy: what's the diagnosis?"

"I don't know. I didn't stick around long enough to find out."

"What do you mean?"

"I walked out."

"Seriously?"

"Yup. Couldn't take his attitude any more."

She whistled. "Well, at least you're getting *your* attitude back. Does that mean we'll see you at college again now?"

"Not yet," I replied vaguely. "There's stuff I need to sort out before that can happen and I was wondering if I could ask for your help."

"Of course! Just say what you need."

"I need you to cover for me tomorrow night – give me an alibi in case Mum starts asking questions."

"You're going out?"

"Yep."

"Where? A date? *Not* with Jake, I hope."

"What? God, no. What gave you that idea? I haven't seen anyone except doctors for ages."

"Well, why else would you need to hide from your mum?"

"It's just something that I need to do. It's no big deal."

"It obviously is if you don't want her finding out and you won't tell me."

I'd forgotten that asking Immy for a favour would involve an interrogation. "Immy – *please*."

"Look, we haven't been out together in months, then you're signed off college so I have no one to have lunch with. And now you're asking me to lie on your behalf. If you want me to help you, you've got to tell me what it is. You owe me *that* at least."

"Fair enough. But don't judge me, OK?"

"Promise."

"And don't think I'm crazy."

"Lindy!"

"Right, here goes. You know Francis Road? Just up from the Co-op?"

"Yeah."

"Well, there's this spiritualist church there, and tomorrow night they're doing this service where they pass on messages from the . . . you know . . ."

"Oh no. I know where you're going with this—"

"I just need to get through to Dad; to know everything's all right. I keep blaming myself—"

"And how will this help? You think that some con artist is going to make you feel better about your dad's death?"

"They're not con artists. They're working in a church."

"That doesn't mean that they're not full of crap."

"They don't take money from anyone, so what would be the point of trying to cheat someone?"

"I don't know. Some people are just twisted."

"Look, I've been trying to teach myself how to talk to spirits, but it's not working. I want to see if this can help. It can't hurt, can it?"

Immy sighed. "Lindy, I'm sorry. I know things are tough, but I'm scared this is going to make things worse. What if they say something terrible? Or what if they don't say anything at all?"

"Honestly, I don't know. But I do know that I have to try this."

"I'll help you, but on one condition."

My spirits lifted. "Anything."

"You let me come with you."

The next day dragged on forever as I waited for the evening to come. Mum was so ecstatic that I was going out with a friend that she let me finish my studies early to get ready.

"Why don't you go into town to pick out a new outfit?"

"We're just hanging out, Mum. Not going *out* out."

"I know, but you wear that same grungy uniform of leggings and a baggy jumper all the time. It would be nice to see you in something colourful for a change."

I tried to ignore the jibe. "No one's going to be concerned with how we look at the Fancier Cuppa café. It's normally full of families having early dinners or uni students."

"Have you thought about what you're going to do with your hair?"

Damn.

"Could you do something with it for me, so the patches don't show?"

Mum shook her head. "The patches are too big now and your hair is too thin to pull over them. You'll have to wear your hat or a scarf."

"What will Immy say?"

"Immy's your best friend. She'll accept you for who you are."

I hoped she was right.

The first thing Immy commented on as I walked through the door was my beanie.

"Is this a new look, Lindy?" she asked, pointing at my head.

"No."

"Aren't you going to take it off? It's boiling in here."

"I know. But it's not as if I'm wearing a balaclava or anything. It's just a beanie."

She snorted. "Since when have you worn one of those?"

"Since I became a Trichotillomaniac."

Immy frowned. "So you stole it?"

"What? No, you idiot. That's a kleptomaniac."

"Oh. Well, what's a trick . . . oh . . . thingy?"

"It's someone who can't stop pulling their hair out."

She tried to hide her shock. "Isn't that some kind of self-harm?"

"Sure . . ."

I looked down at the table – I didn't want to see the alarm in her eyes. The urge to pull started nagging away at me, so I slid my hands under my thighs.

"Is that why you were seeing the psychiatrist?"

"Yes. He thought he could wave a magic curling wand and make it better." I tried to smile, but Immy still looked worried.

"I knew things were bad, but I never thought you'd actually harm yourself. I'm a crap friend – I should have noticed—"

"No, you shouldn't have," I reassured her. "It was easy to hide until recently when I realised that the bald bits were too big to cover up."

"Why did you start doing this to yourself?"

"The sting helps make things more bearable. It distracts me from everything that's going on in my head for a while; comforts me. Does that make any sense?"

Immy considered this, then nodded.

"Sometimes I feel like I'm going mad. The hair-pulling makes me feel in control, for a while, but I know what I'm doing isn't normal."

"What are you going to do if you won't speak to the psychiatrist?"

"I'm taking antidepressants."

"How do you feel?"

"Like a zombie most of the time, so I guess not much has changed." I laughed and she smiled.

"It's good to hear you laugh, Lindy. It's been too long."

"That's why I want to do this thing tonight. I know that if I could speak to Dad to say sorry for the horrible things I said before he died, the pain would go away. Or even hear a message from him that he forgives me. I just need to know that everything is all right, that *he's* all right."

Immy's smile faded. "But what if you don't get a message? What happens then?"

35

"I'm prepared for that. The stuff I've been reading online warns about this – it depends on who the medium picks up on that night. I'll go as many times as it takes."

"Look, don't take this the wrong way but . . . aren't you worried that you'll become a bit, well, obsessed with this?"

"It's too late to worry about that now, Immy. I already am."

7.
THE FREEDA MADILL SPRITUALIST CHURCH

The Freeda Madill Spiritualist Church was a small building, flanked by Victorian terraced houses on either side. I understood why I'd never noticed it before; the only distinguishing feature was a yellow door and a small sign with the name and service times.

"Do we knock or just enter?" Immy asked.

"Dunno. Maybe we should knock."

"You don't need to knock to enter a normal church."

"But this isn't a normal church."

The door swung open to reveal a smiling, middle-aged woman. "Welcome, young ladies," she greeted, standing aside so we could enter.

"How did you know we were here?" Immy asked.

"I'm psychic," she whispered, then winked and laughed at our expressions. "I could hear you arguing outside. The door's not soundproof."

"Oh."

"I think it's safe to guess you've never been to our church before, but have you been to any other spiritualist church?"

"No, this is our first time," I replied.

"Is there any particular reason you're here?"

Immy and I looked at each other. I blushed. For some reason, I couldn't get the words out. The lady patted my arm.

"It's not an interrogation, dear. It's just that we sometimes get teens coming in here as a dare. They think it's all about ghosts and evil spirits, corrupt mediums. We try to . . . *discourage* those who do not believe."

"Oh, I believe," I promised, and the woman nodded, convinced by something in my expression.

"Then welcome. Please go through; the service will start in five minutes."

The room was laid out in typical church fashion, with pews, split by a central aisle, occupying most of the space. At the front was a board with hymn numbers and a small lectern stood in the middle, while two windows at either side of the front wall were covered by black curtains. Around twenty people were already seated, so we slid into the final pew at the back.

"So far, it's not too spooky," Immy jibed, as we took our coats off.

A man entered the room and organ music blared through two massive speakers, making us jump. We all stood and fumbled with the hymnals and tried to sing along, or mime, as best we could.

Towards the end of the hymn, a guy around my age slid into the pew next to us, knocking over my bag with his coat. He picked it up and handed it to me, smiling and whispering an apology. He was nice-looking – short, blonde hair and green eyes that mirrored his smile.

"Please sit," the man at the front of the room said.

The first half of the service was similar to ones I've sat through in church – some speaking and singing but, thankfully, no sermon. In its place was the main event of the evening: the clairvoyance.

The man leading the service introduced the guest medium, Janice Landing – a middle-aged woman dressed in pinks and purples. Her curly, red hair created its own halo as she stood under one of the ceiling lights, and her friendly face beamed at us. Her appearance was surprising; I'd expected her to be like someone out of a ghost story – tall, thin and wearing flowing black cloaks.

"Good evening, friends," Janice said, "and thank you for being here with me tonight. I feel blessed to have such a large and friendly group. I hope to bring as much comfort and joy to as many of you as possible. But I must warn you, of course, that it is not always possible to make contact with the ones we love on a given occasion. The dead, like the living, can be unreliable. Or sometimes just busy!"

Quiet, polite laughter rippled across the room. Immy groaned and whispered in my ear, "Seriously? Was that meant to be a joke?"

I glared at her to shut up.

A hush fell on the room. Janice stood still, gazing into the distance and, for one horrible moment, I thought that she'd heard Immy's comment and was about to throw us out. Instead, she focused her gaze and attention on a woman in one of the front few pews.

"Your mother was a sickly woman, wasn't she?" she asked. The woman nodded vigorously. She was about to reply when Janice held up a hand to silence her.

"It was her lungs, wasn't it? She had breathing problems – emphysema or suchlike. She coughed a lot. Sometimes blood."

The woman kept nodding, while dabbing her eyes with a tissue.

"Well, dear, you don't have to worry about her now. She's breathing freely. She's never felt better, and she wants you to know that she's happy. But she is worried about you. You won't let her go."

The woman shook her head.

"She says you must. She's at peace and wants you to be too. You must eat more and look after yourself."

Janice turned around and took a slow sip of water. "That was impressive," I whispered.

"You think so?" Immy scoffed. "Anyone can see that woman's skinny, so telling her to eat more is pretty predictable."

"What about all that stuff about her mum's breathing problems? She was very specific about that."

"Lucky guess."

This light toing and froing between Janice and various members of the congregation continued for another ten minutes or so before things took a turn.

"My friend in the back row? The young lady – the one wearing the knitted hat?"

I don't know why I looked around – no one else was wearing a beanie in the room.

"Yes, you. I'm talking to you." Janice stared so hard it unnerved me.

"Yes?" My throat dried up and I coughed a couple of times to try to get the saliva going again. Faced with the reality of speaking to Dad I suddenly felt terrified as well as excited.

"There are two people fighting here to speak to you."

"Two?" I repeated, confused, and a man sitting in the pew in front of me turned around and held a finger to his lips.

Janice closed her eyes and placed her fingers against her temples. "Quiet, spirits – one at a time," she whispered. "I've got a young lady here, your sort of age. The initial of her first name is the letter E. Does this sound familiar?"

"No. She can't be for me – I'm here to talk to my Dad."

The man shushed me again, louder this time and frowning in annoyance, but I didn't care. What was this woman playing at? She was supposed to be passing messages from Dad, not from some random girl.

Immy squeezed my hand.

"She used to live in your house, a long time ago before you were born."

I nodded.

"Your bedroom was hers. She says it looks better now that you have removed that picture of a half-dressed young man on your wall."

Muted laughter rippled around the room. My cheeks reddened at the memory of the poster of a shirtless pop star I'd stuck on the wall when I was thirteen.

"She's very animated, this young lady – she's shouting at me. Slower – I can't understand!"

Janice suddenly swayed and her face turned ashen. People murmured in concern – she looked like she was about to faint. Someone in the front pew leapt up, ready to catch her, but instead of pitching backwards, she tumbled forwards and staggered down the central aisle. People gasped and those sitting at the aisle ends edged away from her as she carried on towards the back of the room, stopping when she reached our row.

41

She leant forward towards me, her clip-on microphone amplifying her erratic, ragged breathing.

"You want to talk to the dead, correct?" she rasped.

"Y–yes," I stammered, unsure if I wanted to take this any further now.

She chuckled and her face suddenly looked different. Her plump cheeks had sunk inwards and were framed by deep lines. "Well, deary, you're going to have to do something for me first."

Immy stood up and moved herself between me and the psychic.

"What do you think you're doing?" she demanded. "You're not supposed to ask favours, you're supposed to pass messages on!"

Janice laughed. "I will do whatever I want, young lady."

"Come on, Lindy!" Immy pulled me up. "This is a load of rubbish, just as I thought. She's nothing but a fraud."

At this, Janice roared in rage. "You will not call me a fraud!" She launched herself at us, as everyone gasped in shock. The cute guy at the end of our pew tried to stop her but she shoved him out of the way, sending him falling backwards. Immy yanked me away just in time and Janice lost her balance. She fell, cracking her head against the pew as she crashed to the ground.

8.
THE CHAOS
AND THE CALM

Chaos ensued. Janice was out cold and a trickle of blood had started pooling under her head. A few people had gathered around her, calling for quiet as they tried to revive her, while someone called 999.

Janice's eyes fluttered open briefly but, when she saw Immy, the wildness came back and she started thrashing on the floor, shouting and swearing.

The woman who'd welcomed us to the church ran inside and gasped. "What's happened here?" Her eyes narrowed at us. "*You two!* Have *you* done this? You promised me you were genuine!"

"We are!" Immy huffed. "We didn't do anything! That lunatic came at my friend, screaming and demanding she do her a favour. She's obviously deranged ."

"No, she isn't! Janice is one of our most-loved mediums and she's lying here badly hurt! Nothing like this has ever happened here before!"

The guy from our pew put a hand on her arm to pacify her. "It's

43

not their fault," he said. "We all saw what happened, didn't we?" He looked around at the rest of the congregation.

"Janice did start shouting at the girls, as if she were possessed or something," said someone towards the front.

Everyone was murmuring and nodding. Then the man in the pew in front said, "But she," he pointed at Immy, "provoked the spirit, questioning and doubting everything."

"Don't try to blame this on me!" Immy yelled.

Fortunately, the appearance of the paramedics stopped the argument from developing, as everyone was ordered to clear the space around Janice so they could assess her.

"Come on," Immy whispered. "Let's get out of here."

We slipped out the other side of the pew and crept from the hall into the darkness of the night. I suddenly realised I was shivering, and not from the autumnal temperature.

"Well, I can honestly say, I've never been attacked in a church before," Immy said stoically, doing up her jacket. "Another thing to tick off my bucket list, I guess."

She peered at me. "Are you OK, Lindy?"

I couldn't stop shaking. It was so bad that Immy had to do my jacket up. She put her arm around me. "I'd say I told you so, but that would be mean in light of how upset you are," she said, leading me away from the church.

"Hey! Wait up!"

We turned around and saw the guy from our pew running towards us.

"Are you both all right?" he asked. "That was quite intense."

"It was mad," Immy said. "What's happening in there now?"

"They've revived Janice and she's back to her normal self

but they're taking her to hospital. They say she's definitely got concussion and want to do some other tests on her."

"Psychiatric?" Immy asked.

He smiled, but ignored the question. "I'm Tom, by the way."

"I'm Immy; this is Lindy. She does speak, but I think tonight's events have shocked her."

As we headed towards the main road, Tom asked, "Was this your first time at the church?"

"First and, I think we can safely say, last," Immy said. "What about you?"

"Same. I heard about it and decided to check it out. I'm interested in the paranormal." Tom looked at his shoes, as if embarrassed, and chuckled.

Immy groaned. "Not you, too. I'm trying to persuade Lindy that this is all a load of rubbish, especially after tonight."

"I can see why you'd think that," he replied. "Tell you what – let's find somewhere to have a hot drink and a chat. I can't feel my hands."

Lights from the few remaining open cafés spilt on to the street as we walked. We chose one, parked ourselves at a table and ordered hot chocolates all round.

"So, spill the beans, Tom," Immy said. "Why are you so interested in talking to the dead?"

Tom took a sip of hot chocolate and set his cup down, oblivious to the thin line of foam resting on his upper lip. "I got hooked on ghost stories and started reading more widely about paranormal investigation. When I looked into whether there was anything happening locally, I found the Freeda Madill Church and decided to give it a go. I wasn't expecting anything like that, though."

"What were you expecting?" I asked, finally finding my voice.

"Well, more of what happened in the beginning of the session. From what I've seen and read, mediums usually just pass on messages from the dead. What happened to you, Lindy . . ." He paused and I raised my eyebrows, encouraging him to explain. "Whoever was speaking through her, didn't like you at all." He chewed his lower lip. "It was really weird. I've never seen anything like it."

"Look – both of you – it was all put on for effect," Immy said. "There's no such thing as the afterlife or ghosts."

"But Janice was right about the type of house I live in," I argued.

"Loads of people live in Victorian terraces in Oxford, and everyone in that audience would have been there because they'd lost someone, right? Guessing those details weren't too difficult."

"I could have lost my mum or a sibling," I said. "There was no way of knowing it was my dad."

"You're forgetting, Lindy – you were the one who told her that you had come to speak to your dad. She didn't mention him at all."

Sometimes I hated when Immy was right, which happened to be most of the time.

"And don't forget that she also said some wrong things. She asked if you knew anyone with the initial E. She was obviously just fishing for clues."

Tom shook his head. "I disagree. I couldn't see any signs of cold reading tonight."

"Cold reading?" I asked.

"It's when a psychic tries to make someone think they know more about them than they really do, through analysing their clothes, behaviour, facial expressions. For example, she might assume that you're shy because you avoid eye contact and you wear a beanie pulled low on your face, even indoors, when it's warm." He grinned at me and I blushed. "How close was I?"

Not as close as he believed he was.

"Analyse me!" Immy begged.

"Well, in the hall tonight, you sat with your arms folded, apart from when you thought Lindy was under threat. Therefore, a clever medium could assume that you're a cynic who was there to look after her more vulnerable friend or to prove a point. Or both." He sat back in his chair and finished his drink. "How's that?"

"I do believe you might be ... smug," Immy said, then laughed – her gaze lingering on Tom for longer than necessary.

I gripped my mug of hot chocolate, welcoming the warmth. I didn't know what to believe. Why were there two competing spirits wanting to talk to me? If Janice was genuine, then who was talking through her when she told me that I had to do something if I wanted to reach my dad?

"Lindy?" Tom peered at me. "Are you all right? Did you hear me?"

"What? Sorry, no. I'm a little tired. What did you say?"

"I said I was sorry about your dad. Did he die recently?"

"Around three months ago." I scratched my fingernails on the ceramic surface of the mug, trying to quell the urge to cry ... or pull.

"I lost my dad, too," Tom confessed. "He died when I was eight."

"That's awful," I said. "Can you remember much about him?"

"Enough." He smiled. "But the memories fade with every year. I don't want to lose them. That's what got me interested in this stuff, though I'm not sure yet if I believe in it. I just want to find out more, you know?"

I nodded.

"We should get together some time and swap experiences – if you want to," Tom added hurriedly. "I don't know about you, but I find it hard sometimes not having someone my own age to talk to about how I feel. There are support groups but, I don't know . . . they feel wrong, somehow. They're kind of depressing."

"Exactly! You just want to have a normal conversation with someone who understands." The joy at meeting someone who knew how I felt was amazing, almost liberating. It was like he could read my mind.

Immy stood up abruptly. "Sorry, guys, but I'm knackered. I'm going to head off now," she said pointedly at me.

"It's not that late," I replied.

"*Some* of us have college tomorrow."

If looks could kill, I'd be sprawled, lifeless, on the table.

"Let me get your phone number," Tom said, reaching into his pocket for his phone while Immy scowled at me.

I raised my eyebrows at her. *What?*

"Damn. It's dead. Are you on Instagram?" He was clicking the power butting incessantly like that would miraculously recharge the battery.

"Yes. My full name's Lindy Pennyworth. What's your—"

"Lindy! If I don't get home now, my mum is going to flip. Dad's away at the moment, and you know what she's like . . ."

"One second, Immy! Just let me—"

"We're going . . . *now!*" She tugged the arm of my coat and hauled me outside, leaving Tom standing alone and puzzled at the table.

"That was rude," I snapped, as Immy let go of my coat and stormed ahead of me down the road.

"I don't know what you mean," she tossed back, not bothering to turn her head.

"You couldn't have waited a couple of seconds more? You had to drag me out of there like that? It's humiliating. You're not my mother!"

"In case you've forgotten, I was doing you a favour tonight!"

"I know, but – look, can you slow down a bit? I can't keep up with you."

I stopped to zip up my coat against the cold wind. Immy spun around and glared at me.

"It's freezing out here. We'll die of hyperthermia if you don't get a move on."

"What the hell is wrong with you?" I demanded. "Why are you in such a bad mood?"

"I'm not!"

"Uh, *hello*? You are!"

"Look, I'm glad you've found someone who knows what you're going through and can identify with your grief or whatever, but how am I supposed to join in these conversations when all I've got is a dad who's always away with work and a mum who's always on my back about why I'm not getting the best grades? Tonight is the first time I've seen you in ages and suddenly you're all over this new guy and both of you are acting like I don't even exist."

Immy's strong point was her loyalty; her weakness was jealousy. It had unfortunately reared its ugly head a few times during our friendship. She was always worrying that I would ditch her if someone 'better' came along and didn't understand that I wasn't looking for another best friend.

"You're being petty, Immy – like you always are whenever we meet someone new. You've got to stop being so possessive of me—"

"*You?*" She laughed. "Haven't *you* got a high opinion of yourself! If you must know, I wasn't thinking of you at all when I decided to leave. Well, not in that way."

"Then what were you thinking?"

Her cheeks reddened. "I was thinking how much I liked Tom and how, every time I like a guy, they turn their attention to you and ignore me."

"I don't understand—"

"I never stand a chance whenever you're around. They're attracted to you like bees to honey and I never get a look-in. Tonight, it was all about *you* again: *you* were yelled at by the psychic, *you* bonded with Tom over the deaths of your fathers. He'd more or less forgotten I was in the room."

"What . . . ? You're jealous of us because we can commiserate with each other over our fathers' deaths?"

"No, it's not that, and you know it."

"No, actually, I don't know it. If I'm such a bitch, then I don't understand why you keep telling me you're missing me at college. Things must be so much better without me around."

We were both breathing hard, glaring at each other under the streetlight. A few people scurried past, hats pulled tightly down over their ears and scarves wrapped around their necks to keep out the worst of the weather.

Immy sighed. "Look, I'm sorry. I shouldn't have talked to you like that – I don't mean it. It's just that I always feel like the Ugly Duckling next to you."

"Why? Especially now, with me being partially bald?"

"At least your hair doesn't look like you've been electrocuted."

"What? I've always loved your curls – they're cute."

"Cute? Great – now I sound like a six-year-old!"

"I didn't mean that, Immy. I've always envied your curly hair – it's beautiful. It's so soft and—"

"Frizzy. I look like I've got a sheep on my head."

I couldn't help laughing at the image that conjured up, and Immy grudgingly chuckled too.

"Don't be so stupid, Immy. You're stunning, and I don't see a sheep in sight when I look at you."

"Then why does no one ever ask me out?"

"Well – and I say this with all the love in the world – sometimes you're kind of fierce. Maybe they're a little scared of you."

"They're scared of me? Why?"

"You have a hot temper. Sometimes, you react really quickly and angrily—"

"You're saying I overreact!" She looked at me and her face fell. "Like I'm doing now, right?"

"Right."

"Great."

"But that's OK, Immy. This is exactly what I love about you. You're fierce and strong and true to your beliefs in a way that most

51

of us girls aren't because we're all too easily swayed by what others think. That might be what keeps some of the boys back, but that's because they're just too weak to handle it. You'll find someone soon enough – someone who truly deserves you."

"Shut up! You're making me teary!"

I was, as well. She pulled me into a bear hug and, as she let me go, said, "And you've got to stop being so hard on yourself, too. You still look gorgeous, no matter what you say."

"No one looks gorgeous in a beanie."

"Cute, then." She raised an eyebrow.

"Well played, Immy."

Taking each other's hand, we started walking again, slower this time.

"Back to this evening – I still believe that you should give up on this rubbish now," Immy said.

"I can't. After tonight, I'm even more convinced that there's something to it."

"You're going to get hurt. Please listen to me, Lindy," Immy begged. "All this psychic stuff is nonsense, and the people who believe in it are weirdos."

"Do you think Tom is a weirdo?" I asked slyly.

"Well, he might be, but he's still gorgeous." She paused. "Tom seemed familiar to me, but I can't think where I've seen him before."

"I know what you mean," I agreed.

We kept walking in silence and soon reached my house. We paused in front of the door.

"Look, when do you think you'll be back at college?" Immy asked. "If you don't hurry up and get better soon, I am going to be permanently stuck with Jessica. You know what she's like."

I laughed. "I promise I'll do my best, if only for your sake."

We hugged and agreed to meet up again soon. Immy set off down the road, texting as she walked – a skill I've still not mastered. As I turned around, the door opened, showing Mum's silhouette against the hallway light.

"You've been gone ages. Why didn't you call?"

"Sorry. I lost track of time. We were too busy talking."

She stood aside to let me pass, a triumphant smile on her face. "I knew you'd have a good time. All you needed was a night out with a friend. Where did you go?"

"Just to a café, as planned."

I felt bad about lying but if I'd told her the truth, she'd have gone crazy. "I'm tired, so I think I'll get ready for bed now. See you in the morning."

At least one good thing had come out of this evening: I hadn't pulled all night.

4.
KNOCK-KNOCK

The noise woke me up at two in the morning. At first, I thought it was a branch tapping on my window, but when I drew back the curtains, I could see by the moonlight that the trees were still. I listened. Again, the noise – a knocking. It was getting louder, and I knew it wasn't coming from anything in my bedroom.

Bofur and Bifur stood like sentries at my door; Bifur, always more neurotic than his brother, was growling.

I turned on my lamp. Was it a burglar? My hand reached for my mobile, ready to dial 999.

The next time the sound came, I could tell that it was coming from the attic. If someone had broken in, why would they bother going upstairs when the television and other valuables were downstairs? It didn't make sense. And it didn't really sound like someone rummaging through things; it sounded more like a deliberate tapping – there was a kind of rhythm to it, like a heartbeat.

Knock-knock.

Trying to be as quiet as possible, I eased myself out of bed and put my dressing gown on then made my way towards my bedroom door. Bifur and Bofur hissed and shrank back, hackles raised and tails obscenely fat. I tried to shush them with a gentle pat on their heads, but they ran under the bed. Not much use if there was a burglar, then.

I crept along the landing and paused at the foot of the stairs leading to the attic. The thumping sounded again, more insistent this time. I shivered. What was up there? Who was up there? Should I wake Mum? Nothing good ever happened to people who investigated dark attics in the middle of the night on their own.

"Mum?"

My voice came out as a squeak that I could barely hear myself. I cleared my throat and tried again.

"Mum!"

I heard her shifting in her bed followed by a faint mumble.

This was no good. If someone was upstairs, then I'd already given the game away that I was up and on to them, and they might try to come down those stairs at any moment. I hurried to her room and switched on the light.

"Mum! I think someone's upstairs."

"What?" She squinted against the glare of the overhead light and propped herself up on to an elbow. "What did you say?"

"I heard some noises – they woke me up. They're coming from your office."

A frown creased her face. "Are you sure?"

"Yes! Should I call the police?"

"No. We don't know what it is."

"But what if it's someone up there? They're going to have to come down to escape. What if they try to hurt us?"

She got out of bed and went straight to her wardrobe where, to my surprise, she pulled out a baseball bat.

"I'll check it out."

I followed her along the landing and we waited at the bottom of the stairs. There was no noise this time – no thudding. I kind of wished it would happen again just to prove that it *had* happened, especially since my mother was looking at me expectantly. "I can't hear anything."

"I know, but I swear I heard noises."

"All right. Well, I'd better go up and make sure everything's fine."

She headed upstairs and I followed close behind her. At the top, she switched on the light and we peered inside.

The room was empty.

The only place to hide was the space under Mum's desk. Holding a finger to her lips, she tiptoed over and bent down to look.

"There's no one in here, Lindy."

"I don't understand it. I know I heard something."

"Maybe it was a leftover from a dream. You know? When you wake up and still think you're in your dream world."

"But Bifur and Bofur were terrified – growling and hissing. They've hidden under my bed!"

"Those two will run at the sight of their own shadows. You know they always startle easily."

She had a point, but I still wasn't convinced.

"Do you think we should make sure, though? That there isn't anyone downstairs? They might have crept down while I came in to get you."

She sighed and nodded. "That's probably a sensible idea."

Mum led the way downstairs, less quietly and carefully than she had moved when going up into the loft, which told me that she was only humouring my anxiety. A quick survey of all the rooms proved her right: there was no one there. I blushed.

"Sorry, Mum, but I know what I heard. I don't understand it."

"It's OK," she replied, yawning. "Better to be safe than sorry. I'm going back to bed, now we know everything's all right."

I followed her up and we said goodnight as we went to our separate bedrooms. Two fat tails were still sticking out from underneath my bed.

"Thanks a lot, you two," I murmured, as I took off my dressing gown and turned out the light.

I was just about to drift off to sleep when there was a bone-rattling crash directly above me. I bolted upright, heart racing. Surely Mum had heard that?

A duet of growls rumbled up from underneath the bed and one of the cats let out a long, low yowl, setting the hairs on my arms on end.

My mother hadn't appeared – surely if she'd heard it, she would have said something or come running into the room? So why was it only me and the cats who could hear this noise?

Maybe it was coming from the house next door?

Bifur and Bofur shot out from their hiding place and ran to the door, pawing it frantically. I got up and went to them, bending down to stroke them.

"Hey, guys, it's OK. Nothing's wrong—"

Bifur turned towards me, ears flattened, his back arched. He hissed and spat at me, baring his teeth. I jumped back – he'd never been like that with me before. Like his brother, he was always gentle with humans.

I opened the door and the two streaked down the the stairs, their claws scrabbling on the wooden floor.

I looked towards Mum's room. Not a sound. How had she not heard any of this – the bangs, crashes, the cats yowling and clawing? It didn't make any sense. I would have dismissed it as my overactive imagination, but the cats had heard it too – or, at least, *something* had terrified them.

I made my way along the landing and tiptoed up the attic stairs.

The room was bathed in moonlight apart from the walls and corners, which hid in the shadow from the low eaves.

Knock-knock.

I jumped and barely stopped myself from squealing. The noise seemed to be coming from the back of the room in the right-hand corner. I turned on a lamp and angled it towards the wall. Some of the wooden floorboards lay higher than the others.

Knock-knock.

Fighting the urge to run downstairs again, I walked towards the boards. As I reached them, they knocked – hard and insistent.

Knock-knock.

Nothing good is ever hidden in attics.

Hands trembling, I pulled up the loose floorboards to reveal a shallow space. Lying there was an oval-shaped object, wrapped in a light, gauzy cotton. Coughing on the dust I disturbed, I lifted it out of its hiding place and carried it to the lamp to get a better look.

Underneath the faded material was a picture frame made from dark, heavy wood, the length of my forearm. Beneath the glass lay a delicate border of dried grasses, arranged into flowers, butterflies and leaves. There was a faint, oval outline in the middle, suggesting a picture had once been there. The frame looked antique, like it was from when the house was originally built.

The sound of Mum coughing jolted me into action; I had to get out of there in case she got up again and started asking questions I couldn't answer. She'd be as surprised as I was about the discovery of the picture frame, but she'd never believe that it was the cause of the noise that only I had apparently heard. I moved to return the frame back to its hiding place but the floorboards slammed shut – one by one – until there was no sign that they had ever been loose.

I had no option but to take it back to my room. I clicked off the lamp and crept down the attic stairs. At the bottom, I paused and listened. The house was quiet once more, apart from Mum's gentle snoring. Returning to my bedroom, I put the picture frame in my wardrobe, out of sight, before climbing back into bed. I wished the cats were still with me to keep me company, but the chances of them returning to my room tonight were very slim indeed.

10.
BLUEBERRY PANCAKES

My alarm clock woke me far too soon.

Despite now doing my college work from home, Mum insisted on keeping to the regular college day in an attempt to 'maintain normality', so I was expected to rise and shine at seven every morning.

I dragged myself out of bed and made my way to the bathroom, thinking that a hot bath would wake me up. I ran a deep one, adding plenty of bubbles, before stepping into the soothing water. My mind wandered as I let the heat work its way into my skin and muscles, and felt my body go limp and heavy.

I am standing at the edge of a deep pit, surrounded by mounds of freshly dug earth. To my right, a misshapen tree towers over what looks like a line of bodies, tightly wrapped in cotton and bound at the feet and above the head, guarded by a group of gravediggers, scarves tied around their

noses and mouths. To my left, in the distance, is a knot of crying people standing behind a priest holding a Bible and reciting a prayer.

Two of the gravediggers pick up either end of one of the white shrouds and heave it into the pit, creating a slick smack as it lands on wet ground. A mourner wails as the diggers shovel white powder on to the corpse before another body is added, followed by more powder, until all the bodies are stacked on top of each other.

The priest crosses himself and closes his Bible, ending his prayers for the dead. The mourners melt away, but one man remains, his pale, drawn face a picture of agony against the darkness of the yews behind him. He sinks to his knees and sobs, "My darling Esmerelda! Forgive me!"

"Lindy! Open the door!"

I was shrivelled and shivering. Cold water and bubbles were pouring over the bath's edge, flooding the floor, and both taps were turned on full.

I'd turned them off before I'd closed my eyes. How had I fallen asleep?

Mum pounded on the door. "Let me in!"

I pushed myself to sitting and fumbled with the taps, but they refused to turn. My fingers, numbed by cold, just kept slipping on them uselessly. I yanked the plug out and tried to stand, but my wet skin kept slipping on the ceramic surface of the bath, throwing me down on to my back, legs kicking to stop myself from going underwater. Eventually, I managed to grab the edge of the bath and heave myself up, sliding in a wet mess on to the floor.

Mum was still hammering on the door, her voice getting louder and higher with every shriek. I got up and grabbed my towel which, luckily, remained dry on the heated towel rail. As I wrapped it around me, I stopped short as I caught a glimpse of something strange in the mirror.

The face that stared back at me had a blueish tinge around the lips and nose. The skin was bloated, mottled, and the eyes were dark hollows – empty apart from worms wriggling their way out of the sockets.

I opened my mouth to scream but no sound came out. Instead, a tide of maggots swarmed from the darkness.

"I'm breaking this damn door down!"

"Wait!" I cried, before she could hurl herself at the door. I fumbled with the lock and opened the door, bracing myself for a tirade of fury.

"Shit!" Mum gasped at the scene in the bathroom and then up at me. "How did you do this?"

"I must have fallen asleep in the bath. I was tired this morning – I thought that it would wake me up. I—"

My words were gushing out like the water from the taps. Mum pushed past me and turned them off – experiencing none of the resistance I had struggled with moments earlier. She looked at the mess on the floor and looked up at me, before quietly saying, "Get into some dry clothes before you catch your death."

We both winced at the unfortunate expression.

"I'll try to soak this up. The water's coming through the ceiling in the kitchen." She opened the airing cupboard door, reached in and pulled out a pile of towels before throwing them over the floor.

Half an hour later, I was sitting at the kitchen table, cradling a hot cup of tea as the washing machine spun its heavy load. I was still shivering, and Mum kept casting worried glances at me as she made breakfast. "You're looking very pale, Lindy. Forget about studying today. You need to rest."

I looked at her in disbelief. This was a huge turnaround from yesterday's lecture about moving on with my life. When she then passed me my favourite breakfast, a plate of fat, fluffy pancakes oozing with blueberries, I nearly dropped my mug.

"What's the special occasion?" I asked, staring at the stack.

"You need feeding up. You hardly eat any more."

"Aren't *you* going to eat anything?"

"I had some toast earlier."

She sat down opposite me, twisting her wedding ring absent-mindedly. It was a sure sign that she had something difficult to talk about.

"The thing is, Lindy . . . especially after this morning . . . you . . . I . . . *we're* not doing very well here. I know that it's hard getting over a loss, but it's affecting you very badly. I thought maybe you were getting better after last night, but today you've flooded the bathroom and, well, you look like a ghost. I can't see how we can remain in a house where we are constantly reminded of your dad every time we turn a corner or sit in a chair."

I put down my fork, feeling sick. "What are you saying?"

She cleared her throat. "I'm putting the house up for sale. An estate agent's coming tomorrow to do a valuation. Of course, I'll have to explain the water damage on the ceiling—"

"No!"

"Yes. I've decided. The pills don't seem to be making a difference and you refused the psychological help you were offered. It's time to take more practical action instead of all this faffing around."

"Why are you doing this to me?" I asked, fighting down a strong urge to pull. "Why are you punishing me for how I'm feeling?"

"I'm not – I'm trying to help you get over this. Being here reminds you of him. In a new place, with a new start, you might be able to move on. Here, you're just obsessing with death all the time – it's all you think about."

"No, it's not!"

"Yes, it is." Her voice was gentle now, as she reached across the table to take my hand. "I've seen the little shrine you've made to your dad in your wardrobe—"

I snatched my hand away. "*What?* You went into my wardrobe?"

"All those photos and candles on that velvet cloth . . ." She shuddered. "And that book about speaking to the dead . . ."

"You had no right to invade my privacy like that!"

"I'm afraid I had to. Dr Greenwood warned me to keep an eye on your behaviour, to make sure that you wouldn't do anything dangerous. To make sure that you're not getting worse."

Tears were running down her face now, but I couldn't feel any sympathy for her when she'd betrayed my trust.

I stood up, sending my chair crashing backwards. "OK. We've heard all about your theories and your worries about me. Do you want to hear mine about you?"

She shrank away, shaking her head.

"Tough! You're going to anyway. I think that you've been

wanting to cut Dad out of our lives for ages because you couldn't cope with how close we were. And now he's dead, you don't have to. I think you're *glad* he's dead!"

I hurled my plate. Blueberry pancakes slid down the wall and mingled with the pottery pieces on the floor.

The fury left me as suddenly as it had gripped me. What was I doing? That wasn't like me – I never shouted and threw things. I should have pulled my hair instead, got rid of the rage in that way, then this wouldn't have happened.

"Mum – I . . . I . . ."

She looked at me as if I'd stabbed her, or ripped out her heart. Perhaps, metaphorically, I had. Her face was drained of all colour and her body seemed to have collapsed in on itself. She got up slowly and moved towards the kitchen door.

"I never thought I would say this, but you're really starting to scare me, Lindy. If you can't see how much this has affected you, then it really was a mistake to walk out on Dr Greenwood."

"Mum! Honestly, I didn't mean it . . ."

She shook her head sadly, as she walked out of the kitchen. "Please clean all that mess up before Bifur and Bofur cut themselves on it."

I knelt on the floor and looked at the mess. I was a wreck. A pathetic, balding teenager who couldn't talk properly to anyone.

Even the dead.

11.
PAPER CUT

Back in my room, I grabbed my hair with both hands, swirling and knotting it in between my knuckles, pulling as far as I could to get the relief of the pain without any loss of hair.

I didn't know who I was any more. Every time I thought I was feeling better, something else happened. But this was the first time that I'd ever been violent. Was I actually losing my mind?

Knock-knock.

I can't deal with this now!

Knock-knock.

"Go away!"

The anger and frustration swelled up inside of me again and I yanked my fingers out of my hair. I hadn't meant to pull but some strands came away, detaching themselves from my fingers and floating down on to the carpet. Normally this would have calmed me down quickly, but with the knocking – which by now had become persistent – anger was still raging inside of me. I tugged at the wardrobe doors and pulled out the frame from its hiding place, a teddy bear toppling over in the process. I ripped off the protective cotton cover and glared at it, the urge to destroy it overwhelming. However, the sight of the delicate tapestry of butterflies, flowers and grasses under the glass produced an instant wave of calm. I didn't want to destroy this any more – I wanted to touch the embroidery on the mount. As I removed the front frame from the back, I felt a stab of pain in my finger – I'd sliced it on the frame.

Entranced, I watched as my blood dropped and pooled outwards on to the mount, dyeing the flowers and grasses a pale pink. I'd never really examined my blood before, and I loved how thick and richly crimson it was . . .

"Suck a cut to make it stop."

The voice was husky, low, persuasive.

I pulled my finger away from the frame and held it up. Warm blood trickled down my arm.

"Suck a cut to make it stop!"

The voice again, more insistent. I held my finger to my lips and sucked. At first, there was that familiar, unpleasant metallic taste but, suddenly, an explosion of warm blood filled my mouth.

How badly am I bleeding?

Gagging in panic, I ran to the bathroom and spat into the sink. I exhaled as I bent over and tried to catch my breath but again my mouth filled with blood. Where was it coming from? I'd cut my finger, not my throat.

More poured out – faster and more viscous. Thick clots thudded into the basin. I was drowning in my own blood.

I was going to die.

"Mum!"

It came out as a gurgle and the room spun. I collapsed to the floor.

When I came to, Mum was bending over me. "Are you all right? Did you hit your head?"

I was lying on the bathroom floor, which was still damp from the bathwater incident.

"Lindy! I asked if you hit your head. Can you remember?"

I looked at Mum, trying to piece together what had happened, and then it came to me.

"I cut myself. I cut my finger."

She frowned, then examined my hands.

"You've got a little paper cut here," she said, showing me my left index finger. "They can bleed a lot sometimes, but that doesn't explain why you're on the floor. You're not phobic of blood, are you?"

"No! You don't understand – when I sucked it to stop it bleeding, all this blood came into my throat and I had to come in here and spit it out into the sink, but it wouldn't stop coming. I couldn't breathe!"

Even in my confused state, I could see the doubt and fear in her eyes.

"If you don't believe me, look in the sink," I begged. "There was loads of it in there."

She stood up and looked. Her expression didn't change, which wasn't good news for me.

"All I can see is a clean sink and both taps running. *Again*. Only this time, thank goodness, you didn't put the plug in the sink. I'm going to call Dr Greenwood—"

"No! Please, Mum – don't call him. I don't want to see him!"

"I need to know what to do, Lindy. Your behaviour is very worrying. You're *hallucinating*, you've nearly flooded the bathroom twice in one morning—"

"I swear what I said is true!"

"That's why I said you're hallucinating. These visions you're having seem very real to you but they're not. There's no blood here—"

"The taps were on full, you said. They must have washed it away."

"I don't think there was any blood."

I looked down at my forefinger, at the neat flap that stung when I pressed the skin.

"Then why did I end up on the floor . . . unconscious?" I whispered.

"You must have fainted. You were cold from falling asleep in the bath and then you didn't eat all your breakfast because you . . . "

She didn't finish the sentence, choosing instead to reach into the bathroom cabinet and produce a plaster.

"Here, put this on the cut; it will stop it hurting for now. But I'm going to have to call Dr Greenwood. He prescribed these tablets so he's going to have to recommend what we do from now on."

I scuttled back to my room and looked for the frame. It was still there but the picture mount was spotless. There was no trace of my blood . . . anywhere.

"These medicines have side effects, Mrs Pennyworth. In teenagers, it's important to look out for hallucinations, confusion, suicidal thoughts. If Lindy starts acting strangely, you must let me know."

I sank to the floor, tears sliding down my face. The self-doubt and confusion were almost overbearing. Were the pills making me see and hear things, as Mum thought? But what about the night before, at the spiritual church? *That* wasn't my doing! I hadn't imagined the medium's odd behaviour – Immy and Tom had seen it too. I needed to pull myself together.

I put the picture frame away and decided to concentrate on my real-world problems. Mum was selling the house and I had to come up with some sort of plan to stop her. I'd lost my dad and I was damned if I was going to lose my home as well. If Mum wanted to sell it to strangers, then she was going to have to fight me all the way.

12.
OPEN DOORS AND NOISY ROOMS

"Dr Greenwood recommends that you halve the dose. Cut the pills in half and try that for a week."

Mum was standing in the doorway to my bedroom and I was shocked at how awful she looked. Her jeans were hanging off her waist and her face was haggard. I'd been so busy lately, trying to find Dad, that I'd not noticed how Mum was starting to fade away in front of me. Lines of exhaustion framed her normally bright eyes and her complexion was dull.

"Of course, he also recommended that you restart your counselling sessions and very kindly offered to find a different therapist," she added. "But I suppose you're going to refuse?"

My cheeks burned with embarrassment. "I'll think about it, Mum. I promise."

"All right. I need to get back to work now – I'm already behind on a deadline and I can't afford to lose this commission. Are you going to be OK?"

"I promise I won't do anything stupid," I said, then added,

"I really am sorry, Mum."

"Oh, and Lindy? Considering what's happened today, please don't lock the bathroom door any more. Or any door, for that matter. I need to make sure you're safe and I can't if I can't get in."

Great. I was now a prisoner in my own house.

As she left me alone – bedroom door open wide – to get some work done, I heard my phone vibrating. I hadn't looked at it since the previous night and couldn't see it anywhere. A quick glance around the room and I spied the charger cable dangling down from underneath my pillow and I remembered I'd tucked it under before going to sleep. Immy's name was flashing on the screen and her voice came through loud and clear when I accepted the call.

"Hey, Lindy-Lou," she said. "How're you doing after last night? Offended any more mediums?"

"Very funny."

"Sorry. Seriously, are you OK? Did it upset you? I *did* warn you, I said that—"

"No, I'm fine. Promise. Well, apart from Mum announcing this morning that she's putting the house up for sale."

"*What?*"

"She says it's too upsetting for me to be here with Dad's memories everywhere. She doesn't get that I don't mind them; that they're the only thing giving me any comfort. *She* certainly isn't. She just keeps going on about me being obsessed with death—"

"Hmmm . . ."

"Yes, I know that part is true, but if you were her, wouldn't you at least try to sit down and have a conversation? You know, talk about your feelings instead of just pretending that everything's OK and ignore that Dad . . ."

I couldn't finish. A sob was fighting its way up my throat.

"I know it's hard, Lindy," Immy said, her voice gentle. "But everyone has different ways of dealing with their feelings. She's the more traditional 'stiff upper lip' type, I guess."

"Well, she could at least try to see things from my point of view instead of running away to her study every time I say something she doesn't like."

"I'm more worried that she's planning to move away from Oxford. Please tell me that she isn't. I won't let you go."

"We didn't get that far – we had a row – but she's got an estate agent coming over tomorrow, so I guess that shows how determined she is to get things started."

"Is there anything you can do to change her mind?"

"I doubt it. Apart from making a miraculous recovery, and even then, I doubt she'd stay. I'm really not her favourite person at the moment."

"Why?"

"I threw a plate of blueberry pancakes at the wall."

She whistled. "Yeah, my parents would be pretty mad if I did that."

A group of people started shouting in the background and Immy yelled at them to shut up.

"Give me a sec, Lindy – I can't hear you in the lunch hall, it's too noisy."

A door slammed and the racket of people talking was replaced with gusts of wind hissing through the earpiece.

"God, it's so noisy in there," she complained. "Anyway, I've been dying to speak to you. I remembered this morning where I've seen Tom before."

"Where?"

"Here. At college."

"What? When was this? I don't remember him."

"He wasn't here for long. I think he spent a term here last year and then disappeared. He was in the year above us, which is probably why we didn't recognise him straight away."

I racked my brain, trying to remember him, but couldn't place him anywhere. "Are you absolutely sure?"

"Yes," she insisted. "I held off texting or calling you till I'd asked Jessica. She knew him, of course – she always notices hot guys – but she didn't know his last name."

"Why did he only stay a term?"

"No one knows. Apparently, he joined the college after moving to Oxford. He didn't hang out with anyone. Then he just upped and left suddenly, and no one saw him again."

"That's sad. Why didn't he have any friends? He seemed nice enough last night."

"I don't know. A boy with his looks would have been popular. He must have wanted to keep to himself."

"Well, maybe that's why he wants to make friends now," I suggested. "He recognised us from college and decided to make an effort. We should be nice to him."

"Hey, I'm OK with that," Immy said. Of course she was. I rolled my eyes.

Shortly after we hung up, I noticed that I had an Instagram follow request on my screen from '@Tom_Abel'.

He'd found me.

My finger hovered over 'Confirm'. Should I let Immy know his username so she could make contact first?

She'd be going to class now though, and it would be a couple of hours before she could check her phone again. I could accept Tom and then send her his details so she could request him. There was no harm in that – and I could always use this opportunity to talk Immy up to him.

Accepting him, I decided to face whatever consequences came my way.

13.
PULL OUT
THE MADNESS

After accepting Tom, a couple of hours passed and I still hadn't heard anything from him, so I took out my Art coursework and turned my phone off so I wouldn't be waiting and watching it. Art was the only way that I could be free of distractions of any type – I normally became so absorbed in whatever I was drawing or painting that I didn't even feel the need to pull.

The assignment sheet my teacher emailed me the previous week said to sketch a monochrome family portrait, paying as much attention to the border as to the people because *"the frame can give vital clues to the family's personality"*. The possibility of subverting posed happiness or seriousness interested me, so I grabbed my sketchpad and pencils and set to work.

It wasn't easy. With Dad dead and Mum not really speaking to me, I didn't know where to start. What border could possibly represent our bizarre existence? I tapped my pencil against my knee in frustration until I heard the now familiar sound.

Knock-knock.

Not again. My art was my sanctuary – this wasn't fair!

Knock-knock.

Leave me alone!

Knock-knock.

Then it occurred to me.

I could use the frame as inspiration for the assignment.

Even though I was spurred on by the frame, I didn't want to look at it – there was something odd about it that I couldn't put my finger on. Thankfully, I'd stared at it long enough to remember the shape of the frame, as well as the intricate details of the border and the flowers behind the glass – or, at least, I could recall it well enough to draw a near-likeness. It didn't have to be perfect.

Whether the knocking continued or not, I didn't know, as my art took over. A family of three emerged in a flurry of lead while my hand danced across the page, until cramp forced me to rest. I'd never worked with such speed and confidence before – normally I was a hesitant perfectionist. I looked at my watch and was amazed to see that it was nearly six o'clock; I'd been drawing for three hours.

A father, a mother and a daughter were looking up at me from the page, sketched with an almost photographic quality. I should have felt amazed and proud of this achievement ... but instead it scared the life out of me.

Who were these people?

Instead of Dad's usual outfit of jeans and a jumper, the father in the picture wore a smart suit – a jacket with tails, a waistcoat and cravat. His dark hair was wavy, and a thick, oiled moustache framed his serious mouth. Dad's fair hair was always mussed up, much to Mum's exasperation, and he had a full beard.

The mother also looked nothing like mine. Mum preferred jeans and casual shirts, the woman in my drawing was wearing a floor-length dress. She had a skirt that billowed out from her tiny waist and a collar that came right up her neck. Her expression was also strange – her lips were pursed, and she looked angry – as if she really didn't want to be there.

The daughter had fair hair arranged in ringlets that draped over her shoulders and finished midway down her back. Her white dress sat slightly off the shoulders and she wore a crucifix tied on a ribbon around her neck. She was sitting on a chair in the middle of her parents, with their hands resting on her shoulders.

This was a family portrait all right . . . but it wasn't my family.

The kitchen was silent when I went downstairs to check on the dinner situation. Bifur and Bofur hadn't been fed and they weaved around my legs as I peered into the fridge to see if there was anything to eat. I'd have to ask Mum what was happening. Hopefully she had forgiven my earlier outburst.

I climbed the stairs to her attic office and knocked on the now-closed door. Not a promising start.

"Yes?"

"May I come in?" A pause.

"Yes."

I opened the door to see Mum was sitting at her computer, typing ferociously. She never liked being interrupted when in full flow – she suffered a lot from writer's block, so when she was hitting the keys this quickly I knew she must be on a roll. Unless she was just pounding some random keys to make me think she was busy.

"Uh, do you want me to make dinner for us tonight?" I asked.

"No, thanks. I'll make myself a sandwich later."

"I can make some pasta?"

"No, thanks. I want to carry on working for a while longer. I'm so far behind, I'm worried I won't catch up. You just get yourself something, OK?"

That was the end of the conversation. I shut the door and headed back downstairs, trying to avoid Bifur's attempts to trip me up.

"Stupid cat. Don't you know that if you kill me, I won't be able to feed you? And *she* won't come down to do it either," I muttered, so there would be no danger of her overhearing. I was in enough trouble as it was.

As I placed two smelly bowls of tuna down for the cats, I wondered how Mum could be so undemonstrative about Dad's death and then accuse *me* of being unbalanced. It was all right for Immy to say that different people grieved in different ways but surely, if you loved someone for a long time, you'd show some signs of mental anguish? Mum had always just looked . . . uneasy. Possibly worried, too. But never grief-stricken. Why? Did she think it was weak to show sadness? This possibility made me feel even worse – as if my own struggles were nothing more than an irritation or inconvenience to her.

I yanked a thick strand of hair out and stared at it. Suddenly, I wanted to pull it all out, to feel the raging sting all over my head as I remembered how Dad used to be – before that night.

Fury and despair welled up inside of me and I sat down,

bending my head over my knees, sliding my hands into my hair and knotting it around my fingers. Hot tears dripped down on to the kitchen tiles as I tightened my grip.

Pull out the madness . . .

A deep growl stopped me. Bifur and Bofur were facing me, hackles up and tails like fat brushes. Bifur bared his teeth and hissed.

"What's the matter, guys?" I whispered. "I'm just doing a little grooming. I'm moulting, you know. Just like you do, only I need a little help."

I gripped my hair again and Bofur, ears flattened against his head, batted my leg with his paw.

"Would you prefer it if I brushed it like normal?"

As if he understands me!

I stood up and left the kitchen, not bothering with my own dinner. I called Bifur and Bofur and they followed me to the foot of the stairs, then stopped.

"Come on, guys! Come and give me a cuddle. I need it tonight."

They stared at me. What was their problem? They normally followed me around the place like furry shadows.

I bent down, picked up Bofur and started climbing the stairs, calling for Bifur to follow. He stayed put, while Bofur emitted a throaty growl that he normally only uses when unsuccessfully trying to stand up to the neighbour's tiny cat, Mittens.

"What's up with you two?" I demanded, before letting out a yelp. Claws fully out, Bofur had swiped me across the face, drawing blood from my cheek. I dropped him and he raced down the stairs, hackles up and ears flat on his head. Bifur followed him into the kitchen.

Now my own cats are turning against me.

Inside my bedroom, I closed the door and let out a quiet moan of frustration and sadness. The now ever-present knot in my stomach reminded me that I'd still not released the tension that had built up over the day, and I didn't want to start throwing plates or other stuff around. Without thinking, I searched for a hair at the back of my head, underneath the top layers.

Knock-knock.

"Shut up!" I screamed, and yanked. Several strands of long, dark hair escaped in my hands and the sting in my scalp warned me that I'd been too vicious. I threw the hair against the wall and reached up to touch the spot where it had come from. Faint traces of blood dotted my fingertips. I anticipated my mum's heavy footsteps trundling down the stairs to demand why I had screamed.

I waited.

She never came.

I cried myself to sleep.

14.
QUEEN ROSE

The house was in darkness when I awoke, drenched in sweat and itching all around my neck and ears. Something soft was nestling against me. Bifur or Bofur, no doubt, coming to spend the rest of the night with me. I must have reopened the bedroom door before I went to bed, though I couldn't remember doing that. Maybe Mum had come in and checked on me before going to bed and left it open. It didn't matter either way – I was just glad that they were coming into my room again after refusing to come upstairs, though I was still wary of Bofur's earlier swipe.

Sleepily, I reached out to stroke whichever cat was with me, but the fur felt different. Longer and thicker. There didn't seem to be any warmth of a body underneath it.

I scrambled for my bedside light and switched it on. There was hair.

Everywhere.

Wavy, golden hair, flowing from the wardrobe – flaxen tresses meandering across the carpet and snaking up the bed.

That's when it hit me. It wasn't grass in the picture frame. It was hair. *Human hair.*

I fought the urge to vomit, to scream, as the hair insinuated itself over and around me, caressing me as it moved up my arms and over my shoulders. If I tried to struggle against it, it wrapped itself tighter around me, squeezing me like a boa constrictor. It slid up my neck and crawled along my scalp, stroking the bald patches with a silky touch. A sweet, young voice began to sing:

> *"Queen Rose of the rosebud garden of girls,*
> *Come hither, the dances are done,*
> *In gloss of satin and glimmer of pearls,*
> *Queen Lily and Rose in one;*
> *Shine out, little head, sunning over with curls,*
> *To the flower, and be their sun."*

When the singing ended, the hair unravelled itself and silently slunk away, disappearing under my wardrobe door. I kept still, hardly breathing, terrified that it would come back again.

It's the medication. It's a side effect of the tablets. Forget halving them – I've got to stop taking them completely before I go insane . . .

Knock-knock.

The wardrobe door rattled from the inside.

I yanked my duvet over my head and curled up in a ball.

Had I taken my meds that day? Had I taken too many? Not enough?

Knock-knock.

"Go away!" I shrieked, pressing my hands against my ears. "Leave me alone!"

Footsteps hurried along the corridor and Mum flung my door open.

"What's the matter? Are you all right?"

I couldn't tell her. At best, she wouldn't believe me; at worst, she'd think I was having some sort of breakdown. That night, I didn't even know what was going on. Perhaps I was having a breakdown.

"I–I must have had a bad dream," I said, unable to think up a better answer. "Sorry."

She rubbed her eyes. "I think we'd better book an emergency doctor's appointment tomorrow. I don't think these pills suit you at all – you're seeing and hearing things and this morning, with the plate . . . I don't know what you're going to do next."

"I'm sorry," I whimpered.

"It's all right. Now, are you OK? Do you want me to get you some warm milk?"

"No, I'm fine, thanks. Sorry to have woken you."

"See you in the morning. Try to get some sleep."

I nodded and she padded out. Maybe she was right – maybe if I changed or stopped the medication all this would go away. Maybe even the compulsion to contact Dad would disappear; it had definitely got stronger since I'd been taking the antidepressants. It wasn't exactly going well, anyway, so I wouldn't be losing anything.

Eventually, I succumbed to sleep and dreamt of nothing. No hair, no blood, no graves.

The sleep of the dead.

15.
DEATH IN THE TIME
OF CHOLERA

I slept long and late, not waking up until I heard the Hoover downstairs.

Mum was getting the house ready for the estate agent.

I pulled open the blinds and let the morning sun into my room before turning back to examine it. Everything looked normal.

Apart from the picture frame, which was propped against my beanbag.

How did it get there? I'd left it in my wardrobe!

Hadn't I?

I knelt and, as I picked it up, the glass came away from the back and the mount fell out on to the floor beside me. Tucked into the back part of the frame was a folded article, discoloured with age, from the newspaper *Jackson's Oxford Journal*, dated 3 September 1849.

A photo, taking up a quarter of the page, made my stomach lurch in disbelief.

A man and woman, in old-fashioned clothes, either side of a pretty young girl seated between them.

The family portrait that I had unwittingly sketched yesterday.

Except someone had blacked out the man's face with ink, using such force that the paper had torn and left him virtually headless.

Underneath the photo was the following article:

Daughter of Esteemed Doctor Dies of Cholera

It is with deep regret that this newspaper announces the death of Esmerelda Pennyworth, 17, daughter of esteemed cholera expert Dr Charles Pennyworth.

In what can only be described as a dreadful and cruel coincidence, the young lady succumbed to the same malady that her father has been working so tirelessly to eradicate in Oxford during recent weeks. Dr Pennyworth – a cholera physician of great repute from London – came to Oxford after his presence was requested by our city's doctors. His expertise was sought in the matter of how to contain the rapid spread of the disease through our city in its current outbreak. Dr Pennyworth concentrated his work in the district of Jericho, a neighbourhood characterised by narrow streets of workers' houses that reek with the stench of disease and decay from the open drains. Eschewing the more prestigious housing offered to him by various university colleges, Dr Pennyworth took up residence in Richmond Road, near the epicentre of the worst-struck area of Oxford.

"I want to be as near as possible to my patients, so I can monitor their progress day and night," Dr Pennyworth informed Jackson's Oxford Journal, *shortly after his arrival in the city.*

Alas, it was to be this act of supreme altruism that unfortunately and inadvertently led to Esmerelda Pennyworth's premature death – for the family's proximity to the miasmic neighbourhoods of cholera-infected Jericho proved an irresistible temptation to Miss Pennyworth. An unfortunate mixture of adventurism and curiosity led Miss Pennyworth to abandon the safety of her home one afternoon, while her mother rested. It is believed that her brief sojourn into the surrounding streets exposed her to the disease that would so rapidly and devastatingly end her life.

"Even though we took all the necessary precautions to ensure that Esmerelda did not venture out again into Jericho, it was God's will that this one, brief exposure would infect, and ultimately take, our beloved daughter – our only child," Dr Pennyworth revealed to this newspaper, adding that he and his colleagues believe that Miss Pennyworth must have come into contact with infected water while exploring the streets.

Despite his most skilful and valiant efforts, Dr Pennyworth was unable to save the life of the victim who meant the most to him.

Even in the midst of his distress and lassitude, Dr Pennyworth insisted that his only daughter and child be buried without delay to reduce the risk of further contagion. This newspaper has therefore learnt that Miss Esmerelda Pennyworth was laid to rest in a mass grave in St Sepulchre's Cemetery last Saturday with other unfortunates taken by this dreadful disease.

When asked about the impersonal nature of this burial, Dr Pennyworth, visibly distressed, insisted that since we are all loved by God, it is immaterial how and where we are buried.

"Of course, I would have preferred that Esmerelda have her own grave to serve as a private place to grieve but equally it is important that I can show solidarity towards my less fortunate patients and their families."

It would, of course, be inconceivable that Dr Pennyworth

and his wife, Georgina, would want to remain in the city where their daughter perished. Therefore, the grieving couple will be returning to their home in London shortly, in order to try to regain some sense of normalcy in this tragic situation.

On behalf of this newspaper, and the city of Oxford, we would like to thank Dr Pennyworth for his tireless efforts in helping to bring the recent cholera outbreak under control. We would also like to offer our sincerest condolences at the loss of his daughter. Miss Esmerelda Pennyworth was buried here in Oxford and, therefore, will always remain an Oxford citizen. We will always remember her.

I sat back, stunned, as the realisation hit me.

Janice had said that a young woman around my age with the initial E was trying to communicate with me and that she had lived in the same house, on the same road, and had the same bedroom as me. This newspaper article proved that a young girl called Esmerelda lived in a house in Jericho.

The man's family name was Pennyworth, just like mine.

Dr Pennyworth was portrayed as an Oxford hero because of his work with cholera. However, it was clear from the piece of paper I was holding that not everyone loved and admired him. In the margin of the newspaper article, someone had scrawled *LIAR! MURDERER!* Perhaps another one of his patients had died under his care and their family was furious. Still, it wouldn't be his fault, would it? Cholera was difficult to treat in those days. Who would deface the article like this? And how had they managed to hide it in our attic?

I had to crack on; I had my own problems. In a couple of hours, my mother would be showing an estate agent around the house and I needed to think of a way of stalling her or, alternatively, making the house so undesirable that no one would want to buy it. I didn't fancy my chances with that – if Mum suspected for one moment that I'd screwed up her plans she would be furious, and she was already pretty mad with me.

Taking care not to touch what I now knew was hair, I picked up the picture frame and the newspaper article, ready to hide them under my beanbag till later. But as I tried to put the frame down, a long plait flew up like a whip and wrapped itself around my right hand, unravelling and weaving itself between my fingers. The more I tried to pull away, the tighter it tied itself, cutting off my circulation. I pulled at it with my left hand, but it split into tendrils, binding first my wrist and then my fingers. My hand and arm throbbed, my skin went red, then purple, as the blood pooled. The last thing I remembered before hitting the floor was seeing white ligatures forming where the strands cut into my skin.

"Stop struggling and I'll let you go."

"What?"

I was lying on my bed. How had I got here from lying passed-out on the floor? I started to panic again and tried to pull my hand free from the tight braid.

"I *said* stop struggling."

It was the same voice that had I'd heard singing the night before.

"Who are you? You're hurting me!"

16.
E

"Do as I say, and I'll stop." The female voice was soft, reassuring.

I forced myself to take a few deep breaths. The hair relaxed, unravelling itself from my hands, and I rubbed my wrists and fingers, trying to get the circulation moving again.

"Where are you? Why can't I see you?"

"Says the girl who has been using Ouija boards, tarot cards and a medium to speak to the dead? Look in your mirror."

I hesitated, frightened of what I would see.

Then, driven more by curiosity than fear, I got up off my bed and went to sit in front of my dressing table, holding my breath as I looked in the mirror. At first, my own reflection greeted me, but, the more I stared, the more my facial features started blurring, transforming themselves into different characteristics.

This was too much. I spun around in my seat and faced the opposite wall, not daring to look in the mirror.

"Do not dismiss me. You started this process yourself when you attended the spiritual meeting the other night. You invited *me* into *your* life, not the other way around."

"There's been some sort of mistake. I agree, I was looking for someone to help me – but the person I wanted to speak to was my father. I don't know how you got here instead, or why, and I'm sorry for inconveniencing you, but please just go."

"But you *must* speak to me in order to get through to your father."

"Why? You're not real. You're a hallucination."

"Lindy, you know that's not the truth. Do you really want to risk never speaking to him by sending me away? All I am asking for is one chance to prove who I am. If you look at me and decide that I am unreal, I will not trouble you again. Now, please – turn around!"

Slowly, I turned back, leaving it till the last minute to look up at the mirror. Facing me was a pretty girl, around my age, with long, fair hair, which lay in soft curls down her back. Her blue eyes shone in an ethereal way and her full lips formed a friendly smile.

The girl from the portrait I drew.

She sensed my shock. "Your drawing is a very good likeness of me.

"My name is Esmerelda Pennyworth, but you can call me Esme," she continued. "I am the girl in the newspaper article you have just read. The girl with the initial E that the medium mentioned. The girl who lived in your old house and slept in your bedroom."

"Your last name is Pennyworth?" I was incredulous.

"Yes. As you will have correctly surmised, you and I are related on your father's side."

"How old are you?"

"Only seventeen. Well, that was the age I reached when I died."

"That makes us the same age!"

"Exactly. There is a good reason why you and I have been

91

brought together. We're both victims of the Pennyworth curse, which afflicts all fathers and daughters in the family line and prevents them from communicating with each other when either or both have passed into the afterlife."

"Only fathers and daughters?"

"Yes. You are the first daughter to be born of a Pennyworth male since me, so the responsibility falls on your shoulders to relieve us of this burden. I need your help, Lindy, so that we can both speak to our fathers once again."

"Why does it only affect fathers and daughters?"

"Because that is the nature of this curse."

"This is ridiculous! Curses aren't real."

"Yes, they are. Look at Snow White, Sleeping Beauty—"

"They're fairy tales!"

"In which curses were broken by a true love's kiss."

I grimaced. "I have to kiss someone?"

She laughed. "I'm afraid not. Our situation is much less romantic."

We both sat and stared at each other. I really didn't know what to think or say, and Esme must have read my mind because she pleaded with me, "You're not having a breakdown. Please believe me."

"I don't know what to believe! I don't know what is real any more and what isn't."

I put my head in my hands and tried to calm my breathing, tried to resist the urge to pull.

"The newspaper article is real, isn't it?"

"I suppose."

"Will you at least listen to what I have to say?"

"Sure," I said in resignation.

After all, with my sanity on a knife-edge, what did I have to lose?

17.
THE PENNYWORTH CURSE

"It all happened as the newspaper article said," explained Esme. "I died from cholera and I was entirely responsible for being infected by the disease. I disobeyed my parents and ventured outside the house – had I stayed inside, as instructed, I would not have been exposed. My poor father held himself responsible because he could not cure me. He was a great physician, not God!

"After I passed into the afterlife, I could see that he was torturing himself for what had happened to me. I desperately wanted to talk to him – to tell him that he was in no way to blame. I tried to communicate with him psychically but, being a man of logic, there was no way of establishing contact with him, especially in his distress, so I had to consider other means.

"I picked up a strong spiritual wave from a lady in Oxford who was reaching out to the spirit world. It was at this point that I encountered the medium, Freeda Madill.

"I visited her in a dream one night. I told her of my predicament and begged her to visit my father. She was reluctant at first but then she agreed and asked me for a piece of information that would prove that she was genuine – in case Father did not believe her. I advised her to quote my favourite song – 'Queen Rose of the Rosebud Garden' – as evidence that she had spoken to me."

"I heard someone singing that song the other night! Was it you?" I asked.

"Yes. I love that song because Father would sing it with me and call me his 'Queen Rose'."

"So, what happened? Did Freeda do what you asked her to?"

"Yes, she was true to her word. She visited Father the day after I had approached her to give him the message. But Father was so distraught that he flew into a rage, thinking that Freeda had read about my death in the newspapers and had planned to use her reputation as a talented medium to make money from his grief."

"But what about the song? That should have been proof enough that she was genuine?"

"Unfortunately not. It was much-loved in those days and many people knew the words. I should have thought of something more distinctive, but I doubt that would have made a difference. Father was trapped in a state of mental anguish and was unreachable by anyone – living or dead."

"What did he do?"

"Banished her from the house and then reported her to the police. They warned Freeda to stay away or face prosecution."

"And did she?"

"She did not turn up in person again but she did write to my father. She reiterated what she had said before and repeated that she did not expect payment if he would like her to try to establish a psychic connection with me."

"That sounds reasonable. He could hardly have accused her of profiteering if she offered to do it for free."

She shook her head. "I regret to say, Father failed to see it that way. Instead, he saw the letter as further proof that Freeda would not leave him alone and made it his personal mission to destroy her. He took the letter to the police, who issued her with a final warning. Then he went to the newspaper and revealed how Freeda was trying to profit from his tragic situation."

"Didn't they try to get her side of the story?"

"No. My father was a man of high standing in society – they would naturally have taken his word over hers, as would the police."

"What happened next?"

"Soon, his accusations of fraud spread and Freeda's regular clients stopped seeing her. No one wanted to be tainted by association with her name. She lost her income, her house and everything else in her life. She was cast on to the streets and lived her last days in the Debtors' Tower of the prison, where she succumbed to tuberculosis."

"That's awful," I said. "She died in poverty and pain and all she was trying to do was help you. Why was your father so vengeful? She hadn't even asked him for any money."

"His intentions were good, Lindy," Esme said defensively, "but his instincts were wrong. He did not want others to be duped. All this was happening at a time when he was suffering from exhaustion and immense grief."

She stopped and wiped a couple of tears away. "I feel dreadful that I was responsible for this miserable chain of events."

I was speechless. This sounded like a plot from a soap opera, yet it was a story about my own ancestors in my own house. But I still didn't understand how all that could affect me and my family.

"When Freeda died," Esme continued, "her son, Linwood, put a curse on our family – the Pennyworth Curse – banishing my father to a state of limbo, where he cannot communicate with the living or the dead. Linwood set this curse so that any father figure in our family, who acts in a similarly dishonourable way, would suffer the same fate . . ." She paused, before adding hesitantly, "Your father is there, too, Lindy."

My blood ran cold. "My father? But he did nothing wrong!"

"He must have done something," she replied quietly.

"No! He slapped me across the face the night before he died but that's because I came home from a party drunk. If anything, it was *my* fault."

"The curse is very specific about this—"

"What do you know?" I interrupted, my heart pounding. "There's something you're not telling me, isn't there?"

"Please, trust me, Lindy. I cannot speak any more of this at this time. We must move on, quickly, or neither of us will ever speak to our fathers and they will be trapped forever."

"Why should I trust you? I've hardly asked you for much – just some proof—"

"You will have to ask yourself whether you can afford not to trust me. Can you? For, as I see it, I am the only way you have of speaking to your father at the current moment in time. Turn me away, and you will banish all hope of ever getting through to him in the afterlife."

She'd become fainter in the mirror, her face flickered like a picture on a faulty TV that was losing signal. "Lindy, concentrate!"

"OK, OK! Just tell me what I need to do."

She nodded, or at least I thought she did – she was becoming even more indistinct.

"After Freeda's death, Linwood visited one of her closest friends – a witch – to learn how to put a curse on our family. She instructed him to fetch an item from our house upon which she could put a spell. Linwood waited until my father was out one day and broke in, stealing—"

"A picture frame!" I concluded triumphantly.

"The witch removed the portrait from the inside. She tore it into two pieces – one containing my father, and the other my mother and me. She cast a spell on the two pieces of the photograph and instructed Linwood to hide them in two separate places that were related to the people in this story. Once hidden, he then had to break into the house again and hide the frame from my father."

"And he hid it under the floorboards in the attic," I finished for her.

"Precisely. Now, in order for the curse to be broken, the two parts of the photograph must be reunited and placed again inside the picture frame before being taken to a final destination."

"But how do I know where to find the two pieces of the photograph?"

The image in the mirror became distorted again and Esme's movements blurred.

"This is where I can help you. For Linwood to put the spell into action, he had to compose riddles that, once solved, gave the location of each piece. I can give you the riddles, but I cannot help you in any other way or else the curse will become permanent."

"Does the curse also apply to you and your mother?"

"No. Mother did nothing to hurt anyone and therefore was saved from the curse. That is why we are together in the photograph and Father has been separated from us."

"What does your mother say about all of this?"

"She says nothing." Esme's voice had an emotional edge, as if she were fighting back tears. "She has been unable to speak since the day she died."

"But then the curse must apply to her, too."

"It doesn't. I don't know why she cannot speak, unless the trauma of my death proved too much for her. She was always of a delicate constitution. I am hoping that when she and I are reunited with Father, it will help her to talk again."

This seemed a little strange to me, but then again, what part of this entire affair wasn't strange?

"Right. Let me write down the riddles."

I got up and grabbed a pen and paper from my bag, but when I returned to my dressing table, Esme had disappeared from the mirror. I called her name and pressed my hand against the glass, but there was no reply. The room was silent. Esme had gone, taking the first riddle with her.

18.
RED FLAGS

Had I dreamt the whole thing?

Downstairs, I found Mum bustling around the house, readying it for the estate agent. My stomach twisted at the thought of anyone else living in my home, but I pretended to be calm. I had to remain on her good side if I stood any chance of persuading her not to sell.

"Oh, good, you're up," she said, taking in my creased joggers and jumper with a slight grimace. "I've made you a doctor's appointment for one o'clock so you'll need to leave soon. Will you be all right going on your own? I have the estate agent coming in an hour."

I clenched my fists in my pockets and nodded.

"Don't forget to tell him about your mood swings these last few days," she carried on, oblivious. "You know, the crying and the violence."

Violence?

Frustration bubbled in my stomach. I'd thrown a plate, not hacked someone to death with an axe.

"Lindy?"

"All right."

"Be honest with him, OK? Tell him how you're behaving. I am sure he'll agree that your reactions are extreme. We need to get you back to the old Lindy."

"I'd better head off," I said, going into the hallway and twisting my hair into two plaits, using soft bands to hold them in place. After I put on my beanie to hide the bald patches, I looked pretty normal.

"Can you pick up some milk on the way home?" Mum asked as she joined me in the hallway. "Here's a tenner – pick up a pizza or something for dinner, as well. I won't have time to make anything tonight."

I nodded and pushed the note into the pocket of my joggers. "Have you got your phone?"

Damn. I'd forgotten all about that. I ran upstairs and grabbed my phone from my dressing table. I turned it on and saw that I was in luck – there was still plenty of battery life, plus a notification that I had a new direct message.

Once I was out of view of the house, I stopped walking and opened up Instagram. Tom had been busy sending me messages in my absence.

> Hi Lindy! Thanks for accepting me. 😊 Can we meet up sometime?

Pretty normal, I decided. I scrolled to the next message, sent half an hour later.

> Hi there – just checking you got this. Phone's been acting up . . .

And then the final one, an hour after that.

> Everything OK? Hope you haven't changed your mind. Here's my number if you prefer to reach me off Instagram.

I stared at the numbers written below and leant against a low wall. Should I change my mind? He seemed a little desperate.

A new message popped up, this one from Immy.

> Tom's just requested to follow me! 😬

> He's sent me one too.

> You going to accept it?

> Yeah – that OK with you?

> Fine. Mrs Warwick's spied my phone. Gotta go. 🏃

I carried on down the road towards the GP's surgery, wondering what to do. If Tom had been in touch with Immy then surely she wouldn't mind if I called him to talk about common interests. I stopped in a bus shelter and dialled.

"Hello?"

"Hi, Tom. It's Lindy. From the other night," I added unnecessarily.

"Hi!" His eager reply nearly deafened me. "I was hoping you'd call. I was worried you hadn't got my messages."

"Yeah, sorry about that. I've been a bit . . . busy at home. Do you still want to meet up?"

"Definitely. When can you make it?"

I hadn't thought that far ahead. "Uh, well, I'm free around now but I guess you're not—"

"Sure I am. I'm home-schooled and Mum's away at a conference today."

"Oh. Right. Uh, where should we meet?"

"Cafe Caffeine in Cornmarket? I can be there in fifteen minutes."

We hung up and I continued walking towards the city centre, filled with both excitement and doubt. Finally, I could speak to someone my own age about how I was feeling, which would be a relief. On the other hand, something felt a little odd about how eager Tom had been to communicate once I'd requested him back. Maybe he was just lonely?

I called the GP's surgery to cancel my appointment. The last thing I needed was for them to call home to ask where I was – then I'd be in even bigger trouble. I could reschedule the appointment for another time – it was unlikely that the doctor would say anything except to keep taking the tablets, anyway.

The coffee shop queue was nearly out of the door with university students and tourists buying their lunchtime coffee while glued to their phones. I couldn't see Tom anywhere, so I joined the back of the line, wishing we'd arranged to meet elsewhere. Here was too public – too crowded – and my scalp itched under my beanie. My usual attempts to discretely rub it through the wool weren't helping and I could feel panic rising inside of me. I knew I had to get out of there. Head down, I walked towards the door but felt a hand grab my upper arm.

"Lindy! I didn't know you'd arrived; I didn't see you in the queue."

I tried a smile, but I was breathing too fast and felt like the walls were closing in on me.

He frowned at me – concern etched on his face. "Are you all right?"

I shook my head. "Can we go somewhere quieter? It's really busy in there and I can't face it."

"No problem." He took my elbow and gently steered me out of the café and down the street. "Let's keep walking, OK? I know a good place and by the time we get there, hopefully you'll be feeling better."

19.
CAKES AND
CONFESSIONS

We walked down the High Street, his hand now in between my shoulders, as I tried to calm my breathing. I was grateful that he'd taken control of the situation so I could just follow him, rather than debate where we should go. The entire time, though, my mind was full of questions: *Had I taken my medication? Had I eaten breakfast? Was this a panic attack or just side effects of the tablets? Was I ever going to feel normal again?*

Soon we reached the Church of St Mary the Virgin, and Tom slowed his pace.

"Is this where we're going?" I asked. It seemed a strange alternative to a coffee shop.

He laughed. "Don't sound so surprised – I'm not taking you here to pray. It has a great café which is normally quiet. I usually come here when Mum's away on business. I like to sit and do my work with other people around."

I wanted to ask him how often his mother left him on his own, but it seemed a little personal since I'd only just met him.

"Do you want to sit outside?" he asked. "It's warm enough."

I nodded, and he went inside to get our drinks while I sat down at a wooden table near the church wall. The top of the Radcliffe Camera rose above the hedge, the golden Cotswold stone and contrasting silver of its upper levels gleaming in the sunlight. Bicycles rattled as they bumped along the cobbled road and I could hear people calling out greetings to each other as they made their way to wherever they were going. I felt like I was sitting in a typical Oxford postcard.

Tom emerged a few minutes later carrying a tray piled high with cakes.

"Hungry?" I stared at the food in awe.

"I'm hoping you'll help me out with some of this. Here," he said, putting the tray down and handing me a teacake. "These are the best you'll find in the city, honest."

My stomach rumbled and I sank my teeth into the butter-laden bun. I groaned with pleasure at the competing tastes of salt, sugar, cinnamon and raisins.

"Told you." He grinned.

With a napkin, I wiped a thin trail of butter from my chin. "I didn't realise how hungry I was."

"It might have been why you felt funny earlier," he suggested, before tucking into his own teacake. "What happened to your face?"

"My face?" I frowned in bemusement.

"You've got a scratch across it."

I'd forgotten about that. "My cat went weird on me – he won't come anywhere near my room since the church incident."

He raised his eyebrows. "That *is* strange. You know that

animals are very sensitive to the paranormal, right?"

My mouthful of cake became a lump in my throat. Should I tell him about Esme? Perhaps it was too soon. Would he think I was crazy?

He must have sensed that I was uncomfortable because he changed the subject.

"I'm glad you got in touch. I was worried you wouldn't when I didn't hear from you in a while."

"It wasn't that long," I said, then softened my tone. "I don't check my phone a lot at the moment. There doesn't seem much point as I only really keep in touch with Immy."

"Immy seems like such a character," he chuckled. "I bet she's not afraid of anyone or anything."

"She's fearless," I agreed, thinking that this was an excellent opportunity to sing her praises to him. "She's always been like that; she's always had my back, even when I probably didn't deserve it."

"I wish I had a friend like that, but people think I'm strange. I must come across wrong." He gave a small laugh. "One of the many advantages of being home-schooled – you cultivate peculiarity."

"How long have you been taught at home?" I asked, finishing off the teacake.

"Since I was old enough to start school." He sipped his tea. "Mum was too scared to let me out of her sight after what happened with my dad."

"What did happen to him?" I asked, before hurriedly adding, "Unless you'd rather not talk about it."

"He died in a hit-and-run accident when we lived in London. A car came racing round the corner just as we started to cross the road. He managed to push me away just as it hit him."

I couldn't hide my horror. "Oh my God. Do you remember seeing that?"

He nodded. "Every detail. I wish I could get it out of my head, but I can't."

"Did they ever catch who did it?"

He shook his head. "No. The bastard got away with it. I was too traumatised to describe the car and the driver – I still can't. He died protecting me and I couldn't even help track down his killer."

Tom paused and picked up a muffin from the tray of food. He plucked out a monstrous blueberry, squeezing it between his thumb and forefinger till it bled. "So, that's why Mum's kept me at home as much as possible. Dad's life insurance meant she didn't have to go to work for a while and she chose to teach me from home instead of sending me to school. Now I'm older, she's started working as a freelancer again so she's home most of the time. But, luckily, she has meetings and conferences occasionally, and that is when I make the most of my freedom."

He suddenly looked up at me, grinned, and popped a piece of muffin into his mouth.

"But you came to our college, didn't you?" I asked. "Immy said she was sure she'd seen you at St Boniface's last year."

The smile weakened and he dropped his gaze to the table, brushing off some crumbs. "Yeah. I finally convinced Mum to let me go to sixth form – I said that it would be best for my A-levels – but it didn't go very well; personally or academically. I was way out of touch with everyone. I didn't really get how people my age talked or behaved. I was kind of like an adult stuck in a teen's body; no one wanted to hang out with me. So, I left. The sad thing is that I prefer being taught at home now –

she gets in tutors for me. I just don't know how to act in a school environment."

"But you'll be going to university soon, won't you?" I pointed out. "And then everyone's new again anyway, so it won't matter."

He shrugged. "Don't know if I want to go yet. There's more to life than studying and if I leave uni with loads of debt and no job to go into, it hardly seems worth it. There's always the option to go later if I change my mind. I think I might prefer to travel."

The more I listened to Tom, the more I liked him. It was such a relief to talk to someone else who felt unsure of their place in the world. Yet on the other hand, he gave out confident vibes that suggested he no longer cared what other people thought about him and his choices. I wished I could reach that level of self-assurance.

"So, what about you?" Tom asked. "Are you taught at home or are you just skiving today?"

"I'm sort of both," I replied. "I've been signed off college for a while because I was finding it too hard after Dad died. Everyone stopped talking to me because they didn't know what to say. I felt like I had an infectious disease because people would walk the other way whenever they saw me coming. Immy stood by me, of course, but I couldn't take everyone else's whispering and gossip."

Especially when the bald patches started showing.

I debated whether to tell him about the hair-pulling. Perhaps it was still too early; it might scare him away . . .

"So, will you stay at home from now on then? Or are you planning on going back?"

"I dunno. At the moment, I can't see myself going back. But my mum wants me to get back to reality. She thinks it's unhealthy, me staying at home all the time."

"So, your mum hasn't become overprotective since your dad's death?"

"No. If anything, she wants us to carry on as if nothing has happened. She has no time for grief. She thinks it's self-indulgent."

Tom laughed. "We should get our parents together. They sound like a perfect match – your mother could teach mine how to let go of the apron strings, and mine could teach yours how to . . ." He paused, thinking.

"Behave like her husband's died?" I suggested.

Tom frowned. "Everyone has different ways of coping with grief. Maybe she carries on like she does to avoid feeling anything."

"These days, I'm wondering whether she really has a heart."

We sat in silence for a while. A sparrow hopped on to the table and eyed up the muffin that Tom was absentmindedly crumbling. Tom gently pushed the plate towards the bird, and we watched it take a few tentative tastes of our leftovers. Another sparrow came along and the two sat silently, mirroring the tension between Tom and me. Laughter floated over from a couple of tables away where two women were having coffee and a gossip, their conversation obviously more cheerful than ours.

"Shall we head off?" Tom suggested. "I could do with some exercise after that carb-fest."

Leaving the sparrows to our crumbs, we walked into Radcliffe Square, where tourists gathered in groups wearing Oxford University sweatshirts and wielding selfie sticks. We skirted around them and walked towards the Bridge of Sighs, trying to avoid the cyclists tearing down the way. Tom seemed lost in his thoughts, his usually open face furrowed and every so often I caught the scent of violets in the breeze.

"So, how did you get interested in psychic stuff?" I asked, trying to lighten the mood.

"Every day, since that car hit Dad, I've replayed what happened in my mind. I wanted to see and hear him again, to replace that terrible image of his broken body on the road with something good. I thought that if I could contact him again, through a medium, I could gain some peace from what happened."

"I know what you mean," I said. "I went for the same reasons."

"But at least *you* didn't cause your father's death," Tom said.

"Neither did you. And you didn't have a fight with your father on the day he died," I shot back. "My dad was probably distracted by the horrible things I said to him. At least your father knew you loved him."

I stopped walking and Tom paused too.

"Sorry – I didn't mean to upset you," he said, then smiled. "Don't you think it's stupid that we're both fighting over who should feel the guiltiest? It's a bit of a morbid competition."

I half-laughed and swiped a few stray tears off my face.

A foreign couple approached us. Through a mixture of mime and the odd understandable word, we worked out that they wanted us to take a photo of them in front of the Bridge of Sighs. Tom did the honours and, when he finished, we carried on walking down the road in silence, past Wadham and Trinity Colleges with their perfectly manicured lawns. Leaves scattered like confetti, dropping a crunchy, golden carpet at our feet.

At Keble College, we crossed the road to get into the University Parks and I asked, "So, have you ever received a message from your dad?"

Tom zipped up his jacket as the wind picked up. "No, he's never come through to me. I keep telling myself to stop trying all this paranormal stuff, but I can't – it's like I'm addicted. I figure that he'll have to appear some time soon. Law of averages, right?"

"I guess some people would say that there are no such things as ghosts so they'll never come to us anyway, regardless of averages," I replied. "But that's their opinion – I know what I believe."

We carried on walking and I wondered again whether or not to tell him about Esme. There was no reason not to – after all, he believed in all this psychic communication too and wouldn't think me delusional. But something held me back. I still didn't know him that well, and my conversation with Esme felt private. I wasn't even sure if I'd tell Immy.

We did a circuit of the Parks, chatting about more normal, everyday stuff like college subjects, films and music, before I felt my phone vibrate. I checked it and swore – it was Mum, asking where I was. I'd been out for over two hours without realising it.

"I'm really sorry, Tom – I've got to get back." I turned around and started jogging in the opposite direction.

"Wait!" he called, coming after me. "What's the rush?"

"My mum. She doesn't know I've come to meet you. I had a doctor's appointment, but I cancelled it. I've been out way too long for that. I hope she didn't call the practice to see where I was."

"Just tell her that there was a wait. Our doctors are always running late with emergencies."

"Still, I've got to get back. She's been showing an estate agent around our house today and I want to know what she's doing next."

"You're not moving away, are you?" he asked, with a shocked expression that I didn't understand. We'd only just met – surely it made no difference to him where I went.

"Hopefully not, but I've got to get back now to check. I don't trust her."

We reached the main entrance to the Parks. "I'm going to cut through the Lamb and Flag passage, across to Jericho," I told him, "so I'll say goodbye here. Thanks for the tea and cakes."

"Can we meet again?" Tom asked, his eyes like a hopeful puppy.

"Sure!" I called as I hurried away. "Send me another message."

20.
HEART OF JERICHO

I put the milk and the pizzas in the fridge and gave Mum the change. At least I remembered to do all that in my rush to get back.

"Where did you go after the doctor's?" she asked. "You were ages."

She obviously hadn't called them, thank goodness. I decided to use Tom's excuse.

"Well, the doctor was running really late – some sort of emergency. I was there for at least an hour. Then I just went for a little walk – it's so nice today. I kind of lost track of time."

"What did the doctor say? Did he put you on any other medication?"

"Nope." I grabbed an apple from the fruit bowl, noticing some strands of hair dangling off my my arm. Were they mine, or Esme's? I pulled them off and flicked them on the floor. "He said these things sometimes take a while to work and, as long as I didn't have suicidal thoughts, I should try it for a little longer."

"Maybe he has a point," Mum said after a short pause, and I nearly choked on my apple in surprise.

"Really?"

"Yes. You look different today, Lindy. You've got more colour in your cheeks and you look – dare I say – a bit more like your old self?"

"Must be the good weather," I replied. She was right, though. I did feel different. Not cured or anything, but the heaviness in my heart felt a little lighter.

Maybe it was the talk with Tom – actually being able to speak to someone about Dad without worrying about boring them or making them feel uncomfortable. But then I had a pang of guilt – Immy really liked him and there I was, going out for hours with him and talking to him like we'd known each other all our lives. Was she right? Did he like me, or was it just that we had something in common?

"Things went well here, too – with the estate agent," Mum said. "He has arranged a first viewing tomorrow at ten."

"Tomorrow?" I gasped. "But it hasn't even been advertised yet, has it?"

"He knows a couple who've wanted to move into this area for a little while and thinks our house will be perfect for them. We can find a different house to make a new start in, can't we?" She paused. "Lindy? Are you listening to me?"

Just when I was starting to feel better . . .

"Are you planning on moving just to another house or to another city?" I asked, as she poured the dregs of her morning coffee down the sink and rinsed out her mug.

"I thought we could stay in Oxford. It's better for when you go back to college. All your friends are there and moving during A-levels would be too disruptive."

"Thanks," I muttered, leaving the kitchen for the sanctuary of my room. After all, it wouldn't be mine for much longer.

I could tell Mum had been in there; everything was tidied away and straightened up. My bed was expertly made, the shelves were dust free and the windows were open, blasting fresh air into the room. Flowers sat in a vase on my windowsill and all the clothes I'd left on the floor had found their way into my chest of drawers or wardrobe.

The carpet was fluffier too – evidence that she'd hoovered.

The picture frame!

I'd hidden it under the beanbag that morning. Had she found it?

I yanked the beanbag up and heaved a huge sigh of relief. I was lucky – she'd just hoovered around it. The frame was just where, and how, I'd left it.

I dropped the beanbag back on to the frame again and lay on my bed, overwhelmingly tired from everything that had happened so far that day, coupled with the worry that was eating away inside that this house might not be my home any longer. When I was a child, Dad had told me that it had been in his family for years – since before my grandpa and his, too. Little did I know then that after my father's premature death, I would be speaking to the ghost of a distant relative. But that was another strange thing. Charles had left this house after Esme's death, so how had it passed on down the family line to us now?

Plugging in my headphones, I closed my eyes and listened to some music. I needed to shut the world out for a little while – both the real world and the afterlife.

I'm standing in a long, dark corridor that stretches so far ahead that I can't see an end. There are doors on both sides with identical handles. It's silent and still.

Am I in a hotel? An office building?

I turn around and the same scene plays behind me. It's like a never-ending road with no destination.

The temperature is neither cool nor warm. There is no smell, no breeze, no sounds from the other side of the doors. The ground under my feet is neither hard nor soft.

It's all non-descript; bland. Devoid of colour but not exactly bleak, either.

I have no memory of how I got here.

Am I in a hospital? Has Dr Greenwood sent me here to recover?

Did Mum hear me talking to Esme? Have they drugged me?

Why am I alone?

One of the doors opens ahead of me and I back away, frightened that someone will appear and try to restrain me or drag me off.

"Hello, Lindy. Welcome to my side."

It's Esme. She's in her pretty dress and looks the same as she did in the mirror.

"What is this place?" I whisper.

"We're beyond the grave."

"Heaven?"

She laughs, and gently shakes her head.

"Hell?"

"Neither. This is a holding area. The true afterlife cannot be entered by the living."

"So, why am I here?"

"This is a chance for us to get to know each other. Ask me anything you like about this place and I will answer."

"Why are there all these doors? Where do they go?"

"They're the entrances to the next step in the afterlife. Everyone has one they can go through."

"But how do you know which one is yours?"

She smiles. "You just know."

"But they're all identical. What if you choose the wrong one?"

"Then you will enter another person's afterlife."

"Is that dangerous?"

She considers this for a moment. "Not really. But what lies beyond that door will mean nothing to you. Your own door leads you to the world built from your memories when you were alive, so it's important to go through the right one. Fortunately, it's not hard to choose correctly."

"Is the rest of your family behind your door?"

"All except my father. He's . . . in another holding place. When you break the curse, he will join my mother and me."

She has too much confidence in me.

"What do you do – behind the door?" I ask.

"We exist. We travel. There isn't a room beyond the door – there's an entire world constructed from our experiences and dreams and desires. We can communicate with others we have known before, if they accept our invitations. It's just like being alive, only more . . . fluid."

"What is the point of dying, then?"

Esme thought about this briefly. "What is the point of living?"

"Lindy! Wake up!"

The endless corridor was gone and I was back in my room, staring blearily at Mum's figure framed by the doorway.

"Get up or you won't sleep tonight."

She turned on the light and I held my hand up to shade my eyes from the glare.

"What the . . . what on earth have you done?" Mum gasped, staring at the wall beside my bed.

"What? What are you talking about? I haven't—"

I stopped talking as soon as I realised . . . I was clutching a marker pen in my right hand. The lid was off and the ink had bled on to my skin, turning my palm black. I pushed myself up on to my left elbow and looked where my mother was staring.

Spidery letters were scrawled across the wall next to my bed. "What? I didn't do that!"

"Lindy – you've got a bloody marker pen in your hand and there's no one else in your room!"

She was looking at me with a mixture of fear and fury.

"But I've been asleep. I only woke up when you came into my room."

She obviously didn't believe that and pressed the palms of her hands against her eyes.

"Did you do this to try to stop me selling the house?"

"No! I promise you! I didn't—"

"It just seems like such a coincidence. Why would you start drawing on the walls otherwise? You didn't even do this as a child and yet, as soon as I am ready to start showing the house to potential buyers, you suddenly develop a new . . . I don't know what to call it . . . symptom? A hobby? What is this?"

I didn't know what to say.

"For goodness' sake, how are we going to get rid of this?" She ran her fingers through her short hair, so that each strand stood up as if in fear of what I had done. "You're going to have to figure out how to cover this up before tomorrow," she continued. "I can't have prospective buyers seeing this."

Muttering to herself, she stomped away, slamming the door behind her.

In panicked disbelief, I looked at the wall beside me. The handwriting wasn't even like my own, so how could I have done it? On the other hand, there was clearly no one else in my room, so who else could it have been?

When I read the words, it all suddenly made sense. I knew who the words had come from, even if *I* was responsible for writing them.

Beneath a gnarled and blackened tree,
With other bodies lyeth she,
Wrapped in cotton, swaddled so,
In the heart of Jericho.

21.
MATCHMAKER

This was Esme's first riddle, containing the location of the first piece of the photograph. It was just a shame that, in getting this, I'd given Mum – and myself – another reason to doubt my sanity.

I thought back to the dream. Esme had taken me there to convince me that all this was real. But was she real?

I couldn't keep going round in circles about this. The newspaper cutting existed, as did the picture frame. If I could solve the riddle and find the first missing piece of the photo, then I could prove to myself that I wasn't imagining all this.

I've never prided myself on my riddle-solving ability, but this one didn't look too difficult. Bodies suggested a graveyard, and the dream I had the other night came flooding back – people watching a mass burial from a distance, corpses wrapped in white shrouds, a man crying . . .

There was only one cemetery in Jericho: St Sepulchre's. A Google search brought up its own website. There were pages linking to its history, notable burials, maps . . . and an A-Z archive.

My hope peaked. This might be easier than I'd thought. I clicked on the "P" section and started scrolling down, keeping my eye out for Pennyworth.

Nothing.

I tried searching for 'cholera' and found some useful historical information that confirmed what I already knew about the disease from the old newspaper article. The city's third cholera epidemic started in Walton Street – where St Sepulchre's was located – and there were at least two people buried in the cemetery who died from the disease with their own burial plots and headstones. But there was no mention of a mass grave, nor of the Pennyworth name.

So, where was this lost grave in St Sepulchre's? The riddle gave some ideas – *beneath a gnarled and blackened tree.* I supposed I was going to have to trust my luck.

My phone vibrated, making me jump. There was a message from Tom.

Was your mum mad?

No. She was too busy talking about the estate agent. 💀

Oh. How did it go?

Depends on your point of view.

A couple already want a viewing.

Bummer. 😟

Look, can we meet again?

I hesitated. I liked Tom, but he seemed a little persistent.

On the other hand, it would be good to have someone else with me at St Sepulchre's, just in case there were any undesirables hanging around the graves.

But what about Immy? Her reaction at the café the other night showed that she wouldn't be very happy if I met with Tom again so soon, before she'd had a chance.

Lindy? You still there?

Can you meet me tomorrow?

Yes! What's the plan?

Grave-hunting at St Sepulchre's Cemetery.

Spooky, cool. 🪦

Any grave in particular?

I'll tell you more tomorrow. Meet me there at 9:30?

Sound.

I'd have to tell Immy – emphasise that I just wanted him there for extra safety and that I had no intention to steal him away.

My phone vibrated again: Immy this time.

Hey, finally out of college.
What are you doing?

Not much. You?

French homework 😔 What
happened with the estate
agent?

He's bringing someone to see
the house tomorrow.

No way!!! That soon?

Yep. 💀

Didn't you try to do something
to put him off?

💀

Fair enough.

What did you do while he
measured your floorboards?

I had a Dr's appointment but I
skived and met with Tom
instead.

What?

I know. But I needed to get
out and he was around and I
talked you up, I promise.

123

Did he say anything about me?

That I was lucky to have you in my corner. 💪

Wow, what a compliment. I sound like a guard dog.

He really thinks you're great – honest.

Yeah, right. 😜

Look, do you think I should ask him out or not?

Dunno. Why don't I arrange to meet him again and sound him out on it?

No! He'll think that you're after him!

Hardly.

I want some company tomorrow when I go to St Sepulchre's Cemetery to look for a grave.

?!?!?!

Let me call you. This is too hard to do by message.

In the end, Immy insisted on joining Tom and me.

"How are you going to get out of college?" I asked.

"I'll call in to say I have an orthodontist appointment and will be in later," she replied. "That's the good side of having braces – no one gets suspicious if you have lots of appointments."

"You've bunked off college before for that reason?"

"Yeah, but I'm careful. I spread the fake appointments out so they're every couple of months."

I was relieved she was coming – Immy always seemed so strong and that was one of the many things that I admired about her. She never panicked, whereas I was always terrified of what might happen. While I froze in fear, she walked straight into whatever trouble was facing her. Any strangers hanging around the graves tomorrow better be careful.

By ten o'clock that evening, I was ready for bed. It had been a tiring day and the meds were still making me drowsy. Before I turned the light out, I covered the writing on the wall with a poster. As I lay in the darkness, my mind kept wandering to the cholera pit and the thought of Esme dumped in there with all the other bodies. It must have been awful for Charles – leaving his daughter slung in a heap and covered in quicklime to speed up the decaying process. At least Dad had been cremated and his ashes buried in a peaceful memorial garden.

Thoughts of his funeral resurfaced. It was at St Nicholas's

Church in Old Marston, where Dad had been baptised forty-two years earlier. His parents were regular churchgoers and were disappointed when Dad married Mum – an atheist. They believed that she would lead him off the spiritual path, and they all fell out for a while when my parents refused to have me baptised or confirmed.

They made an uneasy truce over the years, but there was a strained atmosphere each time we met up. When Dad died, as a peace offering, Mum suggested that we bury his ashes in the church's memorial garden, next to his father's. Gramps had passed just a year before.

I couldn't speak or do a reading at the funeral. I felt bad about that, but I couldn't trust myself not to lose it. Mum didn't want to say anything either, so she asked Dad's brother to say some words and got a couple of old university friends to do readings.

At the wake, I managed to avoid people most of the time by frequent and long trips to the toilet, when I had first discovered that a quick pull on a strand of hair would temporarily quell the pain surging inside of me. I didn't know what was worse at that moment in time: the hard realisation of Dad's death or the sympathetic, pity-filled glances people shot my way when they saw me. Those awful smiles that flatten the lips and turn down slightly at the ends – the ones made when you don't know what other facial expression to pull.

Each week, I cycled up to the memorial garden to spend half an hour reading aloud from the book of nonsense poetry Dad and I used to read together – usually our favourites by Edward Lear or Spike Milligan. I liked the garden because it was quiet and well kept, and I didn't have to worry about stepping on anyone like I do in graveyards. I usually took along stuff that he liked – marbles, Lego – things we used to play with when I was younger.

I miss him so much . . .

I squeezed Dad's watch in my hand and fell asleep, hoping that tomorrow would bring me one step closer to being near him again – even if it was a brief glimpse or a stolen word. I had to make things right.

22.
INCORPOREAL

I'm at the edge of the deep pit again, surrounded by mounds of freshly dug earth. Worms wriggle, desperately trying to return to their homes underneath the surface.

The handkerchief-wearing gravediggers move out from under the shelter of a tree; their breath appears in small clouds as they blow on their stiff, muddied hands to warm them up. They approach the pit again, keeping their heads down as rain runs in steady rivulets off the peaks of their caps. They can hear the muffled sobs of the mourners watching from a distance but pay no attention to them. They're used to grief – immune to it now. This is just another day, another grave, albeit a massive one – harder to dig, especially with the soil threatening to slide straight back into the hole they have created under the weight of the rainwater.

I leap out of the way and apologise as one of the gravediggers walks up to me. He walks through me. I am not only invisible – I'm incorporeal.

There is a sudden and intense scent of violets as two diggers pick up a body wrapped in a white sheet, knotted at the top of the head and ankles, and carry it towards the pit. With a mighty swing, they throw the body into the pit and it slides around a little on the slick earth before folding in on itself. One of the onlookers wails as the diggers shovel quicklime on to it. The process repeats again and again until five corpses are stacked on top of each other. Then the diggers start filling in the grave with the mounds of earth around me, working steadily and silently.

The onlookers melt away, but one man remains, his face ashen against the darkness of the yews behind him.

"Wait!"

The man is moving forward, stumbling along the soft ground, muddying his expensive shoes and formal trousers. One of the gravediggers swears and throws down his shovel, running towards the man with his hands up.

"Stay back! It ain't safe!"

"Please! My daughter's in there—" His voice becomes lost in the wind and pouring rain.

"Sorry, guv, but the cholera—"

"I know about the cholera! I'm a doctor – I . . ." he breaks off and starts sobbing. "I should have saved her."

"It ain't your fault. It's in God's hands."

The man is desperately digging around in his pockets for something and I wonder if he's going to offer the gravediggers a bribe. But what would he want to do that for? What would he want in return? It's too late to pull his daughter's body out of the grave – it would already be decomposing.

"Look, sir, you've got to move away." The gravedigger is becoming impatient. "We've orders to bury the victims quick to prevent further infection. If you don't move . . . Well, let's say, I'll have to make you – and I don't want to do that after all you've been through."

The man nods then hands over a small object wrapped in an embroidered handkerchief.

"Can you put this in the grave? It is . . . it was . . . her favourite doll. I want her to have it – seeing as she's in there with all the others; no grave to call her own—" His voice catches in a sudden sob.

"This should have been confiscated with all her other belongings!" The digger's eyes flash with anger, then soften. He shakes his head. "No matter now. It'll go in the grave with her, yes. But make sure you ain't got no more stuff like this lying around or I'll be digging your pit next."

"It would be a blessed relief," the man whispers, as the gravedigger strides back to his workmates and tosses the doll into the pit, muttering something as he picks up his shovel and starts his job again.

23.
GRAVE SECRETS

I woke up early from the dream, shivering in sweat-soaked pyjamas, fingers tangled in my hair. I untwisted each of them carefully and then turned on my bedside lamp. It was only five o'clock and, after a failed attempt to drift off, I decided to get up, get ready and think of a reason why I needed to leave the house early today. I had to come up with something convincing enough to prove to Mum that I was making progress but not enough to send me back to college. I definitely was not ready for that yet.

In the end, she was so busy getting the house ready for the viewing that she nearly didn't notice me until I joined her in the kitchen, kitted out in my gym wear.

"Why are you wearing that?"

"I thought I'd try jogging," I said, taking a bite of my toast. "Exercise releases endorphins . . . I probably need some, huh?"

She raised her eyebrows. "What's happening to you?"

"Is this a bad thing?"

"No." She shook her head. "It's great – it's just so sudden."

"Does that mean you'll reconsider selling the house?"

Her smile dropped. "No. Oh, Lindy – this isn't just a show, is it? You're not just doing this to stop me from selling the house?"

"'Course not," I lied, through gritted teeth.

"Well, as long as we're clear," she said doubtfully. "I'd better run the Hoover around again. How tidy is your bedroom? Have you covered that writing?"

"I've put a poster on it and I've hardly touched the rest of the room since you went through it yesterday."

"I guess it will have to do. It is a teenager's room, after all."

She was no longer talking to me as she grabbed bleach from under the sink and headed out of the kitchen. "I'll just give the loos another scrub . . ."

I gulped down the rest of my orange juice and put my plate in the dishwasher before heading upstairs to hide the picture frame somewhere else. I didn't want to run the risk of her finding it today, should she decide to hoover under the beanbag. Yesterday was a lucky escape, after all. Briefly, I toyed with the idea of taking the frame with me but decided it was too large and bulky to carry round all day, so I put it away in the wardrobe, under some books and teddies. She wouldn't go in there – it was out of sight. Grabbing my rucksack, I bounded down the stairs, hoping she wouldn't ask why I was taking it on my run. I needn't have worried – she barely responded as I called goodbye from the hall and hurried on my way.

I saw Tom before I spotted St Sepulchre's Cemetery. He was glancing up and down the street and his eyes lit up when he caught sight of me as I rounded the corner on to Walton Street. I was glad that he'd arrived before I did because I probably would have missed the entrance otherwise, hidden as it was down a narrow lane between two shops.

"Good day for graveyards, isn't it?" Tom asked, looking up at the leaden sky as the heavens opened. "Ready to go in?"

"As soon as Immy gets here."

Tom raised his eyebrows. "Oh, Immy's coming? I didn't think she believed in this stuff."

"She doesn't, but she's curious."

He nodded. "I've got to admit, I am too. What are you looking for, exactly?"

I couldn't keep him in the dark any longer about what was happening, especially now Immy knew, so I told him everything – from discovering the picture frame in the attic to the cryptic clues Esme was giving me. His eyes grew wide as he listened, but he didn't interrupt, just nodded occasionally. When I finished, he stated, "Wow. This is incredible. Have you ever experienced anything like this before?"

I shook my head. "Never. I spent ages trying to contact Dad and nothing happened – it's just Esme driving this, not me." I sighed. "Trust my family to be cursed in the afterlife."

"That writing on the wall is interesting, too. It sounds like you've done something called automatic writing."

He must have caught my confused expression because he chuckled and explained.

"It's when ghosts or spirits use humans as conduits to write down messages."

"Really? This is something that's happened before?"

"If you believe what they say in books about the paranormal. Sir Arthur Conan Doyle even wrote about it – he said his wife wrote fifteen pages of messages from Harry Houdini's mother under the influence of automatic writing. Though Houdini later discredited it," he added, with a shrug.

"Well, whatever it is, I need to find out how to get permanent marker pen off a wall sooner rather than later."

Five minutes later and I was getting antsy. Where was Immy? She was usually annoyingly punctual, but it was already nearly quarter to ten and she still wasn't here. I was just about to pull out my phone when I saw her speeding around the corner, her dark, curly hair bouncing in time with her feet.

"Sorry," she panted. "My dad insisted on dropping me off at college today, would you believe it? The one bloody day I didn't want him to. I had to wait till he'd driven away and then run back here." She coughed, then looked at Tom and her cheeks darkened. "Hi, Tom."

He smiled. "Good to see you, Immy. Ready to start?"

She nodded, then took a puff on her inhaler. I'd never seen Immy behave so weirdly around a boy before, and nothing had ever stopped her talking. She'd changed from a fierce Rottweiler to a shy puppy over the course of a 'good to see you'.

After passing under the Victorian archway into the graveyard proper, we found ourselves in a sea of crooked graves, with headstones distorted by age and weather. Some looked like people with their backs turned to us, others like miniature houses of the dead. The main pathway into the graveyard – the 'Avenue of Yew Trees' as the map at the entrance described it – was the only sign of order in an otherwise chaotic landscape. It was beautiful but confusing. How would I find Esme's grave among all of this?

I looked around. It all appeared very different to my dream.

Modern housing developments backed on to the graveyard on two sides; a stone wall separating one from the other. At least the layout was still the same.

We kept walking down the Avenue, dodging drops of cold water that dripped from tired boughs. Birds darted across our path, trying to avoid the wet as they shrieked at one another.

"So, where is Esme's grave?" Tom pondered, as he tried to avoid all the overgrown nettles.

"I don't know. She was buried in a communal cholera pit so she doesn't have her own grave and the pit isn't marked on any of the graveyard plans as far as I could see."

Immy stopped and looked at me in disbelief. "You're kidding, right? How are we supposed to find her?"

"The riddle mentioned a gnarled, blackened tree. Look, I took a picture of the words before I left," I said, opening the photos on my phone to find the one I'd taken of the writing on the wall. "See?"

Immy looked at me and then at Tom.

"That's your writing on the wall, isn't it?" she asked.

"I told Lindy that this could be an example of automatic writing," Tom said. "When a living person writes down messages from the dead."

Immy frowned and looked again at Tom. I felt my cheeks burn.

"Let's just take a look around," Tom suggested.

We wandered down the central path for a few minutes, spotting lots of old and decrepit trees – none of them particularly blackened.

"Do you have any more clues?" Tom prompted. "Anything at all?"

As I considered this, my dream flashed through my mind. "I think we should head towards the bottom left first," I said.

We kicked our way through soggy leaves towards the back end of the graveyard. Tom laughed at me every time I tiptoed across graves and apologised to the dead underneath my feet. Headstones lay like broken limbs all over the place, making it hard to differentiate between a proper plot and general grassy area.

Soon our shoes were damp from the leaves and grass, and water had seeped up my tracksuit bottoms. The rain had become heavier and I regretted not bringing an umbrella. I stopped and surveyed the ground before me.

"I think the bodies were lying there . . ." I walked over to a clump of knee-high weeds, ". . . so the burial pit must be around here." I took five steps forwards and slightly west. There were no gravestones in this part so a pit there made sense in an otherwise crowded cemetery.

"Great," Immy sighed. "Now all we need is an industrial-sized lawnmower to clear this jungle."

24.
AUTOMATIC WRITING

We spent a couple of hours crawling through long, wet grass on our hands and knees, searching for anything that might look like it belonged to an old pit or grave, or some kind of marker, like a special stone. By midday, we were wet, cold and grumpy.

Immy groaned. "This can't be right. Surely we would have found the pit by now if you've remembered your dream right."

"I think we should take a break for some lunch," suggested Tom. "I can hardly feel my fingers."

Giving in, we trudged back up through the cemetery to the closest café for massive bowls of vegetable soup. Even our soaking clothes felt less uncomfortable with the warmth spreading through us.

"Aren't you going to take your beanie off, Lindy? It'll dry quicker that way," Tom suggested, breaking the silence.

Immy and I looked at each other. I hadn't confided about my trich to Tom and he'd not asked before why I always wore my hat out and about.

"Uh, well . . ."

"Lindy had a terrible haircut recently and she's feeling self-conscious about it," Immy jumped in. I shot her a grateful look.

"I'm sure it can't be all that bad," Tom reassured. "Anyway, you're among friends. We won't judge."

"I'm fine how I am, thanks," I mumbled, killing the conversation.

We ate the rest of our lunch in silence until we just had the dregs to mop up with thick crusts of bread.

"So," Tom said. "It's clear we need more information if we stand any chance of finding this photo."

"Or maybe it's time to agree that there is no grave and no Esme," Immy said quietly, avoiding eye contact.

"Are you suggesting that I imagined all this?" I demanded.

"Not necessarily imagined it," Immy replied. "Just, you know . . . well, you said you had a dream and sometimes dreams can seem real—"

"What about the picture frame?" Tom said. "Have you got it, Lindy? I'd love to see it."

I shook my head. "Sorry. It's bulky, so I didn't want to bring it out with me, especially in this rain. But I showed you the writing on the wall—"

"The writing that you wrote," Immy cut in.

"I'm going to the loo." I pushed my chair back and squeezed my way through the maze of occupied tables to the back of the café.

The loo was bone-numbingly cold and damp, and I winced as I sat down on the freezing toilet seat. I was shivering so much I couldn't even pee and I swore as I sat there uselessly, waiting. I removed my beanie, which was sodden from the rain, and ran my fingers through my damp hair, trying to curl a few strands around them.

Suddenly, I noticed water trickling down the cubicle's partitions – dripping on to the floor. Where was it coming from? There was no leak in the ceiling, no broken tap on the wall. The water seemed to be seeping through the swollen wood.

A sudden wave of dizziness swept over me and I leant forwards, putting my head between my knees to try to stop the vertigo. I hadn't taken my antidepressants today because I wanted a clear mind. Was this a side effect? I'd read that the withdrawal symptoms could be bad.

My ears started ringing, making the dizziness worse, so I covered them with my hands. I needed to get out of there and back into the warmth of the café, but the room was spinning violently and I couldn't even stand to pull my trousers back up. I shook my head, hoping that the ringing would at least stop, but it kept getting louder until I thought my head might burst with the noise.

Silence.

A tiny whisper.

"Don't look up – look down. The tree lies among the dead: a violet marks the grave."

"Lindy? *Lindy!* What's going on? Open the door. Now!"

Where was I?

I was sitting on a toilet, tracksuit bottoms around my ankles and my forehead resting on my knees.

"Lindy!"

The toilet of the café. How long had I been in here? I raised my head and saw that I was holding a pen again, with no idea where it had come from. My head was throbbing, and my eyes felt heavy; I was exhausted.

Not again . . .

I wanted nothing more than to curl up on the floor and sleep forever.

There was some swearing and scuffling. Seconds later, half of Immy's face peered up at me from the floor underneath the cubicle door.

"Are you all right? What the hell are you doing in there?" she demanded.

"I don't know."

Why did odd things keep happening to me in bathrooms?

"Are you sick?"

"I don't think so. I just feel really tired. I haven't taken my medication today, though – maybe I'm getting side effects."

"I gotta get up," she muttered, then grunted in disgust. "I can't believe I just laid down on this manky floor."

I thought she must be soaking from all the water dripping down the walls, but the floor looked dry. I ran my hands along the partitions, and they were dry too. The room now felt warm and smelt faintly of soap, rather than damp.

I dropped the pen on the floor, not wanting to think about where it might have been before I picked it up, and pulled up my bottoms. Opening the door, I saw Immy trying to examine the back of her head in the mirror over the sink.

"Can you see anything disgusting on me?"

I shook my head. "You look pretty clean to me."

"Well, I'm showering as soon as I get home," she muttered, pulling her curls into a messy bun and fastening it in place with a hair band. "So, why did you stop taking your tablets? That seems a stupid thing to do."

"I need a clear head. I can't think properly when I take them. Was I gone for long?"

"Tom and I reckon at least twenty minutes, but it might have been longer."

I turned on the taps to wash my hands, but the water came out scalding hot. I yanked them back in pain.

"What's that on your left hand?" Immy asked, pointing.

"What are you talking about?"

"You've drawn something on the top of your hand. See?"

She took my left hand in hers and held it up for me to look at.

"I . . . I don't know – I didn't even know anything was there."

Confused, I looked at the line work. There was a strange shape sketched out in black biro. I held my hand closer and realised it was a tree lying horizontally, with a fat, short trunk that tapered to a long, thin fork with no side branches.

"Well, it wasn't there earlier – I would have seen it otherwise," she insisted. "You must have drawn it in here."

She was biting her lip – a nervous tic she'd been doing since we first met in primary school.

"I don't know any more than you, Immy. I can't remember drawing it."

She walked over to the cubicle I'd been in and peered inside, before bending down to retrieve something. The black pen – the one I'd dropped.

"Look familiar?" she asked, holding it out towards me.

I shrugged, trying to pretend that it wasn't a big deal. "It's not my pen."

"But the drawing on your hand is in black biro and, er, this is a black biro."

"What are you trying to say?"

We looked at each other in silence. Immy had obviously been holding her breath because she exhaled noisily and shook her head.

"I'm not trying to say anything. I don't know what is happening. All I know is you disappeared for ages, locked yourself in a cubicle and have come out with something scrawled all over your hand."

"I think I fell asleep."

"In a *toilet*?"

This was getting us nowhere. I didn't understand what had happened and, even if I did, how could I explain it to Immy?

"Maybe it's narcolepsy?" she suggested, her expression brightening. "Yes, that would explain you suddenly falling asleep in, uh, a toilet cubicle. Anyway, we'd better get back to Tom. He thought you'd done a runner on us."

We made our way back through the crowded café and Tom's expression changed from anxious to relieved when he saw us approaching.

"I'm glad you're OK," he said. "Why were you gone so long? Are you ill?"

"She fell asleep. We're thinking it could be narcolepsy," Immy said.

Tom looked surprised and I shook my head.

"I don't know what happened, but I lost consciousness and then apparently drew this shape. I think it might be the tree we should be looking for in the cemetery, actually. So that should help us when we go back there."

He shot a look at Immy and I realised that now *he* had been infected by her skepticism. What had made him suddenly change his mind in this way? Why talk to me about automatic writing as if he truly believed in it and now look at me as if I had lost my mind?

"Why don't we all go to the cinema this afternoon?" Immy asked, too brightly.

"Immy," Tom began, shooting her a warning look.

"What's wrong?" I demanded, and then, when no one spoke, I understood. "You think I'm losing it, don't you?"

"No! It's just . . . well, I told you before that I don't believe in all this ghost stuff. And since it's raining out there, why don't we go and spend the afternoon somewhere warm and, you know, not a graveyard?"

I grabbed my rucksack. "You two go if you want. I'm going back to St Sepulchre's. I didn't even ask you to come along today, you insisted."

"That's because I wanted to look out for you," Immy protested. "Come on, Lindy, don't get so worked up about things. You know I'll always be here for you, whatever happens."

"Do I?" I got up and pushed my chair back against the table. "Because, as I remember it, you wanted to come along today for very different reasons—"

"Don't you dare!" she interrupted. Tom looked on in confusion as people nearby turned to stare.

"Don't worry. Your secret's safe with me. Unless I go crazy and start telling everyone I meet."

I tried to ignore their expressions as I left the café, but their uncertainty had rooted itself firmly in my mind.

Was I losing my mind?

25.
THE VIOLET

When I returned to St Sepulchre's, the rain had lessened but a low fog was hugging the graves. It was no longer beautiful, but sinister.

In the middle of the graveyard, I stopped and tried to get my bearings. We'd been in the lower left corner earlier and, from the vague memories I had of the dream, that was definitely the right area, as there was an old group of yew trees clustered towards the bottom of the site.

The peace of the graveyard was shattered by a sudden uprising of crows from a copse of trees further down the path. They cawed rapturously as they flapped their wings, heading towards the area of the graveyard I'd just been pondering over. As they flew, I caught a sudden scent of sweet violets on the wind, just as I had the previous day.

I started walking, following the scent, and headed straight on to the grass, ignoring the graves this time as I hurried. The smell was growing stronger, almost cloying. A few times, I nearly tripped over hidden brambles and broken pieces of graves, but I managed to keep my balance and continue running.

It wasn't long until the smell became so intense that I stopped and took stock of my surroundings.

Then I saw it: the tree I'd drawn on my hand. There was no mistaking its peculiar shape. No wonder we'd not seen it earlier; it had obviously fallen at some point and was now another dead inhabitant of St Sepulchre's.

I bent down and started crawling through the grass, looking for a clue to suggest the whereabouts of the mass grave. It was cold and unpleasant work. The ground was completely saturated, and the long grass had soaked through my jogging bottoms again. My hands quickly became caked with mud and the coldness had made them stiff and painful. I should have worn gloves, but I wasn't expecting this to be so difficult. To be honest, I wasn't really sure that I'd find anything.

Just as I was about to admit defeat, I spotted a lone, untouched violet – vibrant against its dark background. Next to it was a small stone slab, almost totally swamped by overgrowth, with a smooth shape to it, set into the ground. There seemed to be something cut into it. I turned on the torch on my phone and saw what looked like Roman numerals carved into the stone:

MDCCCXLIX

1849. The year Esme died.

Lifting the stone up was difficult, as my hands were slippery and nearly numb with cold, but I managed it eventually. I bent down to see what was underneath and recoiled at hundreds of woodlice, worms and spiders wriggling in panic at being disturbed.

It was starting to reach twilight, the fog was thickening. I shone my torch down again, and the beam reflected against something in the mud. I moved the stone more to the left, balanced my phone on it, then dropped to the ground, plunging my hands into the soil, trying to ignore the squirming insects that my fingers occasionally touched.

My mud-caked hands hit something solid, but I couldn't grab enough of it to pull it out of the ground. I scrabbled around for something to act as leverage and found a short, stubby stick lying in the grass.

I used the stick to chisel away at the ground around the object and, as soon as I had enough depth, I wedged the stick underneath and levered it upwards as hard as I could. With a loud sucking noise, a bottle popped free.

"Found something interesting?"

The male voice, which sounded like a whisper on the wind, came from behind me. I would have screamed, but shock had stolen my voice and all that came out was the tiniest of squeaks. As I whirled around to see who was with me, I slipped on the wet ground and fell backwards into the mud. A tall, thin figure was standing over me. A black hood hid the man's face apart from a very sharp and white chin that jutted out.

"I'm sorry," the man said. "Did I give you a fright? There is no need to be afraid. I won't hurt you. I just wanted to see what you were doing here all by yourself. Graveyards are lonely places."

There had been news stories of girls being attacked when walking alone in parks, and here I was, scrabbling around a deserted graveyard on my own. I wished I hadn't ditched Immy and Tom now. I looked at my phone and wondered how to get hold of it without him stopping me.

"So, what have you got there, then? In your hand. Buried treasure?"

I shook my head.

"Must be something precious if you don't want to show it to me."

"It's just an empty bottle that I tripped over," I whispered. "It's nothing. But I've got a few pounds in my purse, if you'd like them."

The man threw back his head and laughed, a slow and disturbing noise. "No. I don't want your money." He leant closer. "Let me see what you've found."

I knew I should have done the sensible thing and shown him but I couldn't let it go. The man hawked and spat into the grass.

"You're starting to test my patience and, believe me, I don't have a lot to give," he snarled. "Be a good girl and do as I say, or I might have to make you."

I was too scared to move, but too stubborn to give up what I'd just found to a random stranger.

"Right you are. I'll make you then."

He lunged towards me and, bottle in hand, I rolled to the side. He overbalanced and fell on to the ground as I grabbed my phone and legged it. I caught a glimpse from the corner of my eye as he sat up and shouted something at me, but I didn't stop to listen. I ran and ran through the sea of gravestones and the grasping nettles until I was sure I could run no more.

26.
FRAGMENTS OF A FAMILY

As I sprinted into Walton Street, the few pedestrians I passed sneaked alarmed looks in my direction. I'd lost my beanie in the scuffle and wisps of my thinning hair clung to my face. My filthy tracksuit bottoms clung to my legs and my trainers squelched as I ran.

It didn't take me long to get home but, as I closed the gate to my front garden, I realised I was going to have to explain my appearance to Mum – not to mention the fact that I'd been out for more than four hours, allegedly running, in the rain. If I told her that I'd been attacked, Mum would want to call the police and I couldn't stand the thought of having to talk to more well- meaning but doubtful professionals.

As soon as I climbed the steps to the front door, she threw it open.

"Where the hell have you been? Why didn't you return my calls or texts? I was just about to call the police—" Her voice cut off as she looked me up and down. "What's happened to you?"

"Sorry, Mum," I panted, and not just for pretence – I was

completely out of breath from running from St Sepulchre's. "I went on a long run up through Port Meadow and a little way past Wolvercote. I lost track of time. On the way back, I tripped and fell. I twisted my ankle and had to rest for a while until it felt like I could put weight on it."

She shut the door behind me and waited while I kicked off my trainers and dumped my sodden rucksack on the doormat. "So why not call me to come and help?" she demanded. "You had your phone, didn't you?"

"Uh, I lost reception. It's rubbish up in the Meadow – there are pockets where it goes for ages."

She considered this and nodded. "But still, you should have called or texted me when you did have signal to let me know everything was OK. That's two days running now that you've gone AWOL and left me worrying."

"I thought you wanted me to get back to normal?"

"Of course! It's just that you seem to have gone from hiding yourself away in the house one minute to being out for hours on your own the next. You've got to admit that it's rather extreme."

She was right, of course, but I couldn't tell her what was going on – she'd really think I'd lost the plot. Instead, I decided to agree with her.

"Sorry, Mum. I've just felt so much better lately that I thought I would make the most of it, but I guess I took it a little too far. I'll make sure to let you know where I am next time I stay out longer than expected."

She frowned a little, then nodded. "All right. Thanks. Now, what happened to your hat?"

Damn. I'd forgotten about that. "I, uh, took it off when I was resting. I must have left it in the mud. Should I go back and get it?"

"Don't be daft. We'll get you another one – maybe one that's a little cuter."

Ugh.

"So, how did the viewing go today?" I prodded, as I started to remove my drenched coat.

She grimaced. "Badly. It seems we have a rodent problem."

"Rodent?"

"The couple who viewed the house found mouse droppings by the kitchen bin. Though goodness knows how – we've never had a problem before. And I hoovered this place from top to bottom again this morning – there were no signs of mice then. It seems our two resident mousers are being fed a little too well if they're not doing their job properly." She nodded at Bifur and Bofur, who were sitting in the kitchen doorway looking innocent.

Did Esme have a hand in this to help me remain in the house? I said an unspoken 'thank you' to her just in case.

"So, are they coming back?"

"Hopefully not, once I get an exterminator in – oh, you mean the couple," she said, as she saw my puzzled expression. "They might. They have other places to see. Other mice-free houses."

I tried to be sympathetic but not overly so. She would have seen through it, since she knew I didn't want to leave. Inside, I was jumping for joy, grateful that Bifur and Bofur preferred tuna to vermin.

"You'd better take a shower," Mum said. "You look freezing. Give your hands and nails a good scrub, too," she added as I fake-limped to the bathroom. "It looks like you've been rolling in the mud."

In the bathroom, I shut the door quietly and turned the shower on to warm up. I pulled the bottle out of my rucksack and held it up to the light. It seemed to have some sort of stopper in the neck but, when I tried to pull it out, it remained stuck.

There was only one way to open it.

I wrapped the bottle in the hand towel, then flushed the toilet to disguise any noise. Taking a swing, I smashed the bottle's neck against the side of the sink and felt it crack from the impact.

The bottle split into two clean pieces, with no nasty splinters of glass. Carefully, I tipped the piece of bottle I had in my hand upside down and a stained piece of thick cotton slid into my palm.

Unravelling it, I immediately recognised the girl and her mother in the photo.

Esme was wearing a white dress made of lace and silk and her golden hair – the very hair that I'd touched – cascaded down her back. Her face shone with happiness, oblivious to the tragedy that lay ahead. Her mother, wearing a long dress with a high collar, was standing behind her. Like her daughter, she had thick, wavy hair, but this was piled on top of her head, with wisps and tendrils framing her oval-shaped face. Her features were delicate – beautiful – even more so than her pretty daughter's.

The photograph was obviously very formal and deliberately posed but, while Esme's face radiated happiness, her mother looked as if she didn't want to be there at all. Her eyes were gazing slightly away from the camera and she was gripping Esme's chair so hard that her fingers looked like white claws. Her jaw was clenched and her entire body language screamed unhappiness.

It had to be more than just a standard dislike of the camera.

I put the photo back into its protective cotton and returned it to my rucksack for safekeeping while I had a shower. I couldn't wait to add it to the frame. One task down, one to go.

I was a step closer to Dad.

I was just getting dressed when Mum called up that I had visitors. When I went downstairs to see what she was talking about, I heard Immy's voice coming from the kitchen. She and Mum were talking together like old friends, with Mum saying how nice it was to see Immy again and Immy saying how much she'd missed us.

Then I noticed Tom standing behind Immy. He nodded at me when I walked through the door.

"Look who it is, Lindy," Mum said. "Immy's come over to see how you're doing. Isn't that nice?"

I wished she'd stop talking to me like a five-year-old.

I forced a smile. "Nice of you to come by. You really didn't have to."

She smiled back at me, a little hesitantly. "I wanted to see how you were doing. It's been . . . a little while."

"And she's brought a friend with her, too," Mum joined in, indicating Tom. "Sorry, love, I've forgotten your name?"

"Tom," he said and smiled at both of us.

There was a lot of smiling, but only Mum's was genuine – she didn't have a clue what was really going on in the room.

"How did you both meet?" Mum asked.

"Tom used to go to our college a little while back," Immy explained. "Remember, Lindy?"

"No, I can't say I do." I replied

"I didn't stay for long," Tom said. "Just a term."

"Where do you go to college now?" Mum asked.

"I'm home-schooled," he said. "I just couldn't get used to all the people and all the noise."

"Don't you get lonely?" Mum asked. Like Immy, Mum had a tendency to be incredibly forward.

"No. I have enough friends to keep me busy." He flashed another charming smile at her.

"Well, it's a pleasure to meet you, Tom," she said. "And it's always lovely to have you round, Immy – we've missed your bubbly presence. Right, I'll leave you all to hang out while I do some work upstairs."

She left the kitchen, coffee cup in hand, and when we heard her door shut, Immy let rip.

"Why didn't you answer any of our texts? We were worried sick about you."

"You're sounding a lot like my mother, Immy."

"Well, you left the café in such a mood—"

"That's because you said you didn't believe me."

"Not exactly! I said that I thought you might be mistaking dreams for reality – there's a difference."

"Well, whatever you want to call it, you think that what I'm doing is nonsense. There was no point dragging both of you back into the cold, if that was how you felt," I said, looking at Tom. He was watching both of us carefully.

"We would still have been there for you," Immy admitted.

"Humouring me? No thanks. I'd rather do it on my own."

"Why are you limping? Have you hurt yourself?"

"No. When Mum asked why I'd been out for so long, I told her that I was out jogging and fell down. I have to keep up the pretence."

"So . . . did you find anything?" Tom asked, obviously keen to move the conversation on from its impasse. "What happened?"

"As a matter of fact, I *did* find the piece of photograph I was after," I announced, triumphantly, enjoying the look of surprise on their faces.

"Can we see it?" Tom asked eagerly.

I hesitated. I felt like being churlish – they didn't help me find it, so why should I show it to them? But if they saw it, they might actually believe me and stop thinking I was imagining everything.

"I'll just go and get it," I said, and ran upstairs, pulled out the cotton covering and headed back to the kitchen. Tom looked the keenest to see what I'd found so I gave it to him.

He unrolled it and removed the fragment, holding it up to the light. Immy joined him and they stood in silence for what seemed like ages.

"So?" I demanded. "Do you believe me now?"

The look on their faces was not the expression I wanted to see. It was a mixture of confusion, sympathy and uncertainty.

"This isn't a photo, Lindy – it's a piece of blank paper," Tom said, caution in his voice.

"Let me see." I snatched it off them and stared in disbelief. He was right – there was nothing there. It looked like I'd just torn a piece of paper out of my art portfolio and placed it inside the cloth.

"I don't understand." I was stunned. "I just looked at this ten minutes ago. It showed Esme sitting in a chair in a lace dress, her mother at her side, smiling at the camera."

Tom and Immy exchanged a quick glance, then each found somewhere else in the kitchen to focus their gaze. I could feel embarrassed pity radiating off them.

"She was on this photo!" I insisted. "Maybe the light in here has damaged it or something, but I know what I saw!"

"We believe you," Tom murmured, and Immy nodded – though I could tell that they were just saying this to be kind.

I snatched everything away from Tom.

"I don't know what's happening, but I swear that I found a photograph. Maybe I wrapped a piece of paper up in this cotton instead of the photo. Yes! That must be what I did. I'll go back up and—"

"You don't have to do that, Lindy," Tom said gently, as if he were soothing a panicked animal.

"You don't believe me, do you?" I demanded. "Look, I've screwed up – I brought down the wrong thing, that's all."

"We believe you, don't we, Immy?" Tom asked, hoping I wouldn't see the look he gave her, but his face was an open book.

What was going on?

And why could *no one* else see it?

27.
MOTHERS

"Well done for finding the first piece, Lindy."

It was one o'clock in the morning and Esme had done her usual trick of communicating to me in the middle of the night. She was so frustrating; I'd waited – faithfully, and then impatiently – in my room all evening, only leaving for twenty minutes to gulp down dinner. I'd tried everything to summon her, but she'd refused to appear.

"Why can't you visit at a normal time?" I grumbled, as I sat up in bed, rubbing my eyes.

"It is much easier at night," she replied. "You are alone, it is quiet and we are less likely to be disturbed."

"Yes, but I have to get up in the morning."

"And do what? You are not attending any kind of educational institution."

I hadn't seen this argumentative side of Esme before and, in the early hours of the morning, I wasn't too keen on it. She must have sensed this because she changed the subject.

"Lindy, may I ask a favour of you?"

"What, in addition to finding a torn-up family photograph that magically disappears whenever anyone else looks at it?"

She sighed. "I am sorry about that, but the rule is that you – you alone – must find the photograph. You are not allowed any help."

"You could have mentioned this before," I grumbled. "Two of my friends now think I really *am* insane because I dragged them on a wild goose chase this morning."

"But you succeeded, perhaps with a little assistance from a special flower?"

There was a moment of silence before it clicked.

"That flower – the smell of violets – that was you?" I asked.

"I have always been partial to violets. They were my mother's favourite."

"Well, thanks. I'm not sure I could have done it without that little clue."

"You also had a visitor when you discovered the bottle, didn't you?"

"Visitor makes him sound friendly – he was horrible. Who was he? I just assumed it was some weirdo hanging around the graveyard."

"He was Linwood Madill – Freeda's son – the one who cursed our family. He was trying to stop you from completing the task. He will be determined to make things harder for you from now on. You will need to be very careful, both for your own sake and that of the picture."

"How could *he* appear in the graveyard, but you can't?"

"The curse seems to have trapped me inside this house; the only gateway is a mirror," Esme explained. "I have tried to break through from this world into your own but every time I attempt it, I am pulled back. Such a shame," she said, more quietly. "I would have loved to return, if only for an hour."

"Here – I'll show you the photograph," I said, trying to distract her. I got out of bed and took the frame from under the beanbag. When I moved to turn on the overhead light, Esme stopped me.

"No – the light is too harsh. It will dissipate my form. Come to the mirror so you can see me."

"Fine, but how will you see the photo if there's no light on?"

"Have you any candles? They will be gentler."

I pulled out my fake candles. "These will have to do. They're not the real thing, but they're all I've got."

I sat down at the dressing table and turned on the candles, showing Esme the fragment of the photo I'd found. She breathed in sharply.

"This is in remarkable condition, considering how old it is and where it has been all this time," she whispered. She held her hand against the glass of my mirror. "I remember the day this picture was taken. The photographer was with us for quite some time. Mother, at first, refused to pose for the picture and she and Father quarreled."

"Did your parents argue a lot?"

"Well, they certainly did not get along very well. They rarely smiled in each other's company and, therefore, spent much time apart. I believe this is why my father worked so hard and so late. And why my mother was so fond of her laudanum," she added.

"My parents often disagreed about stuff," I said. "Mum was always accusing Dad of being irresponsible instead of helping around the house or making sure that I'd done my homework."

"Was your father not a disciplinarian?" Esme asked.

"Dad? No! He believed that life was too short to waste being unhappy. I can't remember how many different jobs he had when I was younger, trying to find the right one. He worked for himself because he didn't like having a boss. He ran his own bike repair shop before he became a freelance gardener and then had his own mobile coffee shop. That's when he and Mum started fighting more. She said she wanted him to grow up and take responsibility, not fool around. Her words, not mine. She said he was setting me a bad example, but she was so wrong. Because of him, I saw that life could be fun."

So why was he so angry that I went to the party that night?

"To please her, he trained to teach English as a foreign language," I continued, "and that's what he did up until he died."

Why was he driving the morning he died? He always cycled to work.

"He sounds rather impetuous," Esme said primly. "I can see why your mother found his behaviour frustrating."

"What do you mean?" I demanded.

"A father needs to provide for his family. In my time, women did not work. Well, women of a certain *class* did not work."

"Yeah, well, I don't think I would have liked to live in your time," I retorted. "And Mum likes her job – sometimes too much, I think. She always worked longer and harder than Dad did."

"Why on earth would she work so hard? Are you poor?"

"No. We're not the richest people around, but we're OK. I think that Mum just likes working. She's an author and she's always trying to get new jobs, develop her portfolio. You know."

"I'm afraid I do not know. In my time, women of your mother's status would have devoted their time to charitable works not paid employment. That was the domain of the man in the house. For a married woman who was not of the working classes, having a job would have been unthinkable."

"But that must have been so boring!" I countered. "Imagine spending your time cooped up in a house all day or at tea parties with other women. I couldn't stand it."

"I must admit that I thought it tedious," Esme said. "Maybe my mother thought the same because she never seemed happy. She stayed in her room most of the time, just joining us for breakfast, luncheon and supper – and sometimes not even then. Father said she preferred her own company."

"That must have been tough."

"One gets used to situations." She looked down at her hands. A small shudder went through her and the light flickered. "Are you still there, Esme?" I asked, concern rising in me.

Fragments of words came through the mirror but nothing that I could understand.

"You're fading; I can't hear you! Esme!"

The mirror was empty. Esme was gone and, with her, the chance of getting the second clue.

28.
WD-40

"Not again! For God's sake, Lindy!"

I jolted awake, heart thumping so ferociously I thought it would come through my chest. Mum was standing next to my bed, staring at the wall – her hands planted on her hips and an expression of bewildered rage on her face.

What now?

"Seriously? Is this some kind of joke?"

"I don't know what you're talking about," I replied weakly, rubbing my eyes.

She bent down and grabbed my right hand, wrenching a black marker pen from it once again. "Look at what you've done to your duvet cover!"

I looked down. Black ink had bled on to the cotton cover, leaving an ugly pool running through the patterns of flowers.

"This won't wash out, you know," she said. "That cover is ruined. But that's not the worst of it. We can hide this but how the hell are we supposed to hide all that writing on the wall?

You don't have a picture big enough to cover that."

I sat up and looked. This time the writing was much larger, scrawled over a metre across and down, in a spidery style.

"Mum – I promise you that I don't remember doing this."

"Denying that you've been writing on the wall is pretty stupid when you're the only one in the room, but to insist on it when you're holding the evidence is unbelievable."

"I know I'm the only one who has been in the room, but I swear I wouldn't deliberately write all over the wall."

"How can you write on the wall *unless* it is deliberate?"

"Automatic writing. It's when something or someone makes you write but you're not aware you're doing it because you're in a trance or . . ."

I tailed off at her expression. I should have known not to even go there.

"You're telling me that 'something or someone' is making you write against your will."

She said it as if it were a fact that there was no way she could be persuaded to believe. As if I were making it up to get out of trouble or – worse – because I was losing my grip on reality.

"Let's just assume that you did this knowingly; *willingly*," she said, struggling to keep her voice even. "You did it because you wanted to stop me from selling the house because how can I possibly show it to people when you're writing strange poems all over the walls in indelible ink?"

"But I'm telling you, I didn't do this on purpose!"

"Are you sure you want to say that? Because if you're insisting that some invisible . . . *force* . . . is making you do this, I might have to call Dr Greenwood and insist that you attend an appointment, even if I have to drag you there kicking and screaming."

What could I do? I was stuck at a crossroads. Was it best to let her think I was losing my mind, or that I'd done something bad? Neither was a good option, so I had to choose the lesser of two evils.

"What even are these odd things you're writing?" Mum was asking me. "Why not just normal graffiti?"

"I don't know," I mumbled.

"Are you making up rhymes like this for an art project?"

That actually wasn't a bad explanation for what I had done. Maybe I should go with it. I was mulling it over when I heard Mum speaking again.

"The thing is, Lindy – if you were just trying to stop me from selling the house, I reckon you'd be drawing pictures or writing obscenities all over the place. But this . . ." She looked at the writing again. "This is almost formal writing, as if it has some sort of meaning."

Maybe she was coming around to the idea of automatic writing after all. Should I tell her? Hope rose in me, but I squashed it.

No. I tried to think of a way of explaining the riddle, but I couldn't. Nothing would sound sane or sensible, so I opted for silence and, in the end, she gave up waiting for me.

"You're either going to have to find something to put on it or you're going to have to repaint it," she said. "There's still half a pot of paint from when you decorated in the summer. I just hope it will cover it up."

"I could try removing it?" I suggested. "There must be a way of getting marker ink off a wall. Kids draw on walls all the time."

She shot a meaningful look at me. "Exactly. It's what *kids* do, not young adults."

I childishly stuck my tongue out at her as she left the room. I knew she had a point and that my behaviour was weird, but I didn't need her to be so patronising about it. I'd rather she screamed at me and got angry than acting all hurt and disappointed.

I read the writing on the wall.

> *AnotHer trip to sacred grOund,*
> *is where the next cLue can be found,*
> *beneath a hollY beside a Wall,*
> *this is your sEcond port of caLL.*

The second riddle. Esme had left it with me, even though she'd disappeared before she'd had a chance to tell me in person. I wrote it down on a scrap piece of paper in case the photo that I took of it did a disappearing act from my phone, like the picture had done.

It was obvious from the 'sacred ground' that I was looking for a graveyard but there were so many in Oxford that I had to work out which one the riddle meant first. The reference to 'holly' meant a tree, surely, and there was a wall . . . but this could apply to anywhere! My eyes lingered on the randomly sized letters.

I groaned and rested my head on my arms. I was too tired for this.

"Logic is of capital importance."

It was a whisper that felt more like a breeze, scented with violets. The only explanation could be Esme.

"Capital importance?" I murmured to myself. "Cap . . . CAPITAL!"

I felt stupid for not seeing this obvious clue before. I grabbed my pen again and jotted the capitals down in order:

H-O-L-Y-W-E-L-L

I googled Holywell Cemetery and the first hit was a Wikipedia page that confirmed it as a graveyard in Oxford, situated next to St Cross Church. Like St Sepulchre's, it had been built in the nineteenth century to cope with the victims of the cholera epidemic as all the older graveyards became full.

Clicking on a map and then on street view, I realised why I'd not noticed it before when walking down that road – it was hidden away behind the main graveyard of St Cross Church with only a small plaque indicating where it was. It seemed the Victorians enjoyed hiding their cemeteries down random pathways.

All in all, I was feeling smug. Obviously, I still had to work out where the next clue actually was once I was inside the graveyard, but at least I knew where to head . . . whenever I could next get away from the house. Somehow, I doubted Mum would be willing to let me out again when I still had the issue of the writing on the wall to clear up.

My next internet search was on how to remove marker pen from a wall. Apparently, WD-40 was meant to do it. I was pretty sure we had some in the shed from when Dad used it on my bike when the chain got rusty, so I decided to try that before embarking on repainting my entire bedroom.

The WD-40 was high up on a shelf, out of reach, so I had to balance precariously on an upside-down plant pot to reach it, nearly toppling over when a deafening meow startled me from behind. Bofur – checking the place out and announcing his entry at the same time.

"Are you trying to kill me?" I demanded, hopping off the pot and laying a hand over my racing heart.

He yawned, turned around and waddled out again.

I grabbed some old cloths from a bag, shut the shed and went to start on the wall.

Repainting the wall would have been much easier.

I sprayed the WD-40 on the wall and scrubbed and scrubbed, but there was so much area to clean that I was fighting a losing battle. I should have read the instructions on the internet more closely because I sprayed the whole wall, thinking that if the WD-40 had time to soak in, it would make the pen come off more easily, but this ended up causing *another* stain by leaving the chemical on for too long. In desperation, I started spraying the old rags with more and more WD-40, but I wasn't shifting the ink and, instead, was becoming dizzy and nauseated from the chemical fumes in the process. At first, I rather liked it – it smelt vaguely of vanilla – but as it built up in my throat, it began to burn and I started coughing.

I couldn't stop.

I coughed and coughed until I could taste blood.

Everything went black.

I'm lying on cool, damp grass, looking upwards at a leaden sky. Holly trees lean over me like the setting of a Christmas card.

Pretty. I smile.

A weak drizzle dampens my face – a welcome relief from my fume-filled bedroom. My throat and nose don't feel inflamed any more, and I am breathing soft, soothing air.

166

I'm not sure how I got here, but it doesn't matter – it's relaxing, comforting and not at all cold. Strange, because I know it's October and usually I'd be wearing a coat outside. I wouldn't normally lie on the ground, either.

So why am I now?

I try to push myself up on my elbows, but I can't. It's like someone has sucked the energy out of me and replaced it with lead. I don't mind exactly, but it's odd all the same.

Can I turn my head, at least? I can. I look to the right.

Someone's lying next to me, their head tilted towards me.

A thin woman in a torn dress. Her grey hair is matted against her head and a grimace of death pulls at the shrunken lips on her face.

I scream but no sound comes out – only wheezing air that claws my throat, which feels like it's narrowing by the second.

I try to get up, but nothing happens. My shoulder shakes but it won't help me up.

A voice is calling me, but I can't reply.

"Lindy! Wake up! *Please* wake up!"

My shoulder was being shaken violently.

I opened my eyes to see Mum, her eyes wide with fear.

A sudden, huge cough racked her body and she fell back on her heels, choking as she stumbled to her feet and opened the two windows in my bedroom as wide as they would go.

Then she was back with me again, grabbing me under the armpits and dragging me out of the bedroom into her own, as my breathing shuddered and rasped.

"Hello? I need an ambulance!"

I tried to sit up, but the heavy feeling still sat on my chest, pinning me to the ground.

"It's my daughter – she's having trouble breathing. I need an ambulance *now!*"

29.
A DIFFERENT KIND OF NIGHTMARE

I didn't die, but I succeeded in nearly scaring my mother to death and embarrassing myself in front of everyone because I'd peed myself after falling unconscious – apparently a side effect of inhaling WD-40.

When they arrived, the paramedics gave me oxygen as I was still wheezing and disorientated. One of them took Mum into another room and the other started asking me loads of questions: Had I done it on purpose? Was I experimenting with the stuff to get high? Did I know how dangerous it was to sniff toxins?

No matter how many times I insisted that it was an accident – that I had been using WD-40 to try to clean marker pen off my walls – they treated me like a stupid teenager caught trying to get wasted on chemicals. They were nice – don't get me wrong – but they clearly didn't believe that I'd accidentally inhaled too many fumes in a poorly ventilated room.

"Why didn't you open a window?" one paramedic asked – it was a valid question. Why hadn't I? Why had I put myself at risk?

All I knew was that it wasn't on purpose.

They left, taking some of my dignity with them. Mum was sitting in the living room with Bifur on her lap, cradling a mug of sugary tea that one of the paramedics had made her before leaving. I was sitting on the sofa opposite, a blanket wrapped around my shoulders.

"You do believe me, Mum, don't you? I didn't do this on purpose."

She kept her gaze lowered and said nothing.

"Mum? Honestly – I was doing as you asked and trying to remove that pen on the wall. I just forgot to open the windows."

"If you say so." Her voice was dull, her expression defeated.

I think I preferred it when she was angry with me – then she at least showed some spark; some emotion.

"I should have done what you said – painted the wall," I offered, trying to appease her. "I was trying to do things the easy way and it was a huge mistake. I'll paint the wall tomorrow—"

"Just leave it for now," she interrupted, still staring into her mug. "You have to stay away from fumes for a while and paint will make your breathing worse. Anyway, it's not as if we're showing the house to anyone at the moment, so there's no rush."

This new, forlorn version of my mother was scaring me.

I spent the rest of the day lounging on the couch, flicking through Netflix but not really settling on anything. My room was still airing – the windows wide open and the door shut – and Mum had gone upstairs to work. She was still being quiet with me, and when we crossed paths in the kitchen at dinnertime, I caught her shooting me worried looks when she thought my attention was elsewhere.

After dinner, we went to my room to check it was all right. Apart from feeling like a refrigerator from all the cold air coming in, it was fine – no noticeable lingering fumes remained. The scene on the wall of smeared pen and paint made Mum wince, while I blushed with embarrassment.

What a mess – literally and metaphorically.

I switched on my phone – I had it turned off most of the day because I couldn't be bothered to communicate with anyone, and I knew that Tom and Immy would have been trying to message me. I hated the sympathetic, worried expressions on their faces when I tried to show them the piece of the photograph – I've seen that look countless times in films where the character who is losing their mind is desperately trying to convince their loved ones that they're sane. I *wasn't* that character. I *wasn't* losing it.

As predicted, they'd got in touch to see if I was "OK". I switched my phone off and decided to have an early night. I'd had enough of this day.

Something woke me up suddenly from a deep sleep.

It sounded like wailing – a cry of suffering.

I listened again, straining to hear any other noises. A gasp and a choking sound.

Fear and alarm laced their way through my veins, but I didn't know what to think or believe. Was I really experiencing this, or was it some kind of auditory hallucination?

I turned on my phone's torch and got out of bed. When I crept on to the landing I kept the light low, glancing towards my mother's room. The door was part way open and there was silence. No snoring. I had to be quiet, so as not to wake her up.

There was a splash of light spilling up the stairway from the living room below me. I padded quietly towards it and peered over the bannister. The downstairs hallway light was off, but something was in the living room and it was making odd, gurgling sounds as if it were drowning.

I shivered.

Should I wake Mum up? But what if there was nothing there? What would she think, or say, or do? She might cart me off to Dr Greenwood; have me committed . . .

I crept down the stairs, trying to avoid the creaky spots that I'd memorised from years of practice. At the bottom, I tiptoed towards the living room and paused as an awful whining sound, like an animal in pain, escaped. I felt sick.

Oh no – was someone hurting Bifur or Bofur?

The door was only open a crack, so I flattened myself as much as possible against the wall and pushed it, gently, to avoid making any sudden movements or noises. Once the door was far enough open to get a good view of the room, I pressed my face against the gap and peered inside.

What I saw was scarier than anything I'd experienced in the last couple of days.

On the coffee table were two empty bottles of wine and an empty glass – all lying on their sides. Curled up in one of the armchairs was a hunched figure, shaking and crying and making incomprehensible noises that sounded like slurred talking mixed with sobs.

The figure was my mother and clutched in her hands was a photograph of my father.

I didn't know what to do. I wanted to run – this wasn't the mother I knew, the one who was always in control of her emotions, who held things together. This was a mother, a wife, in pain . . . and I had no idea how to comfort her. Should I go in and hug her? Cry with her to show some solidarity?

Or was she only doing this because she thought I was asleep in bed? She was always such a private person. Me interfering with her grief might make things worse. She might become embarrassed, horrified, ashamed.

In the end, I took the coward's way out. I fled.

30.
THE MOTHER OF ALL HANGOVERS

At ten o'clock the next morning, Mum still wasn't up. I didn't know whether to take her a cup of tea and pretend that I'd seen and heard nothing, or leave her to sleep off what must have been the mother of all hangovers.

In the kitchen, Bifur and Bofur were competing to see who could trip me up first, so I decided that I'd better feed them before I did anything else or I would have a feline revolution on my hands. I filled the cats' bowls before I sat down and poured myself a helping of cornflakes to keep them company.

My phone vibrated with a message from Tom.

How are you?

Fine, thanks.

What you up to today?

Want to meet up again?

What was he up to? Surely with him and Immy getting friendlier yesterday, he'd want to concentrate on her. Besides, he seemed as convinced as Immy that there was something wrong with me.

You still there, Lindy?

Yep, sorry. Don't you have to study today?

Mum's away at a client's. 😊

Is she never around?

She's got a big job on at the moment.

Hey, what's up? Are you trying to put me off?

I was, actually. I didn't know what to think about Tom any more. I liked how we'd talked together the other day. I'd felt so relieved to have something so major in common with someone else, but I found Tom's persistence odd. Why was he always so keen to meet with me, especially if he seemed, like Immy, to think that I was inventing ghosts and imagining photos of dead people? Something didn't feel right about him; I couldn't quite explain it but suddenly Tom was starting to give me the creeps.

I had to say *something* though . . .

I noted the kisses, shut off my phone and put it down.

In the end, since Mum still hadn't surfaced and it was nearly eleven o'clock, I braved taking a cup of tea up to her.

The room was dark; her heavy, red curtains blocked out most of the daylight. I switched on the landing light and opened the door wide.

The room was a mess, much worse than mine on a bad day. Clothes were strewn across the floor, papers and books were in high piles in the corner of the room. The stale smell of alcohol nearly overpowered me.

Her breathing was heavy, and she was lying in the middle of her king-sized bed, wrapped up in a mountain of duvet. A leg popped out of one end, the foot hanging over the edge of the mattress, and one arm was flung over a pillow.

Should I wake her? *Could* I wake her?

I set the cup of tea down on the bedside table and lay a hand on what I determined was her shoulder, shaking it gently.

"Mum? You OK?"

There was a snort and a murmur.

"Mum? It's eleven o'clock. I've brought you a cup of tea. Do you want me to bring you up some breakfast? Toast?"

She groaned and turned on to her back. The stench of alcohol was more potent now that the duvet had come away from her face, and I was stunned by how awful she looked.

Make-up was smeared all over her face; mascara sliding away from her eyes in black streaks down her cheeks. Her skin was creased and imprinted from being squashed into her pillow, and her hair looked like she'd dragged a brush the wrong way through it – full of knots and frizz.

She half-opened her eyes and looked at me.

"What time did you say it was?" she croaked, wincing at the sound of her own voice.

"Eleven," I whispered. "I've brought you a cup of tea."

She gave the tiniest of nods. "Thanks. Sorry I'm not up yet. I, uh, I'm feeling unwell this morning. I had a bad night. Must have been something I ate."

Yeah, right!

She tried to push herself up but grabbed her head, moaned, and sank back down again.

I arranged a couple of pillows and helped her to a semi-upright position.

"Do you want some toast?" I asked again.

She shook her head. "No. The tea's perfect, thanks. I'm sorry I'm still in bed. I just feel . . . dreadful today."

I nodded. "I'll just be in my room doing some French if you need me. Don't rush to get up – I can bring you anything you need."

She gave me a weak smile and held out a hand.

"You're a good girl, Lindy," she sighed, then sank lower against the pillows and closed her eyes.

31.
A STAIN ON HUMANITY

The French homework remained untouched once I got back to my room.

Instead, I looked at Holywell Cemetery's website again and worked out the best way to get there. It was only about a twenty-minute walk from my house, and with Mum incapacitated, I stood a good chance of getting out of the house for a while without many – or hopefully any – questions.

Dressed and ready to go, I knocked quietly on Mum's bedroom door and entered. She was still in the same position, tea untouched, head slumped as she dozed.

"Mum?" I whispered, but she was completely out of it and I didn't want to wake her, for both our sakes. I went back to my bedroom and wrote her a note, saying that I was going out for a walk around town and would be back soon. I put it on the bedside table, under the mug of tea. The way she looked, though, I doubted if she'd be awake before I got back.

In the hallway, I slipped on my shoes and packed an umbrella in my rucksack. I also packed a little trowel from the shed, remembering that I'd needed something to dig out the bottle the previous day. Since I'd lost my beanie, I had to make do with an old baseball cap to cover my head. I looked ridiculous but better that than people noticing my bald patches.

Oxford was full of the usual bustle as I walked towards the city centre. As soon as I branched off on to Broad Street, I had to weave in and out of huge tourist groups, led by umbrella-touting guides. I couldn't count the number of people posing in front of the Sheldonian Theatre with selfie sticks; dodging away from them to avoid being in their pictures became a chore. Luckily, the crowds thinned as I headed on to Holywell Street and it was a short walk along St Cross Road to my destination.

As with St Sepulchre's, the entrance to Holywell Cemetery was not easy to find, so I was glad that I'd looked it up before heading off this morning. I spotted the small, nondescript wooden sign announcing the entrance, sandwiched between two massive hedges.

My heart raced as I followed a dark and narrow footpath leading into the graveyard, which was completely hidden from the main road by dense foliage. If anyone with bad intentions was lurking, no one would be able to see what was happening. I increased my speed and breathed a sigh of relief when I emerged into a large clearing marking the main area of the graveyard.

I looked again at the final two lines of the riddle:

> beneath a hollY beside a Wall
> this is your sEcond port of caLL.

It looked like it was going to be another long day.

Sighing, I sat on a bench and closed my eyes. *Come on, Esme*, I urged. *Give me something else.*

I wasn't expecting a reply; talking to the dead had never worked for me before – well, whenever *I* wanted to instigate a conversation. However, this time a sudden cold breeze tickled my forehead, bringing with it the familiar scent of violets.

Standing, I followed the flowery perfume. At first, I was relieved to be walking through a well-kept part of the cemetery – the lawn was neatly mown and the graves stood in ordered lines – but soon I entered what looked like an older section, with graves packed in tightly and undergrowth forcing its way around the headstones. As I stepped gingerly through knots of weeds, I discovered a dense cluster of violets, softly dancing in the wind. I knelt down, grateful that I was wearing jeans that day so I wouldn't scratch myself too badly on any thorns lurking among the overgrown grass. I really needed a pair of gardening gloves but at least I'd brought the trowel, and I used it to poke the ground in front of me until I hit something hard and solid.

It was a crudely cut wooden cross and the years hadn't treated it well. The damp had eaten away at it and the wood had split under clumps of moss and lichen. Praying there were no hidden stinging nettles among the taller blades of grass, I squashed the surrounding greenery down with my hands and tried to see if there was anything written on it. It was hopeless – the damage was so extensive that nothing was visible.

I couldn't see anything buried next to the cross but I knew from the violets, that this was the location of the second half of the photograph. Had Linwood buried the picture in with the body itself?

There was no way that I was going to start digging down into a proper grave.

Instead, I got to my feet, took a couple of paces forward and looked down into the space between the cross and the wall behind it. Beside the thick holly trunk was a mossy stone. I picked it up, recoiling in disgust as worms swarmed out from underneath.

Thankful I'd brought the trowel, I set to work. I didn't have to dig for long before it hit something just under the surface, and when I shone my torch down on to the area, I saw another glass bottle. It was stuck fast into the soft earth but, with a little more work and perseverance, it escaped with a suck of air and mud.

I'd been concentrating so much on the task at hand that I hadn't been aware of anything else around me. As I lifted out the bottle I realised with a jolt that the sky had darkened and a colder wind had picked up, carrying on it not the pleasant scent of violets but a stench of decay.

The hairs on the back of my neck rose. Something wasn't right. I had to get out of there.

The earth in front of me started to writhe, squirm and roil, turning into a seething mass of liquid. I tried to turn around but I slipped, and my right foot was sucked downwards. Trying to pull it out I fell to my knees. The wind picked up with such force that it ripped holly leaves off branches and hurled them down, scratching the skin on my hands and arms as I shielded my face.

"You cheated. You were supposed to do this on your own." The familiar, hooded figure towered over me.

Linwood.

Just as suddenly as it had started, the storm subsided. The holly leaves dropped from the air to lie on the ground around me.

"Are you deaf, girl?" he spat. "I said you were *supposed* to do this on your own!"

"I *did* do it on my own!"

"Liar! Esmerelda was only meant to give you the riddles but she has also been helping you find them."

"That's ridiculous. You have no—"

He held up a hand and I saw a small bouquet of violets wilting in his fingers.

"They were her favourite flowers. Funny that they should always be around where you need to dig, isn't it?"

"I-I don't know what you're talking about," I stammered. "They're just wild. They can grow anywhere."

"I don't see any others around here."

"It's a coincidence—"

"Just like it was a coincidence in St Sepulchre's, I suppose?"

He threw the dying flowers down and squashed them under his boot.

I had to get him onside – distract him from his current train of thought.

"Whose grave is this?" I asked.

"My mother's . . . and about four other people's."

I must have looked surprised because he added, "You didn't think it was a Pennyworth's, did you? Apart from Esmerelda, they built mausoleums for their dead. My mother died a pauper, and she was buried with other people who couldn't afford their own plot of land. One on top of the other."

"I'm sorry. That must be awful for you. But, as you said, Esme didn't have her own grave, either."

He laughed maliciously. "There's a good reason why, too."

I frowned. "Well, of course. She had to be buried in a hurry because of the cholera outbreak."

"Whatever you say."

He sneered at me and I tried to edge backwards, but I was trapped. There was a high wall behind me that I couldn't climb to escape. The only way was forward, towards him.

"I made that cross myself."

Linwood nodded at the rotting piece of wood.

"It's very good," I said, trying to appeal to his vanity.

"I like carving things. Just as well, really," he added. "Couldn't afford a headstone after Charles Pennyworth had stripped us of all the money we had."

I spotted an opportunity.

"What he did was truly awful," I sympathised, hoping that might soften him some. "I feel embarrassed that he was a member of my family."

I really hoped Esme wasn't listening – she'd never forgive me.

"So you should. The Pennyworths are a stain on humanity."

"Not all of us are. But tell me more about your mother," I said, trying to steer him away from his hatred. "It sounds like she was a brilliant woman – wise, clever and compassionate."

"She was." His voice softened. "She always cared for her clients, gave them great comfort when they visited her – she passed on hope that their loved ones were at peace and free from suffering."

"I wish *I* could speak to her," I said. "She's exactly the sort of person I want to talk to now about my father. Did you know that there's a church in Oxford named after her?" I added.

"It's a shame people didn't think of her like that when she was alive. When Pennyworth started spreading scandal about my mother, all her clients abandoned her in droves."

"I know, and it's so unfair. I asked Esme, *Esmerelda*, why he would have done such a thing, but she doesn't know either – she's trying to understand—"

I'd taken it too far. His eyes bulged and his nostrils flared. I could see the outline of his teeth through his gaunt cheeks.

"There is nothing to understand, except that evil runs in your family!" Linwood roared. "The Pennyworths deserve every punishment they get."

"Please, Linwood! Believe me – we're *all* sorry. If I can do anything—"

"Shut up, you stupid girl! You had your chance – you and Esmerelda had the chance to prove to me that you could be honest and play by the rules. It's heavy to carry a grudge like this for so long, but I should have known better. Pennyworths never play by the rules, so the game is over . . . and you've lost. For good."

But instead of attacking me like I prepared for, he disappeared in a black, swirling vortex.

32.
STALKERS

All I can remember is staggering back through the graveyard and then along the busy streets. I pushed through crowds of people, ignoring their angry comments telling me to watch where I was going. I was too afraid to look back in fear that he was coming for me.

When I shut the front door, the house was still silent. Bifur and Bofur padded into the hallway to stare at me, eyes wide with tragic expressions that spoke of how they hadn't been fed for all of three hours. I ran up the stairs – they still wouldn't follow me, despite the protests coming from their stomachs – and headed straight for the bathroom, where I scrubbed the scratches on my hands from the holly leaves. The sharp sting from soap and water lessened some of the horror I'd just experienced and stopped the swelling urge I had to pull as much hair as I could. After a thorough cleaning, I was sure the scratches were disinfected but they were still angry and swollen, so I dabbed them with antiseptic and took an antihistamine, hoping that it would calm things down – including me.

After the first aid was complete, I turned my attention to my rucksack. Despite his threats that Esme and I had lost the "game", Linwood had not taken the second bottle with him. I wrapped it in my bath towel and smashed the neck against the sink, as I'd done the day before. Taking care to avoid the shards of glass, I shook the bottle upside down and caught the roll of cloth as it slid out.

After ensuring everything was tidy, I went back into my bedroom and closed the door, retrieving the picture frame. I sat on my bed and opened the cloth to inspect the second fragment.

As expected, Esme's father, Charles, stared back at me and, once again, I was startled by how accurate my sketch of the Victorian family had been. Did automatic drawing exist in the same way as automatic writing? Was it Esmerelda drawing through me? I hadn't laid eyes on this man before, but I'd captured all the details – the formal suit with tails and tie, the waistcoat, the extremely astute posture. Charles had dark, wavy hair that was styled away from his face, and the oiled moustache sitting above his rather small mouth was exactly how I'd drawn it. His expression wasn't happy or friendly, as I would expect from a photo nowadays. Instead, he was almost smirking. There was a self-satisfied air about him – a sense of superiority that radiated off the photograph even now. This was hardly a happy family portrait; instead, it showed a group of people who looked like they really didn't belong together.

It was time to unite the two parts of the photograph in the frame. I placed them side by side and sat back, holding my breath.

Nothing happened.

I'm not sure what I was expecting exactly. A flash of light or a disembodied voice making an announcement? That's what normally happens when a spell or curse is broken, right?

But I just sat there in silence, staring at an old photograph inside an antique frame.

Linwood had said the game was over. Maybe everything I had done counted for nothing.

I'd not heard a peep from Mum since I'd been back, so I tiptoed to her bedroom and braved a look inside. She was still sleeping. I'd never seen her like this. Normally, she was buzzing around the house, but she laid there, comatose, her untouched tea had developed a skin along the surface. I didn't know whether I should wake her or leave her to sleep off her hangover – and whatever the emotions were that she'd been experiencing the previous night.

There was a knock at the front door. I wanted to ignore it, but it got louder and more insistent, so I hurried downstairs, cursing at whoever was being so inconsiderate.

Immy was standing on the doorstep, her curls even madder than normal and her face was full of worry.

"It's you!" I exclaimed unnecessarily. "Why are you banging on the door like that?"

"Because you wouldn't answer!"

"Keep it down. Mum's asleep upstairs." She grimaced.

"Sorry. Is she all right?"

"Yeah. Just drank too much wine last night." I led her towards the kitchen.

"Seriously? I don't remember her as a big drinker."

"Well, since Dad died, she's never without a glass of something alcoholic in her hand. Although last night was weird. I caught her crying in the living room. I just don't get it. With me she seems determined to carry on like nothing's happened and refuses to show any emotion, but then she sits downstairs literally drowning her sorrows."

"Maybe she's trying to hide it to help you through it all," Immy suggested. "Maybe she's not as strong as you think."

She plonked herself down on a chair. "Did you go in and talk to her about it?"

"No. I didn't know what to say."

"Well, why don't you ask her about it?"

"Because if she's so desperate to hide it from me that she stays up late drinking and crying on her own, she obviously doesn't want to talk to me about it."

"She probably doesn't want to worry you. Sometimes strong people don't realise when they actually need help."

I didn't know what to say, so I didn't say anything. Immy had a point – but it annoyed me how she was always right.

"So, are you OK?" she said, changing the subject. "Tom told me that he was worried about you."

I gritted my teeth. "I don't know why."

"He said that he'd messaged you today to see if you needed some company, but you brushed him off and said that you had to stay at home because your mum was unwell."

"So? You know she is – that's what we've just been talking about."

"But he said that you'd been out anyway."

I nearly dropped the biscuit tin I'd just taken from the cupboard. "What? How does he know that I left the house?"

She squirmed a little and her cheeks darkened. "Well, he was also out in Oxford and saw you walk past. He called out to you, but you either didn't hear him or you ignored him."

I put the biscuit tin on the table. "I did pop out, yes, if it's any of your business. Just briefly to do some shopping."

"Tom said he saw you down by New College. There aren't any shops down that way."

We stared at each other.

"Well, what was Tom doing down there?" I asked, trying to keep my anger under control. "That's out of his way, too, isn't it?"

Immy was never good at lying and the way she was twisting a ringlet around her finger was a clear sign that she wasn't telling me something.

"I don't know – he goes for walks sometimes . . . he likes taking photos of places—"

"Places I just happen to be at? Seems a bit too much like a coincidence to me," I snapped.

"Look, don't get angry, OK? It's just . . . well, after yesterday, we were worried about you and all this death and graveyard stuff. So, we agreed to keep an eye on you. Since Tom is home-schooled, he said he'd do the college day shift and I could take over in the afternoons."

I was so livid, I couldn't speak at first. And then the anger came out, very loud and very clear.

"The two of you have decided I need *babysitting*?!" I screeched, forgetting about my mother's hungover state upstairs.

"We only have your best interests at heart—"

"No, you don't. You fancy Tom, and the only way you can think of to keep him interested is to concoct some kind of bullshit story about my mental health. I bet you've even told him about my hair-pulling, haven't you?"

"No, yes . . . well, he asked why you always wear a beanie . . . what was I supposed to say? And, no, I do not use your mental health as a way to keep him interested! Why would you even *say* that?"

"Tell you what," I said. "Why don't you tell him that you have some kind of psychological problem and ask him to be *your* bodyguard? Especially since you fancy him so much. That will get him off my back and then we can all be happy."

Immy's mouth set in a line.

"I think you're being really ungrateful," she argued, pushing her chair back and standing up. "We're both worried sick about you and want to help you, but all you do is push us away."

"In case you've forgotten, we've only known Tom for a few days," I said. "He seems like a nice enough guy, but I don't know him well enough to trust him with my life, and it's pretty weird that he cares so much."

"It's because he also lost his father—"

"No, Immy, I think it's more than that," I interrupted. "I don't get why you trust him so much when you hardly know him. It's weird."

"As weird as pulling out your hair?"

The words were out before she could stop them. She clapped a hand to her mouth in horror. "I'm so sorry! I was angry – I didn't mean—"

"Yes, you did. You don't understand what I've been through . . . what I keep going through. I get it, fair enough. But that doesn't give you any right to criticise me or tell me what to do. I'm sick of both you and Tom and everyone else saying they know what's best for me."

She scurried into the hall and picked up her bag before turning around to face me. Tears shone in her eyes.

"I really am sorry, Lindy. I want to help. I know you're angry now, but please – when you've calmed down, give me a call, all right? We can all sort this out together."

"Goodbye, Immy," I said, holding open the door, then slamming it behind her before she could say anything else.

33.
DUVET DAY

What a mess.

In just a few days, after starting to see Immy again and making friends with Tom, I had succeeded in destroying both relationships. My mother was a late-night alcoholic, refusing to get out of bed, and I'd been haunted by the ghost of a girl who had me running around Oxford's graveyards looking for bits of an old photograph. Dad was still dead – of course – and I probably wasn't ever going to be able to contact him.

For the first time, I wondered if it was wise to have stopped taking the antidepressants. It had been a couple of days since I'd last taken one and, while I had more energy, my moods were definitely more erratic. Should I start retaking them? I picked up the package and pulled the strip out containing the tablets, then changed my mind. I was almost done with this curse; I could last a few more days.

There was still no stirring from upstairs and I was getting worried. Sure, Mum sometimes overindulged in alcohol, but she'd

193

never spent all day in bed. I headed upstairs and pushed open the bedroom door. She was still lying immobile with the duvet pulled over her head.

"Mum?" I asked, shaking her shoulder gently.

"Hmm?"

"It's seven o'clock. *At night.* Are you going to get up?"

"Don't know." She shifted and pulled the duvet tighter around her. "No. I don't think I will. The day's nearly over. Why bother."

"I'm worried."

"Let's call it a duvet day."

"This isn't like you."

"I know, but maybe today I just need to feel not like me. Maybe today I just don't want to feel anything."

"Mum, you're scaring me."

She sighed and propped herself up on to one elbow. Half her face was in darkness, while the other half was lit up by the landing light.

"I just feel burnt out at the moment. Everything is going wrong. I needed a day where I didn't have to think about anything. Do you understand that?"

"Yes. That's how I feel every day, but you make me get up and do coursework to try to get on with my life."

She laughed, but it wasn't pleasant.

"Ever since your dad died, it's all been about you, hasn't it? I've had to be strong for you, because there's no one else to do it. I've watched as you've gradually fallen apart and I've tried so hard to help hold you together as you've cried and yelled and got skinnier because you won't eat. You won't make an effort to get any better. You won't try."

"I have been trying! You even said that I've seemed better lately."

She shook her head. "And how long will that last? I heard you yelling with Immy downstairs. I don't know what you two were arguing about, but you've only been seeing her for a couple of days and already you're destroying that relationship."

"Why are you taking her side?" I demanded. "If you didn't hear the argument then you can't possibly know what it's about. For all you know, *she* was the one in the wrong."

"I don't care any more, Lindy," she said. "You just love drama – always have done. Just like your father. Everything had to be a big deal. Neither of you could ever quietly get on with life. If anything went wrong, it had to go *spectacularly* wrong, and if you did something good, well, the whole world had to know about it and applaud rapturously or you'd sulk. Now your dad has gone and you're carrying the tradition on by yourself – missing college, skulking around miserably. You can't just grieve like a normal person, can you?"

"At least I *am* grieving!" I yelled, tears burning my eyes. "Maybe I'm reacting this way because you just go around trying to erase Dad from our lives, as if he never existed. But then, you're drinking more nowadays, too, so I don't know *what* to think! You know, I saw you last night, crying on the sofa and surrounded by wine bottles? That doesn't look like someone who's grieving in a normal way, either, so don't criticise my behaviour. You're no saint!"

She threw the duvet cover off and attempted to stand up but wobbled and sat down again.

"You have no idea what I've been through, you vicious little cow," she said, her voice barely containing her rage. I flinched.

"All this time, I've been protecting you from the truth and you just treat me like I'm a monster . . . You're just like *him*."

"What does that even mean?" I asked.

She started sobbing and collapsed back on to the bed – this was far worse than the anger.

"Your dad loved you, Lindy, but he wasn't the hero you make him out to be. Or, at least, he wasn't with me. Like you, he thought I was boring. I was the quiet, sensible one, who worried about paying the bills and making plans for the future. Even though we own this house outright, we still have outgoings. While your father faffed around trying to decide what job he fancied doing, I had to take whatever boring jobs came my way. Naturally, I was a worrier, and that bothered him. He'd make fun of me for it and involve you in the jokes. Remember? You'd both laugh at me and roll your eyes when I said we couldn't afford to do things. You'd call me 'boring'. And who can forget the Lapland Disaster?"

"You wouldn't let us go."

"That's what *you* think. Your dad promised you a day trip to Lapland to see Father Christmas before consulting me. He'd, yet again, given up his latest job and we had no money coming in, except for what I was earning. There was no way we could have afforded it, but he told you that we'd go. He put me in a terrible situation because I had to say no in front of you, and you both blamed me for being horrible. You never knew the reason why."

"So why didn't you tell me?"

"You were six years old! Unlike your father, I didn't think it was fair to point out your other parent's weaknesses to you. I also didn't want you worrying about money at such a young age. That was supposed to be our responsibility as your parents."

I remembered that evening clearly – how I'd been in tears, how Dad had ranted about Mum being mean. She'd said nothing, which I took as stubbornness. I'd always thought that Dad was under Mum's thumb, but now I wasn't so sure. But why hadn't she said anything? She could have tried to explain what was happening; why she was behaving a certain way. I wasn't a mind reader. How could I have known?

"Why didn't you tell Dad to stop behaving like that, then?" I asked. "Surely if you'd just tried to reason with him—"

"I did try. He always said he would try to be more responsible, but he never changed. And then, before he died—"

She cut herself off, and I knew she was holding something back – something bigger; more awful.

"What did he do, Mum?" I asked, my voice catching in my throat, although I wasn't really sure I wanted to know. Something about the way she was behaving suggested that whatever revelation she had would ruin the idolised picture of my father forever.

"I'm sorry to tell you this, Lindy, but he told me he was leaving me. *Us.* He was leaving us for another woman."

34.
FURY, SADNESS, GUILT, RELIEF

At first, I could do nothing but stare at her.

She was lying.

She had to be. Dad would never have done this to us. She was just jealous that he and I had such a good relationship and had to invent something to make herself look better.

And yet...

When I'd arrived home the night of the party, his suitcase was in the hallway. I'd noticed how odd it was then. We weren't going on holiday and he always kept the bag in the attic when it wasn't needed. Was it packed already?

"When was he going to leave?"

"The day he died – Lindy, are you all right?"

The day after the party, the alarm goes off at its usual time. I pull my pillow around my head to try to block out the noise, but it stops anyway.

Mum's in my room – she turns it off before taking the pillow off my head. "Lindy, time to get up."

"I don't feel well."

"I know, but you can't miss college."

I roll over and squint at her in the bright light. "Please – just this once? Can't you write me a note? I promise I'll never do anything like this again."

I'm serious. I never want to feel this way EVER again.

"Sorry, but if you go out drinking on a weeknight, you have to cope with the consequences the next day. That's what adults do, and you're trying to be one, after all."

So much for the caring, gentle mother of last night.

I'm about to say this, when I notice her eyes are red-rimmed and puffy.

"What's wrong, Mum?"

She blinks away tears and clears her throat.

"Nothing's wrong. You need to get up and go to college. Consider it your punishment for lying to us, and that will be the end of it."

I try to stomp into the bathroom, but the movement hurts my head too much. It's bad enough that the room sways every time I take a step. I run a hot shower and stand under it until I hear Mum calling to me to hurry up from outside the bathroom door. Back in my bedroom, I pull on a pair of jeans and a baggy t-shirt, then twist my wet hair back into a ponytail. I creep gently down the stairs, trying to keep the nausea at bay.

The hallway looks normal and the suitcase is nowhere to be seen. Someone has cleared up the mess I made the night before, although there is still a faint, sour smell in the air that makes me gag a couple of times. I try breathing through my mouth instead.

"Are you coming through for breakfast?" Mum asks, as I grab my coat off the hook.

I grimace. "I can't face it. Sorry."

"In my experience, it's better to have something in your stomach," she suggests. "It calms the nausea. Just try some dry toast if you can't manage anything else."

I follow her into the kitchen but stop short when I see Dad sitting at the table, cradling a mug of tea in his hands. His eyes are bloodshot and it looks like he hasn't slept all night. He stands up and I back away from him.

"Lindy – please come here. I've got something important to tell you."

"Don't you dare," Mum says, casting him a furious look, "not when she's about to go to college."

"It's about last night," he replies, through gritted teeth. "I wanted to apologise."

I wait, not knowing what to do. He's visibly tense and he won't look me in the eye.

He clears his throat. "I guess I just overreacted. I'm not used to you lying to me – we've always been so honest with each other. It hurt my feelings."

Mum gives a weird snort and mutters, "That's rich, coming from you."

He turns to her. "Shut up, Caroline."

"Don't speak to her like that!"

I surprise myself with that comment and Dad spins around to look at me.

"Keep out of this, Lindy. You don't know what's going on."

"You're right, I don't. You're usually this funny and loving father, but, out of nowhere, you've turned into a horrible man – hitting me and yelling at Mum. What's wrong with you?"

My head throbs with every word, but they need saying.

"Don't talk to me like that!" Dad leans towards me and I back out of the room.

"Or what? You'll hit me again? I hate you!"

I run for the door, ignoring the dizziness, praying I'll get out of the house and away before I keel over. Dad's behind me, calling my name, but I leg it down the path and to the end of the street before I check that he isn't behind me. Then, I bend over and vomit all over the pavement.

"Why didn't you tell me sooner?" I yelled at Mum. "All this time I've been blaming myself for what happened to him, and he was going to leave us anyway?"

She backed away from me, alarmed at the fury in my voice. "I didn't want to upset you; you worshipped him. Since he never managed to leave us, I thought there was no point in telling you. Why spoil your memories of him?"

"When did you find out?" I demanded.

"The night that you went to that party. He came in and announced that he was leaving that night, though at least he had the decency to want to see you before he left. But then you came back late, and he'd worked himself into a state by then. Seeing you wasted must have pushed him over the edge."

I started shaking. "All this time, I've been grieving for a man who was a liar – who didn't love me as much as I thought he did."

"Lindy – don't say that. He loved you more than anything—"

"He can't have! He wouldn't have wanted to leave otherwise, would he?"

She shook her head. "It was because of our marriage. We'd not been getting on for ages . . . he felt trapped . . ."

"Why are you making excuses for him?" My voice was getting dangerously high and squeaky. "I hate him! I hate all the time I've wasted mourning him!"

Then, a sudden, terrible thought occurred to me. "Where was he going that day in the car?"

"I don't understand."

"The day he died! I always thought it was strange that he was driving, because he normally cycled to work."

She was twisting the wedding ring.

"He was driving to be with his new woman, wasn't he?"

She looked down, and her silence confirmed my fears.

I couldn't keep the screams down any more. Horrible, strangled noises were coming from my throat and Mum was reaching out to me, but I dropped to the floor and curled into a ball.

Mum got on to the floor next to me and wrapped me in a tight hug, whispering words I couldn't hear through the strange sounds I was making. It felt like all the tension I'd held within me had been uncorked, and fury, sadness, guilt and relief were pouring out of me.

Relief that I wasn't the cause of the accident and I didn't need to mourn him any more.

Guilt for the way I had been treating Mum all my life, not just after the accident.

Fury at his lies and deceit.

And sadness, real sadness, at the realisation that, to me, my father was dead in more ways than one.

We sat on the floor together, crying, for what seemed an

eternity. When there was a lull in the torment, when it felt like we couldn't physically shed any more tears, Mum said something totally unexpected.

"Let's go to McDonald's."

35.
A DIFFERENT BURDEN

We said nothing until we reached the restaurant and only then to place an order. With enormous burgers, piles of fries and a large Coke each, we grabbed a table by the window and tucked in. We gulped down food like we hadn't eaten in weeks – maybe we hadn't.

As we tackled the last remaining fries, Mum sat back and sighed contentedly.

"I really needed that."

"I thought you hated McDonald's?"

She shrugged. "When I'm trying to set a good example and be healthy then, yes, I hate it. But sometimes there's nothing better, especially for a hangover . . ." She smirked and nodded towards my empty packets. "You seemed to enjoy it too."

"I didn't realise how starving I was. It was a great idea."

She smiled at me and I returned it. For the first time in ages, even before Dad died, we were relaxed together.

"I always wondered about the suitcase," I pondered, prompting her to frown.

"What do you mean?"

"That night I came in drunk from the party, I noticed his suitcase by the front door. It seemed weird at the time, but then we had the argument and he died . . . and I forgot about it. I can remember it clearly now, though. Why didn't he just leave that night?"

"He felt bad about hitting you. He also wanted to talk to you when he knew you would understand, and that night you were . . . rather the worse for wear."

"He was going to tell me at the breakfast table, right? Why did you stop him?"

She nodded. "I didn't think it was kind or wise to send you in to college after hearing that. I insisted that he wait till the evening and he was annoyed with me. That's part of the reason he stormed off in such a mood that morning."

"Do you think the accident was a kind of divine punishment?"

"Don't be silly," she reassured. "You know I don't believe in all that stuff. It was an unfortunate coincidence, that's all. He was so angry when he left that he was probably distracted. They say people shouldn't drive intoxicated, but the same goes if they're upset."

"I can't believe you've been keeping all this from me," I said. "It must have been a nightmare. No wonder you weren't grieving for him."

"Oh, but I have been, Lindy," she corrected me. "It's made it *more* difficult, if anything. I don't know how to feel. I see his things and think of the happier times we had together, but the last time I saw him, he was on his way to be with his new woman. And, of course, he's your father and having you was an amazing thing that we did together." Her eyes welled with tears.

"I'm sorry," I whispered. "If I'd known . . ."

"Yes, I know." She held my hand and sniffed. "We've all done our best trying to cope. I think maybe it's time we're kinder on ourselves and do what we need to, to get through this."

"Will you still sell the house?" I asked.

"I honestly don't know. Maybe now we've shared this, I can move beyond it. If he'd left us, we'd have been in the house on our own anyway, so why not stay? But I need to have a think about it. I know you don't want to leave."

"At least I understand now why you might," I said. "And if it's what you need to find some kind of peace after all of this, I won't stand in your way."

It's odd how life sometimes swaps one burden for another – how one morning, I still felt guilty that I'd somehow killed my father and then, by the evening, I was struggling to know how to deal with the knowledge that he'd died on his way to being with another woman. I felt the raw ache that Mum and I weren't good enough for him. I was falling into shock and grief for a second time.

Mum urged me to not let this new information change my opinion of Dad, but it was impossible not to. Yes, I knew he loved me, but he wanted a different future for himself; one that didn't have me in it so much.

Then there was my guilt over Mum. She'd hidden this from me to protect me and I'd been so hard on her. I'd held Dad up as some kind of martyr when Mum was the one who'd had my best interests at heart, all through my life – not just now. All those times we'd teased her and pretended to yawn because we thought she was boring, yet she was the one holding the family together.

I'd lost the will or desire to talk to Dad in the few short hours since learning about his indiscretions. I needed some time to try to forgive him for what he'd planned to do to us, and I wasn't sure how long that would take. So, the first thing I did when we got back home was remove the picture frame from under my beanbag and take it into the garden shed. I toyed with the idea of throwing it away but that felt too permanent. Then again, after what had happened in Holywell, would Esme still be in touch? I was worried for my friend, but I couldn't keep holding on to a relic in case something might happen. I had to move on, return to normality, whatever that was now.

I hid the frame behind some folded-up lawn chairs, under a can of petrol, and murmured an apology to Esme.

I hoped she was still able to hear it.

36.
FREEDOM AND FLAMES

My sleep was blissful for once – uninterrupted by nightmares, ghosts or crying mothers. It was as though Mum's confession had soothed something in me, that by breaking a barrier I didn't know existed, I finally felt free.

I started doing my coursework again and Mum occasionally popped into my bedroom to leave me drinks and food. I found comfort in analysing Shakespearean monologues and memorising the conditional tense in French. It felt good to be away from the afterlife and, for the first time in weeks, I genuinely didn't feel the need to pull. Bifur and Bofur started coming upstairs again and stretched themselves out on my bed, basking in the sun.

Even though I knew that this serenity wouldn't last forever, I was happy in my newfound sense of domestic wellbeing. Well, until I received an email from my art tutor, asking me about the picture frame assignment. I'd not looked at the portrait I'd unwittingly done of Esme's family for a while and, of course,

I didn't want to now that I'd abandoned the plan to break the Pennyworth curse.

I opened my portfolio and stared at the picture. If anything, Charles looked even more smug, Esme's mother more tense and Esme, herself, more hopeful. I could hardly look at her. I felt guilty for abandoning her, but what else could I have done? Linwood had said, more or less, that it was all over now, so was there even any point speculating about her?

While I'd finished the portrait, I still needed to add the frame to the artwork. I started sketching a rough outline of the border from memory, incorporating the effect of the wood grain into the shading, adding as many of the swirls and flowers as the original. But as I worked, I became aware of a tickling sensation in my ears, forcing me to scratch at them in irritation. This seemed to make it worse, prompting a new sensation to emerge – less the feeling of a tickle and more the obvious whisper of breath in my ears. I jabbed my forefingers into them to try to block out the sound, but I could still hear a voice inside my head.

I'm in danger . . .

I looked down at the portrait and froze. Esme had become paler and her facial features had started sliding down her face – her eyes and nose melted into her mouth, as if she were a waxwork figure on fire. Her body bled black blood into the paper and, when I tried to reinforce the lines, they blurred and faded just as quickly, leaving a grey sludge as a reminder that she'd once been there.

Help me!

What was happening to her?

Then the stench of burning – not a smell like wood smoke on

a cold winter's day, but sweet and putrid – assaulting my nose. I didn't understand why this new smell was relevant – could I not go a day without this damn curse affecting my life?

I felt an overwhelming urge to look towards the window.

Black clouds of smoke billowed up and towards me, carried on the wind.

I got up and looked out, all my senses alert, my heart racing. The smoke was coming from our shed and, standing just in front of it, was my mother.

I recalled the half-empty can of petrol for the lawnmower that I had placed on top of the frame. If that caught light, the whole shed would go up like a firework.

Throwing my window open wide, I leant out and screamed at her.

"Mum! Get away from the shed! There's petrol in there! Get back into the house!"

She slowly turned and looked up at me, but her eyes were no longer hers and all she did was smile and turn back to the roaring flames.

I raced into the hallway, praying I'd get there before she got hurt. Through the kitchen and out the back door; I stumbled, coughing, as the smoke assaulted me – it was thicker here and stuck to the inside of my nose, not allowing a sliver of fresh air.

If I thought the image of Mum standing motionless in front of the shed was bad, she then did something decidedly worse. She began walking up to the door, as if in a trance, and, as she did so, a sudden wind picked up, feeding the greedy flames as they leapt and licked higher.

"Mum! Stop!"

She reached out to pull the shed door open – she'd burn her fingers on the bolt if she tried to open it. She ignored me and started tugging on it, clearly not affected by the scalding metal that was eating into her skin. She managed to open the door and walked inside just as I reached her.

I ran in after her. The smoke was so thick that I couldn't see her. This was only a small shed, though, and it was packed full of junk. Where could she have gone? I was coughing, spluttering, yelling for her. The acrid smoke burned my throat and my nose felt on fire.

A hand grabbed my forearm, yanking me outside into the blinding sunlight and sent me spiraling to the ground.

"No!" I screamed; begged. "My mother's in there! We've got to get her out!"

Hands gripped me under my armpits, dragging me at speed down the garden as the grass burned my bare feet, before a deafening explosion ripped through the air, blowing wood and glass in all directions.

A heavy body fell on top of me, forcing the air from my lungs. I cried out for my mother, struggling against the heavy weight of the arms and legs that kept me pressed down on the ground. My ears were ringing from the explosion, adding to the heart-stopping panic and disorientation that was gripping me.

I was dragged to my feet, hauled through the back door and into the kitchen. All I was aware of were the tears that were spilling from my eyes, burning as hot as fire, as I screamed for my mother entrapped by flames.

And then she was in front of me, reaching out for me, and

hugging me close to her. The rougher, stronger hands had let me go and I was in my mother's embrace, smelling the sweet, familiar scent of her perfume.

37.
THE OTHER
WOMAN

Mum insisted that she had never been in the shed.

From the kitchen window, she'd seen the smoke and called the fire brigade. She claimed she heard me run down the stairs, yelling for her and watched me run outside towards the shed. She started coming after me when the fire brigade had arrived. They saved my life before tackling the blaze. Now they were in the garden, making sure that the fire was fully extinguished while I watched in disbelief.

Mum sponged my face and neck with lukewarm water, soothing me with absent-minded words that meant nothing to her or me, until one of the firefighters came in to tell us that everything had been made safe.

"Do you have any idea what caused the fire?" Mum asked.

"Nothing can be determined right now. There was a petrol can on its side in the shed, and it looked like the top had been taken off. It's possible, if it hadn't been screwed back on tight enough, that it could have fallen off if the can tipped over, but there's no way of knowing because we can't find the lid anywhere."

There was a pause, during which I felt Mum staring at me. "Lindy – you were in the shed yesterday . . ."

I looked in horror at her. "Are you suggesting I did this?"

"No! Not at all – I just wondered . . . Did you notice anything? Did you touch anything?"

They were *both* staring at me and my face burned. "I just . . . I . . ."

How could I explain I was hiding a Victorian picture frame in there?

The picture frame! It would be destroyed by now.

"Lindy?" Mum's voice was sharper. "What were you doing in there?"

"I just took the bottle of WD-40 back, that's all."

The colour drained from Mum's face. "You couldn't have. I threw the bottle out after . . ."

She stopped herself. The firefighter didn't need to hear about that, too.

Luckily, he stepped in.

"If you were in there the other day, it sounds like this might have been an accident – perhaps you knocked over the petrol can when you went in and didn't notice it. We'll file a report and you can make a claim on your insurance. But you—" he paused to look at me sternly, "no more running into burning buildings. That's *our* job."

What a joker.

Mum thanked him and saw him to the door. When she came back, she was still looking at me weirdly.

"Mum, I know you must think this is all too coincidental, but

I swear I had nothing to do with this. I just . . . I put something in there that reminded me of Dad, that I didn't want in my bedroom any more. I must have knocked the petrol can over without realising, like the firefighter said. I didn't do it on purpose—"

"Oh, Lindy! I never said I thought it was . . . deliberate."

Even better.

We were both startled by a sudden and urgent hammering on the door.

I got up and peeked through the curtains – closed from the eyes and craning necks of our nosy neighbours.

Tom and Immy were on the doorstep.

I tried to close the curtains without them seeing me, but I didn't make it in time. Tom called out, "Lindy! Please open up! We want to make sure you're OK!"

This was not what I needed just now, with Mum suspecting me of accidental arson, but they'd already seen me, so I supposed I had no choice.

When I opened the door, Immy stepped forward and gave me one of her bear hugs, squashing the air out of me.

"Oh my goodness, Lindy! We were walking past your street when we saw the fire engines. We were terrified that they were there for you – and when we saw that they were . . ." She glanced at Tom and then back at me. "We were so worried . . ."

"It's fine," I replied, disentangling myself. "It was just the garden shed. The house is fine. We're fine."

"But all the black smoke," Tom said, eyes wide. "It looked worse than a small shed fire."

"That was the half-full petrol canister exploding. It blew the shed to pieces."

They gaped at me.

I wasn't going to tell them any more than necessary. Besides, Immy and I still weren't speaking, as far I could remember.

"Immy, Tom – lovely to see you again." Mum emerged from the living room. "Lindy, don't be so rude. Invite them in."

"We don't want to intrude," Immy said. "We just wanted to make sure you're both all right."

"That's very kind of you. We're fine; just a little shocked. Come on in – we could do with some friendly faces in here."

Immy and Tom followed Mum into the kitchen and then to the back door to look at the mess in our garden. She talked about how brave the firefighters were in tackling the blaze and that one of them had pulled me out of the shed.

"Did you try to put it out yourself?" Tom asked incredulously.

"She thought that I was in the shed and ran in to save me," Mum replied, before I had a chance. She came over and gave me a big hug, patting my hair. "But she's promised not to do anything like that again!"

They all laughed, while looking at me with concern, and I wanted to scream at them to just leave me the hell alone. But I smiled and went along with it – it was the easiest way out.

"Well, I'm going to have a shower," Mum said, heading for the door. "I stink of smoke. Help yourselves to anything you want."

We stood in silence, listening for her footsteps to recede up the stairs, until I couldn't take it any longer.

"So, who was on guard duty today when the fire broke out?" I snapped.

Immy looked at Tom and then at me before clearing her throat. "Neither of us. Tom met me at college, and we were walking home this way when we saw the smoke and fire engines. Honestly, Lindy – I promise."

"Well, maybe if one of you *had* been stalking me, the shed wouldn't have caught fire," I deadpanned. "Unless one of you did it, of course."

Immy's eyes widened. "How could you even *think* that? I'm your best friend!"

"Who doesn't believe a word I say and thinks I've invented a weird story because I've gone insane."

Anger flashed across her face. "That doesn't mean I'd set your shed on fire. If you think that's true, then you really *are* insane!"

"Stop it, both of you!"

Tom stepped in between us, palms held up. "Look, Lindy, this is all my fault, not Immy's. I was the one who suggested keeping an eye on you after you stormed out of the café the other day. I was worried about you because I know how easy it is to get obsessed about things when someone close to you dies. I've been there, don't forget."

"I don't need babysitting, especially from someone I've just met," I spat, glaring at him.

"I know, but you've been through a really tough time lately. You need some good friends to make sure you're all right. I wish I'd had that when my dad died."

"Which is why I don't understand you," I rebutted. "Remember *where* we first met you? At a spiritualist church, because you also wanted to talk to your dad. You're not so different to me after all."

"But I haven't been trying to solve riddles set by a Victorian ghost and wandering around graveyards," he replied quietly.

"Well, you needn't worry, because I won't be doing that any more."

"Really?" Immy asked. "Why?"

"You warned me that doing this kind of stuff might hurt me even more and you were right."

Immy glanced at Tom and then back to me. She was going to get whiplash if she kept doing that. "I *was*?"

I really didn't want to go into what had happened at Holywell – they wouldn't believe me anyway – so I decided to keep the information to facts they would understand.

"I found out last night that, on the day Dad died, he was leaving us for another woman," I said, ignoring Immy's shocked spluttering. "Apparently, he wanted to go the night you and I were at Jake's party, but I was late home, and then he and I got into an argument. He was going to tell me the next morning, but I didn't give him a chance."

I felt tears prickle in my eyes, furious with myself for wanting to cry.

"The thing is," I continued, in a thick voice, "I've spent all these weeks hating myself because the last words I ever said to him were that I hated him and all along he was on his way to that ... *slut's* house. Here I was, wanting to beg his forgiveness and wasting all those tears ..."

I crumbled, letting the tears flow freely down my face.

"And now I discover that he wanted to leave me and Mum for a new life. So, it's all over. I don't want to talk to him. If I did get the chance, I don't even know what I'd say."

"Oh, Lindy, I'm so sorry," Immy whispered.

She moved to hug me again, but I shook my head and stepped back. I didn't want anyone touching me.

"How did you find out?" Tom asked.

"Mum and I had an argument last night and she told me everything. It explains why she's been so weird since Dad died."

His face had turned a strange shade of grey. "Do you know who the other woman is?" he asked.

I shook my head.

"Do you want to?"

I scowled at him. "No. Why would I want anything to do with her?"

He shrugged. "No reason. I just wondered if, you know, you were ever curious."

"For God's sake, Tom, why would she want to meet the cow who tried to split up her family?" Immy said, looking at him in disbelief.

"Why are you both assuming that she's a cow or a slut? Maybe she didn't even know that he had a family."

I was surprised at how furious he looked; it was as if I'd personally insulted him.

"Tom, will you *shut up*?" Immy turned on him. "You're supposed to be supporting Lindy, not defending the woman who wanted to steal her father away."

He clenched his jaw. "She didn't want to steal Lindy's father. She knew that he was unhappily married but he didn't tell her that he had children, otherwise she wouldn't have considered seeing him. It was just as much of a shock to *her* when she read about his death in the paper."

"What are you talking about?" snapped Immy. "How could you possibly know all of that?"

"Because, that cow, that *slut*, that woman . . . that's my mother."

38.
ROLE REVERSAL

I felt the room spin and Immy's hands on my forearms, steering me to a chair. I put my head between my knees and tried to steady my breathing, while she straightened herself up and launched into an attack.

"Have you known about all this all along?" Immy demanded. "Is this why you made friends with us?"

"Yes . . . and no." He hesitated. "When my mother and I read in Ben's obituary – your *dad's* obituary," Tom corrected himself, "that he left behind a wife and a daughter, well, to say we were shocked would be an understatement. We knew that he was apparently in an unhappy marriage and that he was planning to leave his wife – your mum," he added unnecessarily, "but we had no idea that he had a child."

"Why didn't he tell you?" Immy snapped back.

"How would *I* know?" Tom said defensively. "He lied to everyone and now we're all in this mess."

I raised my head. "So, you've known who I was all this time

and you never told me?"

"I wanted to! Believe me, I did. But I didn't know how. I mean, how do you suddenly drop something like this into an everyday conversation?"

"There were plenty of opportunities." Immy's voice was full of hurt and anger. "You don't string someone along, pretending to be their friend, when you know something major about their life."

"I thought if Lindy got to know me first – and hopefully like me – then maybe she'd be all right. I never meant to hurt either of you," he said, looking at both of us pleadingly.

"How did you know where I lived?" I asked. "Were you following me for a long time?"

"No, I swear I wasn't, although I did see you from a distance at your father's funeral . . ." his voice tapering off towards the end.

I felt sick with disgust and fury. ""You were *there*?"

"Only because I was trying to get my head around everything that I'd just found out."

"Was your mother there too?"

"No. She was a mess after your father died. She was devastated, but also angry about how he'd deceived us. She still is. Mum and I were . . . *are* struggling too."

"Don't you dare compare your situation with mine."

My voice was quiet – calm, almost – but the rage inside me was close to bursting. On instinct, I reached up and yanked at my hair, holding the strands in front of me, perversely enjoying the horrified expressions on Immy's and Tom's faces.

"Lindy – don't hurt yourself," Immy said. "He's not worth it."

"I didn't do it to hurt myself – I did it to stop me from hurting *him*," I growled, with a nod in Tom's direction. "It's my control valve, Immy. Tom's used us both – withheld information and wormed his way into our lives—"

"I wanted to get to know you," Tom said. "I thought we could both feel less alone."

"So, what about when we met you at the spiritualist church?" I asked. "Was that planned, too?"

He bowed his head. "Yes. I followed you to the café first – it was just after I discovered where you lived – and, by coincidence, you went out to meet Immy. Honestly – I hadn't been near you before that."

I didn't know what to say. I felt violated, knowing that he'd been there all along, following me to the café, staging our first meeting. I should have paid attention to the red flags.

"So, it turns out that I'm not the craziest out of all of us," I said softly. "I think you've probably won that competition, Tom. At least I don't stalk people and then pretend to bump into them."

"Look, I know this seems bad but there was no hidden agenda," Tom pleaded. "As soon as I found out that Ben was your father, I wanted to get to know you, Lindy, and look after you somehow. You know, like a brother might."

"A *brother*?"

The voice didn't belong to any of us.

Mum was standing in the door frame – wet, tousled hair framing a face that was white with shock and rage.

"Mrs Pennyworth—" Tom began, but Mum held up a hand. "Why are you talking about your mother and my husband? Did your mother and my husband . . ." She swallowed, started again. "Was your mother the reason my husband left me?"

Tom nodded.

"Get out," she whispered, before she started screaming, "Get out! Get out! *Get out!*"

Tom fled, almost tripping over the rug in the hallway, and crashed out the front door.

Mum turned to us, breathless and borderline hysterical. "I don't *ever* want to see him in this house again! Understood?"

We nodded and she stormed out of the room, up the stairs and slammed her bedroom door before she started hurling things against the walls and sobbing.

"I'd better go and see her," I told Immy.

"I'm so sorry."

"Why are *you* apologising?"

"All of this . . . and him . . . and me saying I was worried about you . . ." She rubbed her eyes and looked at me beseechingly. "Please believe me when I say I had no idea—"

"I do."

She had tears running down her face. "After everything you've been through – and now this." She swiped her eyes with her wrist.

"It'll be all right," I reassured her, as I walked her to the front door.

It'll be all right.

You have to tell yourself this when things are so desperately wrong, don't you? Because if you don't, your mind shuts down and you have a breakdown and throw things at walls.

I watched as a shard of porcelain skittered to a stop at my feet.

I stood in the doorway and listened to her rant about how ". . . that bitch must have sent her son around to spy on us!"

There went her favourite vase.

"It wasn't enough that she had the best of him while he was alive—"

And the Swarovski cat figure.

"She's got to taunt me now he's *dead*!"

When she was holding her framed wedding photo hostage, I rushed over to prise it from her fingers.

"Not now, Mum. If you're still angry, you can chuck it later."

Mum sat on her bed and looked at me through swollen, bloodshot eyes. "It seems these days that you're the adult and I'm the child."

I hugged her. "Sometimes we all need a little looking after. Now it's your turn."

I spent the rest of the evening with her. Between sobs, I cooked our favourite comfort meal – pasta with heaps of butter, black pepper and parsley – and put on *Friends* reruns for two hours. Two cups of hot chocolate later, feeling slightly sick from an overdose of marshmallows, and finally all cried out, we both went to bed, determined to get back to normality the next day.

Instead, I woke up cradling Esme's picture frame in my arms in the dead of the night.

A box of matches was on my bedside table.

Every one inside used.

39.
DARKNESS CONSUMES US

Oh my God.

I didn't do it. I didn't do it.

An anaemic light was coming from the mirror on my dressing table and a weak cough came from its direction.

"Esme?"

I jumped out of bed and ran over, peering into the glass.

Esme was slumped over. When she raised her head to look at me, her bright blue eyes were sunken pools of darkness against a translucent face; her skin papery, like dried petals that had been pressed between the pages of a heavy book for too long.

"What happened to you?"

"Why have you given up on me? Why would you do such a thing when you are so close to the end? You promised you'd help me, Lindy. *You promised.*" Her voice broke.

"Linwood told me it was all over. He said we'd broken the rules—"

"And you didn't think to carry on trying anyway? He doesn't control the curse. The witch who put it on us does."

"But then why doesn't *she* visit us? Punish us? It's always him."

"He's as part of the curse as we are. His fate in the afterlife is as tangled up as ours is – only he never realised it. He was never the most astute of souls."

"I'm sorry, Esme – I never meant to hurt you – but things have changed here. I found out some things about my dad that ... that are so hurtful that I don't want to keep on looking. He was a liar and a cheat and a ... a ... heartless bastard!"

"How can you speak of him in that way?" Esme gasped. "He's your father. Whatever he's done, you owe him your heart and your loyalty!"

"Do you know where he was going the day he died? He was leaving my mother and me for another family. He'd been planning it for a while, apparently. He had two families and he lied to them both. Now he's gone and we've all been mourning a man who was selfish to the core. I'm sorry, but I'm not going to do this any more. I'm moving on."

"I am truly sorry that you've found out about this," Esme said. Her breathing had become more erratic. "But I must beg of you to please finish this for my sake. I know I ask a great deal of you, but you are my only hope – I am throwing myself on your mercy. Please do not abandon me and my father!"

Guilt tugged at my conscience. I didn't want to let Esme down – she felt almost like a sister to me. She was family, after all, and from my own sadness I knew how I would feel if I were in her situation.

"If I do this for you and reunite you with your father, do I have to speak to mine?"

She shook her head. "No. Not if you don't want to. But I am

worried that you will break his heart. He is truly sorry—"

She clapped a hand to her mouth.

I leant forward, eyes narrowed. "What do you mean? How would *you* know that he is sorry?"

Her eyes were wide with alarm. "I . . . I should not have said—"

"What do you know? Have you seen him?"

"Lindy – I'm sorry – I cannot tell you any more than I already have."

"You've told me nothing!" I yelled, gripping the mirror. "If he's spoken to you, then you should tell me! You, more than anyone, should know that!"

"It was hardly anything! He came through my door once and begged me—"

She was cut off, as blackness swarmed around her. She screamed and cowered, covering her head with her arms, trying to protect herself from whatever force was attacking her.

"Esme!"

I banged uselessly on the mirror with my fist until it cracked and splintered all the way down, and blood gushed from my hand.

The room whirled.

I grasped on to anything that tethered me to consciousness. I failed.

40.
FINAL WARNING

Something distinctly feline prodded my face.

I blinked, groaning from the nauseating pain in my head, feeling as if I'd been hit by a lorry. I was lying on the floor and Bofur was staring down at me, puzzled. When he saw me starting to move, he bent his head down and rubbed his cheek against mine before letting out a yawn.

I pushed myself up and examined my hand. It was fine – there was no sign of anything, not even a scratch. I looked around for the mirror. It was in its usual place on my dressing table – undamaged.

Even though I knew I wouldn't see Esme there, I checked anyway. I feared for her safety – how could anything hurt her in the afterlife? What had attacked her last night?

Then I spotted the picture frame lying on the floor. Esme's golden hair had been ripped out of it – the plaits pulled apart and strands splayed all over the carpet.

"No!" I cried, scrabbling over to pick up the frame. The photo was still there, thankfully, but the patterns of Esme's beautiful hair were ruined.

I looked over at Bofur, who was languidly cleaning his face with his paw. Sensing my gaze, he stopped, mid-clean, and stared back. Had he done this?

As Bofur returned to cleaning himself, I saw it – a strand of blonde hair caught in one of his claws.

"Hey, what have you got there?"

I leant forward and stroked him to divert his attention as I started to pull Esme's hair from his paw. But as soon as he felt the tug, he twisted his head around and sank his teeth into my hand, clamping down hard. I screeched in pain and surprise and tried to pull my hand away, but he wouldn't let go. If anything, he tightened his bite, teeth pushing themselves into the soft skin, and flattened his ears as a low, angry growl erupted from him.

Panic rose inside me. Bifur and Bofur were the gentlest cats I'd ever known. They could hardly take care of the mice problem, let alone attack me. My breath quickened as I thought of ways to make him let go.

Keeping still, I waited, hoping that if I gave up resisting he would let go. It stopped the growls – but as soon as I tried to pull my hand away, he clamped down harder. In desperation, I grabbed the scruff of his neck and he froze, allowing me the chance to pull him off of me. Bofur hissed before slinking out of my room, pelting down the stairs as fast as his tiny, furry legs would carry him.

My hand had bloody fang marks, but luckily it didn't look too unsalvageable. I went to the bathroom to rinse the damage thoroughly in hot water, in case of infection, then decided to jump in the shower, hoping that would clear my head and unknot my stiff neck.

Everything started to loosen as I let the hot water soothe my aches and pains. The steam, scented with almond and rose from my shower gel, was a welcome and comforting escape to a world where there were no ghosts or temperamental cats.

At first, it was so gradual that I didn't notice, but when piercing heat subsumed my body, I frantically started fumbling with the shower controls.

It made no difference.

I stabbed at the button to turn the water off but all that did was increase the pressure, shooting scalding jets on to my body. I yelped, diving out of the shower. I couldn't see anything in the steam, not even my hand in front of my face. The extractor fan was only making the situation worse, pushing the steam inside the room rather than removing it.

I groped around, trying to find the bathroom window, but when my fingers found purchase, the latch wouldn't budge – wrenching it this way and that did nothing but tear at my fingernails. It was jammed shut.

My skin was burning from the steam. Heat was making its way inside of my throat, invisible hands threatening to strangle me.

I dropped to the floor to crawl to the bathroom door, but even the tiles were burning my body. I couldn't move; I couldn't breathe in the thick air.

My skin was blistering. I was going to boil to death.

I curled up on the floor, managing choked sobs and praying to make it stop.

The shower clicked itself off and the steam dissipated within seconds, as if someone had hit reverse, escaping through the extractor fan like a criminal fleeing the scene of a crime.

On the wall over the radiator a section of paint was peeling off, revealing dark red writing.

Tears trailing down my face from the pain, I struggled to stand. I peered at the letters but not enough of the paint had come away so, using my damaged fingernails, I scratched away at the flakes.

It was hopeless – they came off in such tiny pieces that it would take me forever to uncover the message. Grabbing my toothbrush, I scrubbed hard.

Within a few minutes, I was able decipher the message scrawled on the wall:

This is your final warning.

My skin crawled. In less than twenty-four hours, a force, most likely Linwood, had tried to seriously hurt me twice.

How could a ghost even harm me?

The burning returned with a vengeance. I looked down at my arms and hands, feeling sick at the sight of huge blisters bubbling on my skin. In the mirror, I saw them coming up on my neck, rising like fluid-filled monsters. At least my face was unscathed, not that that was much consolation.

Swallow the panic.

I told myself that the blisters would vanish once I left the bathroom, just like the cut on my finger had done a few days ago and the gash down my hand from the night before. They were just another symptom of psychic interaction, weren't they?

I wrapped my towel around my body, wincing as the cotton brushed against my skin. I hurried back to my bedroom, quickly closing the door behind me, and threw off the towel, waiting for the blisters to disappear.

Come on, come on, come on – go back to normal!

I blinked hard and opened my eyes again to check.

The blisters were still there, looking angrier than ever, throbbing with every movement.

I groaned and my hand moved towards my hair, but the pain from the blisters was overwhelming.

This can't be real. Side effects, side effects . . . it's all in my head . . .

"Oh!"

Mum!

I opened my bedroom door and saw Mum standing just outside the bathroom in her dressing gown, staring open-jawed at the wall.

The writing . . . the flaking paint . . . none of that could still be there. No one ever saw what I saw . . . that's why they didn't believe me.

Mum turned towards me slowly, eyes nearly out of her skull. "Why? What . . .?"

She stopped, whimpering, and clapped a hand to her mouth as she took in my naked, blistered body.

41.
IGNORANT MINDS

Eventually, the two paramedics agreed that I could stay at home rather than go into hospital, on the condition that I rested, with my arms raised, to prevent further swelling. The "good news" was that the blisters hadn't broken, so the risk of infection was low. They bandaged my arms, hands and neck so I could wear clothes, but I had to have them changed at my GP's until they healed.

While one paramedic stayed with me in the living room, the other took my mother into the hallway where they had a hushed conversation. My paramedic tried to distract me by talking about music and films, but I ignored her. I wanted to know what was being said on the other side of the door. I could only hear the paramedic occasionally, saying things like, "duty to inform social services due to multiple call-outs" and "psychiatric help". My paramedic was fussing over Bifur and Bofur, who were sitting with me on the sofa – she was talking in a raised voice to try to block out the conversation in the hallway.

"My little fella is called Pedro," she said, stroking Bifur, who rolled over in ecstasy. "I adopted him from the local animal shelter because no one else wanted him. He's got epilepsy and needs constant monitoring and medication," she added. "I can't give up the day job even when I'm at home!"

My half-smile faded as soon as the door opened and Mum trailed in behind the other paramedic. Mum looked terrible, like she'd aged ten years in only two days.

"Ready to go?" the paramedic asked.

"Yep. Just let me tickle these two furballs one more time!"

After the two left, Mum sat down next to me and my heart raced.

"Don't send me away!" I begged.

She looked at me in bemusement. "No one's sending you away, Lindy. Whatever gave you that idea?"

"I heard that paramedic saying something about psychiatric assessments."

"Ah. Well, she was pretty worried about you. First there was the issue with the chemical inhalation from the WD-40, then we had the shed fire with you running head first into it and today you burnt yourself in the shower, rubbing off paintwork with a toothbrush. These aren't things that most . . . *stable* people do."

"But I didn't mean to! I mean, I did rub the paint off because I thought I saw something behind it. The burns were an accident. The water suddenly went boiling hot and the pressure increased without warning. I got out as quickly as I could – I swear!" I was rambling; pleading.

She looked down and twisted her wedding ring. "I want to believe you, Lindy, but you keep writing on walls—"

"That wasn't me today!"

"Well, I don't know who else could have done it."

"I can't explain it, Mum, but I promise I didn't do it."

She carried on, not looking me. "And then there's been your hair-pulling, which you've been doing for quite some time now. You've got a history of self-harm since your father died, so it's difficult not to be concerned. I had to tell her about that, of course, which is why she recommended a psychiatric assessment. I said I would arrange that via the GP. We'll book you an appointment for tomorrow. I should have taken you today, really, but . . ."

She pulled the ring right off her finger. "I feel responsible for this latest drama. I shouldn't have told you about your father and his affair, although I suppose you would have found out from that . . . *Tom* anyway." She spat his name out as if it were poison. "Frankly, it's been an awful couple of days for both of us."

"I'm glad you told me," I insisted. I wanted to hold her hand but both of mine were hurting too much from the blisters. "It's helped me to stop blaming myself. And Tom's confession – it was a shock, but I guess I can understand why he's been hanging around. He's just trying to understand all of this, like we are."

"Come off it, Lindy! It's bloody creepy! The way he wormed his way into your life isn't normal – hanging around and following you from a distance. He should have been honest with you from the start, so you could decide whether to let him into your life or not. I don't understand why you're not more upset."

"We were both tricked by Dad," I said. "He can't be blamed for what happened." I was too exhausted to hold any kind of real grudge.

She didn't look convinced. "There's something I wanted to ask about last night, but I forgot. You were all talking about some kind

235

of church you met at?"

I took a deep breath. It was time to tell her, even though she'd probably think I was weirder than before.

The story came pouring out of me like water: trying to contact Dad, meeting Tom at the spiritualist church, finding the photo frame. I kept going despite her increasing expression of disbelief, especially when I got to the part about Esme and attempting to find the missing photo pieces. I ended with what had happened the previous night and this morning – that someone in the afterlife was trying to hurt me and had done something to Esme.

"This whole thing isn't about talking to Dad any more," I finished, "it's about saving Esme – if that's even possible now."

I had to stop talking at some point. I'd been gabbling on, thoroughly frightened of her response. When I did stop, and she just stared at me, I added, "You can check all this with Immy, although she doesn't really believe anything is going on with the ghosts. She's so stubborn that she won't allow herself to look beyond the obvious."

"You're right, she is stubborn. And sensible," Mum said slowly. "It's a shame that you can't see things the way she does."

"What do you mean?"

She leaned forward and took my hand. "I can see why it is so important to you to believe that we all go on to something else after we die. It's a comforting thought, especially when you've lost someone close to you. But even if there is a heaven that we all go to when we die, we can't come back when we feel like it and talk to the living."

"How do you know?" I challenged her. "If there's no proof either way?"

She shook her head but said nothing.

Then I remembered the picture frame. She couldn't deny physical proof.

"Come upstairs – follow me!"

I ran upstairs, ignoring the stinging in my arms and hands, while she followed me, urging me to slow down, warning I'd make the burns worse if I was too energetic. I opened the door to my bedroom and picked up the beanbag, where I'd hidden the frame earlier, announcing, "There's the picture frame! You can see it for yourself!"

But all I was pointing at was bare carpet. The frame had disappeared.

I tried to convince Mum that the picture frame was real by showing her the portrait I'd done for my art homework but she wouldn't buy it, saying that I could have copied it from a picture on the internet. When I asked her why I'd want to lie to her, she said, "I think you believe what you're saying, but it's not true, Lindy. There are no such things as ghosts."

I didn't bother to argue; I knew there was no point. It was hard to change an ignorant mind about the paranormal.

I went to bed early, exhausted and depressed by the day's events. My skin still felt like it was on fire and Mum gave me some codeine to dampen the pain. "It will help you sleep, too," she added as she tucked me into bed – something she hadn't done since I was ten. Was this how things were going to be from now on?

Being fussed over and treated like a child?

42.
APPARITION

I could feel someone sitting at the foot of the bed.

It must be Mum. She was checking up on me; making sure I was not destroying the rest of the walls with my marker pen. All of the writing in the bathroom had mysteriously disappeared without the help of WD- 40, I'd noticed as I'd got ready for bed.

"Mum – you don't need to sit with me," I murmured, yawning. "I promise I'm not going to do anything stupid."

I couldn't really blame her if she didn't believe me. She'd had enough trouble, thanks to me, to last a lifetime.

Still, she didn't reply. That was strange.

"Mum?"

I noticed her breathing sounded more laboured and had a wet quality to it, like she had a chest infection.

Worried, I sat up and reached over to turn on my bedside lamp.

"Leave it off," a voice wheezed.

I felt sick with fear.

"Mum? You're scaring me—"

"I am not your mother."

The voice was female and frail, with a more mature cadence.

A weak glow pulsated, swirling and restless, unable to remain still.

"I haven't much time or energy, so please listen to me. Concentrate."

She started coughing and I winced at the sound of her fighting for every breath.

"You sound like you need a doctor," I said stupidly. The figure chuckled through breathy gasps.

"A doctor. If only I'd had one before this dreadful illness took over me, then my fate might have been very different indeed. But then again, a doctor was the person responsible for my demise, so perhaps a physician is not the wisest choice for me."

I quickly caught up. "Freeda?" I whispered.

"Yes, my dear, although understandably not in the flesh."

"Why are you here? Were you behind everything that's happened to me over the past twenty-four hours? The fire, the burns, the writing on the wall—" Questions kept spilling out of my mouth with no filter.

"I was not responsible for any of those events. They were, I'd say, merely unfortunate occurrences."

"Someone was trying to hurt me," I asserted. "Was it Linwood, then?"

She gave another wheezy laugh. "Linwood? He couldn't do that if he tried. He was always the most loyal and loving son a mother could want, but he could not cast the simplest spell. He lacked the skill – the finesse."

I stayed quiet, not sure where to go from here.

"I want to help you."

"Help *me*? I am a descendent of the man who destroyed you! Why would you want to do me any favours?"

"I am not being entirely altruistic – I will gain from this situation, too. As you can hear, in death I am still riddled with the consumption that took me in life. This is a punishment given to me because Linwood sought vengeance through a witch practising dark magic. If you can break the curse, I will be free of this ailment, you will be able to speak to your father, and Esmerelda and Charles will be together again. Everyone benefits. Besides, I am weary of all this hatred and vengeance. It is time to put the past to rest."

"But why is Linwood trying to stop me from breaking the curse if it would help you? It doesn't make sense."

She sighed. "The situation is . . . complicated. In activating the curse, Linwood made a tremendous blunder. By hiding one piece of the photograph by my grave, he unintentionally tied us up in all this. So, my dear, we are afflicted by the same curse as you and your family. We cannot see each other or speak to each other. If he knew that I was still suffering in this life, then I know that he would immediately help you to break the curse, but he just does not understand the rules of such magic."

"Didn't the witch warn him?"

"The witch was as useless as Linwood. She understood how to cast spells but did not comprehend the consequences. It is all a regrettable mess and, if we do not move quickly, the curse will become permanent."

"But I can't break the curse without the final riddle – and Linwood made it very clear that he would not let Esme give it to me."

"*He* might not be prepared to give you the clue, but *I* am," Freeda replied. "I watched Linwood and that ridiculous witch cast the spells, so I know the riddles, too."

"Why don't you just tell me what I need to do?" I asked. "You need to take the picture frame to its final destination, whose name is given in the third riddle. I cannot merely give this to you because you must solve it yourself, to allow you to move to the final stage. But you have managed admirably so far; I have no doubt that you will succeed."

"Can *I* make one request this time?" I asked.

"Perhaps," Freeda replied cautiously.

"Please don't make me write it on the walls. I'm in enough trouble as it is."

43.
UNHEALTHILY OBSESSED

It was nearly midday when I woke up with a piece of paper pressed against my cheek. I unfolded it and checked that the writing was still there.

> *High in London, on a hill,*
> *Gates protect the dead ones still,*
> *Cemetery residents on the East,*
> *Looking for eternal peace.*

The third riddle, as promised. Freeda had dictated it to me just before she'd faded into the night and I'd written it down the normal way instead of scrawling all over my walls. I looked around me just to double check that I'd not done anything stupid and sighed with relief to see that I hadn't.

My stomach was rumbling so I headed downstairs to the kitchen to fix something to eat. Mum was sitting at the table with her laptop.

"Why didn't you wake me?" I asked, grabbing juice from the fridge.

"I thought you needed the sleep," she replied. She looked better – her cheeks had more colour and her eyes were less sunken. She'd washed her hair and put on a pretty dress.

"You look nice," I said as I sat down at the table. "Are you going somewhere?"

She shook her head. "No. I just thought I'd feel better if I made more of an effort." She looked at me. "How are you feeling? How are your arms?"

"A bit better," I lied.

"I've booked an appointment at the practice today for the nurse to check your burns and redress your bandages. We've got to be there for four o'clock."

"You don't need to go, too," I said. "I'm sure you have loads of other things you'd rather be doing."

She shook her head. "I want to be there with you. I want to see what they do with the bandages and how they think everything is healing. I've been thinking . . ." She paused, as if she wasn't sure whether to continue.

"Thinking what?" I prompted.

"Well, the way things have been here – we could both do with a holiday. There are some good last-minute flights for this weekend. If I can learn how to change your bandages, then we could go away and forget about this place for a little while."

My heart started racing. We couldn't do that – at least not until I took the picture frame to its final resting place.

"There's no need to look so alarmed," Mum soothed. "We won't go anywhere far. I just thought somewhere sunny and warm would do us a world of good: Spain or maybe the south of France?"

"That sounds nice but maybe in a week or so," I said, trying to smile. "I have various college projects to hand in still—"

"I've already rung college and explained the situation. They're fine with it. You just need to submit that picture you showed me for Art and the rest can wait."

Damn her efficiency.

"But won't a hot country be bad for my burns?" I asked. "I think it would be better to wait until they've healed."

Her smile dropped and her tone became icy. "Fine, then we'll go to Iceland. I don't care where we go as long as we get away from here for a couple of weeks. I've told the estate agent to stop advertising the house for a while so we can decide what to do. But I'm insisting on this – you need a change of scenery."

"But, Mum—"

"It's either that or the psychiatric assessment," she said firmly. "Which is it going to be?"

As if I had a choice.

I needed to finish this as soon as possible, for everyone's sake.

Back in my room, I studied the riddle again.

Narrowing down the cemeteries in London was a huge task. I had to think critically. The other riddles had given me clues about the name, so this one had to, too.

I sat staring at the words for ages and got no further forward, so I went for the literal approach, typing "London cemeteries high on a hill" into the search bar of my phone and hoped for the best. The top answer fit perfectly: Highgate Cemetery. When I looked back at the riddle, I felt like an idiot; the answer was right there at the beginning of the first two lines.

I clicked on Highgate Cemetery's website to find out more about it. There seemed to be two sides – East and West. Easy choice. So far, so good. But I had another problem ahead of me. Freeda had told me that my final destination was Charles Pennyworth's grave. Highgate was a huge graveyard, with over 170,000 people buried in 53,000 graves. That was the population of a medium- sized city! How on earth was I going to find a Pennyworth grave in all of that? There was a grave-finding service but they charged and it could take at least two weeks for me to hear back. I didn't have that time to play with, especially if Mum was thinking of whisking me off abroad for a break.

It looked like I was just going to have to take my chances and hope for some sort of spiritual guidance from Freeda – she seemed pretty desperate to get this finished. I decided my only option was tomorrow. The question was: how was I going to explain why I needed to be away for the day to Mum, let alone leave the house on my own? And how was I going to make it in my current physical state? I could throw on a hat to hide my scalp but trying to cover up the bandages on my arms, hands and neck would be trickier – not to mention painful.

I raised this dilemma on the phone with Immy later when she was back from college and I'd had my bandages redone.

"You're not seriously going to carry on, are you?" she asked, exasperated, after I'd explained my plans to her. "I thought you'd dropped all this now."

"This isn't about me any more – this for Esme's sake – and Freeda's," I explained to her.

"You're doing this now to help yet *another* ghost?"

I could hear the disbelief in her voice but chose to ignore it. It wasn't her fault that she was blind to the paranormal. I just needed to do one more thing, then I could get back to normal and everyone else could stop worrying about me.

"All I need to do is return the frame then I can go on holiday with a clear conscience."

"But what if you do this and then something else happens?" she worried. "Seriously, Lindy – just go away and forget about everything. I know I keep saying this, but you're obviously not listening. Whatever is happening with Esme . . . and Freeda, they're *dead*. What more can anyone do to them that would be worse than that?"

"Immy, I know it's hard for you to believe because you haven't met Esme, but please trust me – she looked awful. And don't say it's because she's dead. The first time I saw her, she looked like any normal person except, well, obviously a ghost . . . but you know what I mean . . ."

"No. I *don't* know what you mean," she snapped. "All I know is that you are unhealthily obsessed with some dead girl, who may or may not have been your ancestor."

"She *is* my ancestor!"

"Have you got any birth certificates to prove it? Any research from one of those ancestry websites?"

"No, but—"

"And even if you did," she carried on, not letting me finish, "why would there be an evil curse on all of you that you – *only you* – can lift? Everything you've told me sounds like a plot from a paranormal mystery. It's all very exciting, but none of it's real." She emphasised the last four words slowly and it felt like she was twisting a knife further and further into my heart with each syllable.

"You're supposed to support me. You're supposed to be my best friend."

"I *am* – that's why I'm telling you this. Best friends are truthful with each other and I have to tell when you're being ridiculous! I can't sit here listening to you spout nonsense any more. Seriously, Lindy, I'm going to have to talk to your mum soon. I'm worried about you – you're clearly not well. You're not taking your antidepressants and each time I speak to you, you're more and more deluded. I think you're actually a danger to yourself."

A rage that I never knew I had swept over me and before I knew it, I was yelling down the phone at her.

"I *did* start taking the antidepressants again and they made no difference – I *still* saw Esme! I am going to finish what I started, whether you believe me or not, and if you tell anyone about my plans tomorrow, I will never, ever speak to you again!"

It was at times like these that I wished I had an old-fashioned phone so I could slam it down on her. In the end, I had to satisfy myself with stabbing the "end call" icon on my screen and throwing the phone on to my bed instead.

Suddenly, everything became clear. The only true friend I had was Esme and I owed it to her to save her.

44.
HIGHGATE

The next morning, I was up and out of bed early, packing my rucksack with everything I needed for my day in London. While Mum was in the shower, I sneaked downstairs and used her credit card to book my train tickets. I prayed that she wouldn't need the card or look for it before I left because I had to use it at the station to print the tickets at the machine.

We had a late, quiet breakfast – she was still looking at travel websites while munching on toast and I was racking my brains for an excuse to get out of the house.

"I thought I might go for a walk into town today, if that's OK?" I said casually, drinking the rest of my tea.

"Hmm?" Mum didn't even look up from her screen.

"I said I want to go into town today. I've got some leftover birthday money and I thought it would be nice to buy some new clothes. You know, to cheer me up, make me feel more positive about things – get me ready for our holiday."

She glanced at me and frowned. "Do you feel up to it?"

"Yes," I lied. In truth, my arms were still stinging and itching from the warmth generated by the bandages. I hadn't taken my painkillers because I needed to stay alert. The only positive thing to come out of these burns was that it hurt to even lift my arms to pull.

She leant back in her chair and considered me. "I don't know. I think I should come in with you."

"No!" I said too loudly, then corrected myself. "I mean, why don't you stay here and continue looking at holidays? I'm fine, honestly."

She twisted her wedding ring. "I'm worried you'll have an accident or something. You know . . . with all these pills you're taking . . ."

We both knew that wasn't what she meant – not really. She was thinking of the shower incident, convinced that I wasn't safe to be let out of the house without a bodyguard to protect me from myself.

"Mum, I know you don't believe me, but I really didn't mean to burn myself in the shower. I've been feeling a lot better recently and I'd never do something stupid – if not for my sake, for yours. You've been through enough lately and I don't want to add to your pain. Please trust me."

She thought for a moment, then nodded. "Fine. As long as you are sure you're feeling up to it. Give me a call, though, if you start feeling unwell. Oh, and remember that we have to get your bandages changed again today at four o'clock. Not that you'll be out that long if you go soon – it's nearly eleven now."

I nodded, hating myself for lying, but what other choice did I have? I put on my baseball cap and gave her a kiss. Just as I was about to head out the door, Mum called to me.

"Lindy?"

She was standing in the doorway to the kitchen, looking worried.

"Yes?"

"Be careful, won't you?"

The journey to Highgate wasn't as difficult as I'd feared. I printed out the tickets at Oxford and caught the next train to Paddington, arriving just before one. At first, the crowds overwhelmed me, sweeping me along in a sea of people that were glued to phones while pushing aside anyone who couldn't keep up. I half-ran, trying to avoid being stampeded, and found my way on to the Tube; each train I took seemed worse than the last. The final train was quiet, and I spent the ten-minute journey psyching myself. I wondered what would happen when the photograph was complete.

I'd texted Mum earlier explaining that I'd had a change of plans but that I'd be home as soon as possible – something urgent had come up but, once it was done, I could relax and try to lead a normal life again. Not that I was sure what a normal life *was* any more. If Dad's death taught me anything, it was that the best we can hope for in life is to just get by day-to-day, because we never know what's around the corner.

When I finally arrived at Archway Station, I pulled my rucksack higher up my back and, ignoring all the texts from Mum demanding to know where I was, I checked Google Maps to work out the route to Highgate.

Highgate Hill was a busy, steep road but the walk was pleasant enough, once the shops and takeaways gave way to houses and flats. I turned left on to the smaller Dartmouth Park Hill – a pretty, tree-lined lane – and wandered down the road, admiring the older houses and buildings. The park bordered Highgate Cemetery, so I knew it couldn't be much further to the entrance. There was a small admissions hut at the East Cemetery and a middle-aged woman sat behind a till. None of the other graveyards I'd visited had ticket offices but, then again, Highgate was nothing like the other graveyards.

I walked inside and pulled out my purse. "One ticket, please." The lady smiled. "How old are you, dear? If you're under eighteen, entrance is free. But you can only visit this side. If you want to see the West, you have to book on a tour and we don't have any spaces till tomorrow."

"No, that's fine, thanks. I want this side. One of my ancestors is buried here."

I gave her a big smile, laced with hope. She raised her eyebrows and nodded. "How interesting! Do you know where they're buried?"

"Uh, no. I was kind of hoping you might have heard of him."

Her smile faded a little. "We have so many graves here that it's impossible to know where everyone is buried, unless they're one of our more famous residents. We do offer a grave-finding service but we need a few weeks' notice."

"I understand," I replied. "It's just . . . I'm on a tight deadline and I thought I would come along anyway in case you or anyone else might have heard of him."

"Well, there's no harm in asking but it's pretty unlikely I will know, even though I've worked here for twenty years!" She laughed. "What's your ancestor's name?"

"Charles Pennyworth."

She frowned. "I can't say that name rings a bell. Quite a name, too. Pennyworth . . ." She shook her head. "Sorry, love. I just don't recall ever hearing it. Not that that means anything, of course. We have so many—"

"Graves," I interrupted, then smiled an apology. "Thank you. I understand. I'll just have a wander around today then, since I've come all this way. I can always come back another time."

No, you can't.

"Of course. It's a beautiful place for a walk, but be aware that some parts of the cemetery are rather wild and overgrown. Stick to the main paths as loose stones can be a tripping hazard on the smaller, side avenues." She chuckled. "Goodness, listen to me. I make this place sound like a health and safety nightmare. I suppose it is, in a way," she added. "We try our best here to keep things under control, but nature has a way of asserting itself and we can't keep on top of everything."

"It's OK – I've come prepared," I said. "I'm wearing my hiking boots and thick socks. Thanks for your help."

As I walked through the door, the woman called after me,

"Oh, by the way, the cemetery shuts at four o'clock."

"I should be out of here well before then, but thanks," I said, not feeling full of optimism but deciding to try my best anyway. Freeda had come to my help the night before, so maybe she'd put in an appearance again. If she wanted to me to succeed, she'd have to.

45
WHISPER OF AIR

No inspiration – divine or otherwise – had given me any clues as to which way I should go, so I followed in the footsteps of all the other visitors in front of me, heading down the path towards Karl Marx's monument. Leaves danced on the ground, swirling around the graves that led off the main path like lines of crooked teeth. Crowds of stone crosses and headstones stood in every available space, with the occasional white angel thrown in for contrast.

The air was damp and cool, leaving a fresh scent of greenery that made it soothing; the sound of birdsong drowning out distant traffic noises, made it even more peaceful. Rays of weak, autumnal sunshine stretched lazily through the trees. This wasn't a graveyard from classic horror stories or films – instead it resembled a wild and romantic garden.

The only thing that was distracting me was my phone, which was constantly vibrating with notifications.

I hadn't been walking for very long when a knot of tourists taking selfies confirmed I had reached Karl Marx's monument.

I paused for a moment to take it in, knowing I was seeing something special, but all I could think of was how massive his eyebrows were. Apparently, this wasn't even his proper grave – that was situated further down in the middle of the graveyard, among other less-well-known people.

It seemed that most of the afternoon's visitors were celebrity-grave spotting because, as I walked on, I left most of the crowds behind. The path sloped gently downwards into an area of more densely packed graves, which resembled a jungle rather than a garden. Thick, thorny brambles, covered in cloying clumps of ivy, crept on to headstones and weaved through the undergrowth. Creepers strangled anything in their path and nettles competed with nearby trees for light. I shivered – the air was cooler and damper here, with the light struggling to get through the trees. Perhaps that explained why the birdsong had become quieter in this part of the cemetery – the blackbirds and sparrows preferred it warmer and lighter. I didn't blame them.

My phone had stopped vibrating. I pulled it out of my pocket and saw that I had no reception in this part of the cemetery. I hesitated for a moment – what if something happened to me? I wouldn't be able to call for help. I tried to reassure myself that the ticket lady knew that I was visiting – if I didn't reappear when the cemetery shut, she'd send out a search party, wouldn't she?

She wouldn't think twice about you. She sees hundreds of people a day.

Panic was crawling through me.

I had to pull myself together or I'd never finish this.

The feeling of my fingertips running along my scalp under my hat and twisting delicate strands around my knuckles alerted me to what I was doing before I had another thought. The sting that followed was like a welcome splash of cold water; a slap in the face. My breathing sped up before it returned to normal, and I said a silent "thank you" to whoever was listening. Quite an audience in this place.

I flicked the hairs off and was about to resume walking when I felt something brush against my legs. I jumped and squealed, imagining a corpse, awake and disinterred, grabbing hold of my leg but, to my huge relief, I saw a very fluffy charcoal-coloured cat looking right back at me with large, yellow eyes.

"Bloody hell, you little monster! You scared me!"

I bent down to stroke it, but it trotted off a little down the path, which had become nothing more than a thin line of dirt at this point. The cat stopped and glanced back at me, beckoning me to follow.

I didn't have any better ideas.

It wound its way along the very narrow path for a few minutes until it reached a dense patch of foliage and ran inside.

"Very funny," I said. "Thanks for nothing."

As I turned to go, I was hit by a scent of violets that was so powerful, it made me choke. I quickly spun on my foot, determined to follow my fluffy companion.

Making my way through the tangled trees and bushes was not fun, especially as they pulled on my coat sleeves, which, in turn, rubbed the bandages protecting my blisters. I held my breath to fight the pain, letting out a few strained gasps when the sting became too much to bear, and blinking away the tears filling my eyes. A couple of times, I was smacked in the face by a sharp twig or branch, and the hanging ivy nearly stole my hat, but soon I was in a clearing, facing a dilapidated stone building. The cat, already sitting in front of it, stopped cleaning its paw and looked at me, as if to say, "What took you so long?"

This time it allowed me to stroke it, purring richly as my fingers tickled its ears. I crouched down next to it as I gazed up at what must be a mausoleum. No simple grave for Charles, then, much like Linwood had said – he had a mini-house to call his own. It wasn't as impressive or as well-kept as the ones near the entrance to the cemetery, as if to say that the person buried inside was important but not enough to deserve better care. It looked as if not even the cemetery caretakers knew it existed. Charles would have hated that. In the middle of two stone pillars at the entrance was a brickwork pattern, grey and weathered with age. Settled between was an enormous stone door with a rectangular window the size of a paperback book.

The sound of twigs snapping echoed in my ears, warning me that I wasn't alone. I was sure that none of the tourist groups had ventured this far into the cemetery. My heart stuttered a beat. The only person who knew I was here was Immy – it couldn't be her. She was all the way back in Oxford and wouldn't dare to try and make this journey alone, knowing how her parents would react.

Another snap and crunch. The cat stiffened below my hand, its ears rod-straight, twitching.

I pulled my phone out of my pocket to check it again and cursed silently. Still no reception.

To my right, there was an explosion of leaves and a squirrel scurried up a tree. Taken by surprise, I fell backwards, then laughed in relief.

It's just a squirrel. Get a grip!

The cat ran off in the direction of the squirrel – I was now alone. I got to my feet and walked to the door of the mausoleum, the scent of violets growing stronger with every step. When I reached out to turn the handle, I paused, unsure.

You're almost done.

The door creaked open on rusty hinges – it had obviously been a while since anyone had been inside.

The first thing that hit me was the smell of damp and age, tumbling towards the outside world like a tsunami. I coughed and stepped back to let the air inside settle and clear my lungs before I faced the interior again.

My eyes adjusted to the gloom as I edged into the mausoleum, helped by the light coming through the doorway.

I couldn't place how I felt in this moment, but my breathing had quickened and it felt like someone was wrapping damp, soft fingers around my throat.

I fought to ignore it by setting down my rucksack and approaching a large, stone sarcophagus in the middle of the room. I turned on my phone's torch and directed the beam at the tomb. There was a plaque on the side facing me, with the following inscription:

In memory of Charles Pennyworth, 1823–1864.
Respected medic, generous philanthropist
and devoted father and husband.

Taken too soon by a heart weakened in body and spirit.
Here also lies his loving wife, Georgina, 1825–1862.
May they be reunited with their daughter,
Esmerelda, now and forever.

The perfume of violets was so strong in here that my head throbbed – I felt sick. It was too overpowering; too cloying.

Turn it down a notch, Esme.

I'd made it this far, but I didn't know how to end it. I had the frame in my rucksack, and the portrait inside was complete. Was I just supposed to leave it in here and hope for the best? What a disappointment. After all this intrigue and accusations of insanity and personal risk, I felt that there should be something more momentous to mark this occasion. At least for my mind's sake.

A whisper of air brushed my right cheek as something drifted past.

Scurrying.

Rats?

I set my rucksack down and, lifting my phone with a shaking hand, I shone the torch in the direction of the breeze, the beam hitting a wooden table in the back right-hand corner. There was an old candelabra with unlit candles in it sitting on the left of the table, where a velvet scarf was draped over something on the right.

I slowly edged towards the table, holding my breath, and pulled the scarf away.

Glassy eyes stared out at me from a familiar, waxy face. The head, decapitated from the base of the neck, rested on a cushion – a glass jar over the top for protection.

I opened my mouth to scream but nothing came out.

The face was one I knew very well. I'd drawn it, seen it in my dreams and nightmares, looked at it in the mirror. The hair, that had wrapped itself around me one night, cascaded from her crown and lay in waves around her neck.

How was it here? Had her parents had it cut off and embalmed and just buried the body in the cholera pit? What kind of sick, crazy person did this to their daughter?

I backed away from the hideous sight, fighting the rising bile in my throat, but my left foot became entangled with one of the straps of my rucksack and I tripped, falling backwards against the sarcophagus, hitting my head with a loud crack as I tumbled to the floor.

46.
PAINFUL TRUTHS

"Rise and shine, Sleeping Beauty."

Darkness surrounded me, apart from a flickering light coming from the candelabra on the table. I blinked and turned my head, wincing at the pain, trying to work out what was happening; where I was.

The mausoleum. The damp cold of the stone floor seeped up through my trousers. The owner of the voice grabbed my arms and dragged me to a sitting position. My head spun as my eyes tried to adjust to the darkness.

"I *said*: rise and shine!"

The last time I'd heard this voice, it was weaker – breathier. "Freeda?"

A petite woman with curly blonde hair bent down and shook my shoulders.

"Where's the picture frame?" she demanded.

"It's in my rucksack."

"Well, get it out!"

"You sound different," I said, as I fumbled around trying to open my bag. "You don't sound sick any more."

"I never was sick. I needed you to think that I was a desperate woman who required your help."

"But you sounded so genuine."

"Years of holding séances makes one well-accustomed to fooling others. Now, shut up and show me the frame."

Her eyes sparkled with excitement as I held it up to her. "Perfect! Oh, we are so close now!"

"I don't think we are," I said. "I've done everything the curse asked and, as far as I can see, nothing's happened. It hasn't worked."

"That is because there is one final task. To break this curse, you must pluck out a strand of Esme's hair and place it inside the picture frame to join the others."

"No one said anything about that! I'm not touching her head!"

"It's not real, you fool – it's a waxwork."

"I don't care! It's creepy!"

"You are hardly one to feel squeamish about pulling out a hair when you are such an expert."

I held a hand against my head, trying to contain the dizzying pain. My hair felt wet to the touch and, when I pulled my hand away, I saw blood on my palm.

Lots of blood.

"I'm not feeling well," I mumbled. "I think I need a doctor."

"All in good time. Now, do as I say or you won't ever get out of this place."

I shuddered as I pushed myself on to my knees. Slowly, I straightened to standing, holding the picture frame in one hand

and my head with the other, praying the pressure I was exerting on my skull would contain the pain. It did – marginally.

I stood in front of the wooden table and Esme's face smiled back at me in the candlelight. My vision swam.

I can't do this . . .

"Remove the glass jar from the head and pull out her hair. Come *on*, Lindy – just one quick tug! It doesn't matter if you pull out more than one."

I reached out a shaking hand and removed the glass cover, nearly knocking over the head in the process. Then, I reached out my hand and touched the soft hair. Pulling out my own had felt easy, effortless. Pulling Esme's felt like an act of violence. I snatched my hand back and shook my head.

"No. *You* do it," I said.

"It cannot be me, silly girl," Freeda snapped. "It has to be a member of the family."

Laying my left hand on the head, to stop it from toppling over, I used my right to tug at a few strands. They were surprisingly resistant – much more difficult to dislodge than my own hair. I made several attempts before I finally felt them release.

"Good," Freeda said. "Now put it inside the frame with the other hair."

I did everything she said, hoping that the damage Bofur had done to the hair inside the frame wouldn't render all this pointless. I needn't have worried; as soon as the newly pulled strands touched the damaged ones inside the frame, they slithered and weaved their way into the existing plaits, making them whole and perfect again.

Relieved, I stumbled backwards and leant against the mausoleum wall, waiting for something to happen.

A strange electricity hummed in the air: cracking, fizzing, making the hairs on my arms stand on end. A familiar voice whispered in my ear.

"Lindy – leave this place immediately!"

"Lindy is not going anywhere," Freeda said. "Do not play games with me, Charles Pennyworth. If you do, then I will keep Lindy a prisoner inside your monstrosity of a mausoleum until you do the right thing. No one knows that she is here. It doesn't bother *me* if she dies while we wait. But could you bear another innocent life on your conscience?"

I lunged for the door, groping around for a handle, but, of course, there was none. *The dead don't leave . . .*

I kicked and banged my fists, screaming, tears running down my face.

"Please, Freeda, I've done my bit. I just want to go home."

"Stay where you are, or I will have to make you!"

Her face was contorted into a paroxysm of rage. It looked like it might have been pretty, once, before the ravages of tuberculosis left their mark.

The damp air grew thick with the scent of violets and formaldehyde. Esme materialised, Charles by her side holding her hand: two apparitions that flickered in the pale candlelight. Charles looked over at me, his face creased with concern.

"Miss Lindy, are you all right? You have blood in your hair."

He moved closer to me and peered at where I'd hit my head on his sarcophagus. "What has this monster done to you?"

"The injury was self-inflicted," snapped Freeda.

"She needs to be examined by a doctor, urgently. We have done as you asked, so let Lindy go and leave us in peace."

Freeda shook her head. "Not so fast, Charles. I did not invite you here for a cosy reunion."

"Why *are* you here, Mrs Madill?" Esme asked.

"Your father and I have some unfinished business, young lady," Freeda said, never taking her eyes off Charles, "regarding the circumstances of your premature death. There were some . . . discrepancies."

Charles took a step towards Freeda. He was breathing faster, his chest rising and falling in exaggerated movements, and he had clenched his hands into fists.

"There is nothing to discuss!"

Seeing the rage on her father's face discomfited Esme. She stepped forward and said, in a placatory tone, "Mrs Madill – it's quite simple. I died from the cholera." She reached out to take her father's hand. "I am so sorry I disobeyed you, Father. I should never have left the house."

Freeda raised an eyebrow at Charles.

"You see? The poor child is still blaming *herself* for her death. Do you think that is fair, Charles?"

Her words forced him backwards. The anger in his eyes was gone, replaced by something that looked a lot like guilt.

I could sense she was going to unleash some dreadful truth and, while I was curious, I didn't want there to be any more trauma.

"Esme and Charles have been through enough. Let's just leave it there," I said.

"Impossible," Freeda replied, her gaze still locked on Charles. "Death normally brings resolution to life's mysteries but, in Esmerelda's case, the opposite has occurred. She died thinking that she was to blame for her fate, but I am going to free her from this burden."

"Please stop torturing my father, Mrs Madill," Esme begged. "I know how I died!"

"Oh, but you do not, my dear," Freeda tutted, shaking her head. "It was never *your* fault that you caught the cholera. It was—"

"It was mine," Charles cut in, tears running down his face.

His body sagged, as he put his head in his hands.

"I took a small sample of water from a gutter in Jericho and added a few drops to your water glass one night."

Esme looked first at Freeda, then at me, before turning to her father and giving a nervous laugh.

"That makes no sense, Father. The passage of time has confused you. Why would you deliberately infect your own daughter?"

"I was certain that I had found a cure for the disease. However, I needed someone to test it on – someone I thought was healthy enough to withstand the symptoms – so I picked you. You were young and strong . . . I had no idea that you would succumb to it, nor that my treatment would fail. It was my fault that you died, Esmerelda, but I did not mean to kill you."

SELF-MURDER

Esme swayed in the hazy light, her face a picture of un-comprehending horror.

"Esme?" I asked gently. "Are you all right?"

She turned her glazed eyes towards me and her face blurred into a swirling mass of grey anguish. The outline of her body smeared and faltered. She was disappearing; evaporating. Charles fell to his knees and grabbed her arms, hugging her close in a desperate embrace.

"Don't leave me, Esmerelda! Not like this. It is not as it seems, I promise!"

In his arms, Esme settled, but she still refused to look her father in the eye.

"I love you more than anything, Esmerelda. I would *never* have risked your life had I known that there was even the remotest chance that you would not recover."

I wondered just how good a doctor Charles Pennyworth was.

"While I was working at the hospital in London, I'd secretly been giving a tincture to a group of patients who were severely ill with cholera and the results were favourable. Most recuperated within days."

"*Most* is not *all*," Freeda tutted, shaking her head.

"Be quiet!" Charles yelled at her, then turned back to Esme. "When I was called to help in Oxford, I talked to one of my colleagues and suggested we try my treatment on the patients there. He thought it was too risky and, when I tried to persuade him otherwise, he accused me of seeking to make my name in medicine during an outbreak. So I thought . . ." Charles looked down and shook his head, "I thought that if I could prove that I had cured a member of my own family, then my colleagues could hardly accuse me of opportunism, especially if I had been willing to—"

He stopped himself, but it was too late.

"Put your own daughter at risk by infecting her and using the tincture to cure her?" Freeda suggested. "You are a disgusting specimen of a man, Charles Pennyworth." She spat on the floor where he knelt.

"All this time, I have blamed myself for disobeying you, and it was *you* who killed me." Esme's ghostly eyes shone with tears. "Did Mother know? Did she agree to this?"

"No! Truthfully, she had no part in this."

Esme looked at Freeda for confirmation.

"She did not know at the time, but she soon found out," Freeda confirmed. "I believe she did not take the news very well, did she, Charles?"

Charles glared at Freeda as Esme pushed him away and buried her face in her hands. My heart broke as I heard her sobs; it put my father's transgressions into perspective: at least he hadn't *murdered* me.

"Tell Esmerelda what became of her mother," Freeda insisted.

"After you died, your mother was inconsolable," he began. "She . . . she could not cope with your passing. I moved her back to London, hoping that this would improve her mood, but she became worse and I had to increase her laudanum dosage.

"Your mother still struggled and then, one afternoon, I found her slumped over my desk. She had managed to get into my medicine cabinet, presumably to take more laudanum, but she'd also discovered my diary in there, in which I had confessed what I had done to you. She'd left me a note, declaring her hatred for me. An empty bottle of laudanum was beside her."

"Mother *self-murdered*?" Esme gasped.

"Darling – she was not in her right mind. Please, do not blame her."

"Why would Esme blame her mother?" I demanded, incredulous. "She only committed suicide because she found out that *you* had killed her daughter!"

Charles shook his head. "You do not understand, Lindy. Regardless of the circumstances, self-murder is an act against God. At best, my wife would have been declared deranged if news of how she died had spread. At worst, she would have been branded a criminal."

"That's terrible!" I cried. "The only person who committed a crime was *you*! You deserved the punishment and instead, Esme and her mother suffered!"

"Bravo, Miss Lindy," Freeda said, slowly clapping.

"But Mother is buried here," Esme said thickly, through her

tears. "That would not have been allowed if she died the way you claim."

"Her death certificate states that she died from a weak heart. The coroner, a friend of mine, asked no questions."

"How convenient to have friends in high places," said Freeda.

"Is this why she cannot speak to me in the afterlife?" Esme asked her.

"It is, I am afraid," Freeda confirmed. "By murdering herself, she took something, so she had to give something when she crossed to the other side."

"But that's completely unfair!" I cut in.

"Life *is* unfair, Miss Pennyworth," a new voice said, as a familiar tall, thin figure appeared from the shadows. "I thought *you* would have known this by now."

48.
KEEPING SECRETS

"Linwood!" Freeda exclaimed in delight.

Her son flung his arms around her and she chuckled. When he still wouldn't let go, she prised Linwood's arms off and brushed down her dress, saying, "Let us not be *too* sentimental."

Linwood nodded and tried to regain his composure.

"Sorry, Mother. I have been so desperate to see you – where have you been all these years?"

"Unfortunately, our separation was your own doing. When you buried the second half of the Pennyworth photograph in my grave, you also shackled us to the curse. Never mind – it has all turned out for the best, regardless."

"I do not see how," Linwood said, surprised. "The Pennyworths have been reunited. They were meant to be separated forever!"

"Separating them forever was never the brightest of plans. Look at their faces now they have been reunited! Do they look happy?"

It was obvious to anyone that Charles and Esme looked emotionally beaten and bruised.

"Whatever do you mean, Mother?" Linwood's confusion softened his harsh, angular features. He no longer looked like a villain; he just looked lost – like me and Esme.

"Tell Linwood, Esmerelda, how you feel now that you know how your Father killed you," Freeda purred.

"Charles Pennyworth killed his own daughter?"

The look Linwood shot at Charles almost begged him to deny the accusations. When Charles remained silent, Linwood added, "What kind of monster does that to their own child?"

"You are all right; I am a monster, but not the monster you've portrayed me to be," Charles shot back.

Linwood turned once again to his mother. "When did you discover this truth?"

"She has known all along, Linwood," said Charles. "You see, your mother likes to be selective with the truth when it suits her."

"What? Why did you not tell me?"

"He is lying," Freeda snarled. "This man killed his own daughter – do you not think him capable of bending the truth?"

"You, Madam, are a hypocrite. You have forced me to admit my mistakes to my daughter – to break her heart – and yet you refuse to tell your son what happened at my house all those years ago."

Freeda stepped towards Charles as if to speak, but shrank back in surprise when he boomed, "Don't!" Now that he had a captive audience and a shot at revenge, nothing was going to stop him.

"Freeda came to my house within days of me burying my child, but she did not do so out of the kindness of her heart. The only thing she had on her mind that day was money, and she was determined to exploit my grief for her own financial gain."

"Liar!"

While this revelation came to light, I had managed to attract Esme's attention, indicating the door with a nod of my head. Charles was still in full flow.

"This witch told me that she had had a vision about what I had done to Esmerelda," Charles continued, "and she threatened to go to the police if I did not pay to keep her silence."

Linwood looked at Freeda in disbelief. "You tried to *blackmail* him?"

She threw her hands up. "Yes! And why should I not? He had committed a terrible crime and he had got away with it!"

"That does not give you the right to break the law in return!"

"Oh, don't be such a judgmental bore, Linwood."

"I don't understand – we had a good business. We did not need the money."

"People always need more money," Freeda scoffed. "And I was getting tired of the psychic business, of contacting boring relatives for boring rich women. It was physically and mentally draining. It was time to retire and I could not hand the business over to you. You don't have a psychic bone in your body, as this ridiculous curse has shown. The means to enjoy a comfortable retirement presented itself at the right time and I took it. Charles was both wealthy and corrupt – a perfect combination."

"That still doesn't make it right, Mother," Linwood said quietly.

"Why are you not on *my* side?" Freeda asked through gritted teeth. "*I* was the one who ultimately paid, not Charles Pennyworth. His type always gets away with everything. Charles took my life, just as he took his own daughter's. He's a murderer who was never brought to justice."

I felt a change in the air – a thickening and a cooling; Esme was now standing to my right. I didn't know what we were going to do but at least we could now do it together.

Without looking our way, Freeda flung out her arm and a strange force immediately stopped both of us in our tracks, anchoring our feet and rendering us immobile.

"No one is allowed to leave until I say so!" Freeda barked. "We still have one more father-daughter Pennyworth pairing to accomplish and no one leaves until we do so!"

I felt the colour drain from my face. "No. Please don't; I don't want to speak to him!"

She tutted. "How must your father feel, knowing that one of his children did not want to speak to him when given the opportunity?"

I frowned. "What do you mean by 'one' of his children'?"

She raised her eyebrows. "Oh, dear. It looks like another Pennyworth father has been keeping secrets."

She was playing with me like a cat taunts a mouse. I could see the sick pleasure in her face, and I hated her for it.

"You're making all this up out of a twisted desire for revenge."

"I am not making anything up, Lindy. I agree – you are definitely your father's only daughter."

She paused, letting it sink in, before adding, "but you're not his only *child*."

"What are you up to now, Mother?" Linwood demanded, his voice uneasy, as he cast nervous glances in my direction.

I pressed my palms over my ears as I felt screams coming up through my throat and leaving my body.

Guttural – wounded – I could only hear an echo of what I was saying.

Freeda slapped me square across the face, then forced my hands away from my ears.

"Compose yourself, you pathetic girl! You will thank me in the long run because it also concerns someone else in your life who is close to you – a young man called Tom."

The relief was immediate. "I already know about Tom," I said. "He told me my father was going to leave me and my mum for him and his mum. It's not a secret."

"I'm afraid there is more to the situation than that," Freeda said.

A loaded pause. The nausea returned as she made me wait.

"You and Tom are not just friends – you're siblings."

44.
EXORCISM OF GRIEF

"No – no, you're wrong."

The hysteria in my voice was obvious. "Tom's mum and my dad met a year ago; Mum told me. We didn't know she had a child and Tom said that he and his mum didn't know that I existed."

"Tom's mother, Isabelle, and your father met *again* a year ago," Freeda corrected. "They met for the first time eighteen years ago and had a one night . . . liaison before going their separate ways: Benjamin stayed in Oxford, while Isabelle went to London. It was there that she discovered she was with child, but she did not tell your father. Last year, she found his details and made contact again."

This wasn't true. It couldn't be true.

I felt something in my mind crack – a gaping fissure climbing up my scalp.

"No," I said, shaking my head as I tried to push her words from my mind. "Tom already told me that his father was killed in a car accident – that was before Dad died. It happened when he was a little boy."

"As far as Tom knows, that man was his natural father; Isabelle hasn't told him the truth. When she found your father again, she decided she would break the news once the two had become better acquainted, but she never succeeded in doing so because your father died."

"Did my dad know about Tom?" I whispered, fighting back tears. I wondered just how much more a mind could take.

"No – he didn't, at first. But as time went on, and he saw pictures of Tom with his other father, he realised how much Tom resembled himself. He asked Isabelle, a month before he decided to leave you, and she told him the truth."

Dad knew he had a son – and he wanted to live with him instead of me.

"Do not let her get inside your head, Lindy," Esme murmured.

"Another fine Pennyworth mess!" exclaimed Freeda, a sneer stretched across her face. "One father a murderer; another a philanderer. Aren't family secrets dreadful, Lindy? They lead to nothing but trouble. This is why I am determined to give you the opportunity to tell your father exactly what you think of how he behaved. I would hate to think of you carrying around this emotional burden for the rest of your life."

"No!" I turned to Esme for help. "Isn't there something we can do to stop her?"

She looked at me and whispered, "The door is open. Run!" I felt cold air on my back.

How had she managed to open the door?

"Run!"

There was no time to think. Twisting around, I stumbled out of the door and into the thick undergrowth – brambles and nettles tearing at my clothes and stinging my face and hands. I tripped, swore. It was dark now and a mist had formed, enveloping the gravestones ahead in swirling clouds that were tinged with a sickly, yellow hue.

Highgate Cemetery was officially closed.

In my moment of nervous hesitation, claw-like fingers gripped my hair, my scalp, dragging me backwards.

The pain was excruciating. Mud lodged itself under my fingernails as I grappled for something to hold on to, to stop myself from being dragged back into that dreadful mausoleum.

"It is rude to leave without saying goodbye," Freeda hissed from above me. "It is customary to thank your host."

I screamed in agony and despair.

"I *said* I wanted to make your father face up to the trouble he has caused you. But you Pennyworth girls are so ungrateful."

"I have never done anything to you," I sobbed. "All I want is for you to leave me alone!" My hands moved to release my hair from Freeda's hold, but there was no way out of it.

"And all I want is for your father to face up to the trouble he has caused you!"

"Why? Why does it matter so much to you?"

"Because he's a Pennyworth." She spat my surname as if it were a disease. Still, I fought against her hands, pulling at her fingers to prise them away from my hair, but Freeda's hold was absolute. She yanked, harder.

"Do not fight me!"

"Lindy – please," Esme begged, arms reaching out towards me. "Come back, stop fighting her. If you are not careful, she will destroy you. You will never win against her. She will keep haunting

277

you and me until she gets her way. Just face your father and face your fate, like I did."

"That's better," Freeda nodded at Esme, throwing me against the mausoleum floor. "Finally, you are seeing some sense. Let's hope *this* one," she slammed a boot-clad foot on to one side of my face, ignoring my moan of pain, "will do the same."

She closed her eyes, held up her hands and started murmuring. I shrank back, crying, curling into myself. This was not how I wanted to see Dad – in our ancestor's mausoleum, as part of an evil woman's revenge plan.

A pale light spread in front of me, which gradually took on the shape of a man. Freeda's eyes were wide with greedy anticipation . . . until the light began to dim, collapsing back in on itself, as quickly as it had formed.

"Benjamin Pennyworth! Come back here at once!" she yelled. "Or I will torture this daughter of yours until you do!"

Linwood stepped forward.

"He will not be coming here tonight, Mother."

"Stop interfering, Linwood."

"No. This has got to stop."

She spun around to face her son. "Leave! Let me finish my work!"

"You have done enough work already. You are destroying everyone's lives!"

"Charles Pennyworth ruined me—"

"Only because you threatened him with blackmail. You omitted that part from your story and had me thinking, until my dying day, that my mother was an innocent victim of upper-class injustice. All these years, I was convinced that *you* were the victim."

For the first time, Freeda looked uneasy.

"I *was*!" She rallied. "Charles was a murderer—"

"Yes, Mother, and *you* are a liar!"

Freeda stepped away from me to face Linwood full-on. Esme moved to my side. Charles moved to stand in front of us – a sentinel between us and the battle that was raging between Linwood and Freeda. I didn't care any more. I was cold and tired and wishing that I'd never tried to break the curse in the first place.

"Linwood, a court of law would have seen murder as worse than blackmail. The jury would have handed out a death sentence to him. Yet I was the one who perished!"

Linwood ignored her. "I spent my life, and much of my afterlife, seeking to avenge you and now I discover that I dedicated my life to a liar. Well, I will do so no longer. I will not let you destroy more lives!"

"Oh, shut up, you imbecile—"

Her apparition flickered again. She was weakening.

"Don't call me an imbecile!" he roared and, before any of us knew what was happening, he trapped Freeda's arms behind her back and small flames licked out from below her feet.

"Let go of me!" Freeda screamed.

It started slowly. Freeda looked down in terror and struggled against Linwood's containment but, the more she tried to free herself, the higher the fire grew.

I have never seen hatred like that. Freeda was consumed with rage, knowing for the first time that she had been beaten. She looked towards me.

"You will never be free of this until you face you father, Lindy. The curse is in your bones now, in your very skin."

Only when the inferno reached her hair did Linwood step back, watching and waiting for his action to be complete.

Her final laugh was monstrous. The flames licked higher, consuming her in a final howl of malevolence and fire.

"Burn in hell, you vindictive witch," I whispered.

"She may very well do, Lindy. Or, at the very least, she has gone to a place where I hope none of us will ever see her again," Linwood replied. He suddenly looked years older, as he sank down on to the floor, the energy draining from him before my eyes. He looked at me with remorse and something that resembled sympathy.

"I am truly sorry for all the pain and suffering I caused all of you. If I had known what she did to you, Mr Pennyworth, I would never have done . . . all this." He waved an arm around vaguely towards the frame on the table. "I am actually glad that you have broken the curse, Lindy. It has freed me from its grasp so I can finally rest in peace."

"At least someone can," Esme muttered, and her father looked at her.

"Will you ever be able to forgive me, Esmerelda?"

She shrugged. "What would you do, Lindy? I would appreciate your guidance."

"I don't think that I'm the best person to ask," I admitted. "After everything I've discovered recently about my father, I don't feel very forgiving. But, after seeing what hatred and revenge did to Linwood and Freeda, perhaps the best way forward is to put things behind us. Time, they say, heals all wounds."

I turned to Esme and Charles. The latter looked at me beseechingly, and I felt all disgust and hatred and sadness leave my body like an exorcism of grief. It was like my dad was looking at me through his eyes and, in a way, I suppose he was.

"Forgive him, Esme . . . forgive him," I said. "Not because he particularly deserves it, but because you deserve peace."

Esme was about to reply when there was a rattle and bang on the mausoleum door. Without another word, she, Charles and Linwood disappeared and the candles were extinguished, leaving me drowning in darkness and shivering from the cold.

"Thank you, Lindy." Her breath was the breeze, caressing my face. "Until we meet again."

50.
LITTLE STAR

Whoever was on the outside landed a heavy kick on the door and then turned the handle again. This time it worked, and the door creaked open. I crouched in the corner, out of sight from the intruder.

The shape of a person was outlined in the doorway, but I couldn't make out whether it was male or female – human or ghost. Their figure was lit up from behind by pale moonlight filtered through the clouds.

They began to make their way inside, taking slow, cautious steps towards the table with the picture frame.

I seized my chance. I lurched forward and stumbled outside and away, tripping on the creepers and ivy underfoot. My head was spinning and throbbing and the cold night air chilled the wound under my matted, blood-stained hair. The fog swallowed me, growing denser as I hunted for a way through. I took out my phone and turned on the torch, but the light was reflected back at me, temporarily blinding me with its glare.

I swore as I stubbed my toe against a large rock. Where was that damn cat when I needed him? Probably tucked up somewhere warm, sleeping off a meal.

After an eternity of crashing through weeds and brambles, I sighed with relief when I reached the main path. *Finally.* Then my spirits sank again. There were two branches. Right or left? I couldn't get my bearings and there was nothing visible to navigate by. I still had no reception on my phone to help guide me.

I remembered that I'd walked down a gentle slope to get to the mausoleum, so that meant that I needed to be heading upwards if I wanted to go in the right direction.

I caught a flash of movement out of the corner of my eye. A young boy, who couldn't have been older than nine or ten, darted out on to the path in front of me, dressed in jeans and a Manchester United top.

"Hey," I called.

He turned around and giggled.

"What's your name?" I asked, but he had moved and was now behind me. I twisted and he smiled, somehow amused by our absurd game of hide and seek.

Finally, he beckoned me with his hand before dashing to the left.

I followed, wondering why a boy would be here on his own at night. Maybe his family had private, out-of-hours visiting rights. He certainly knew his way around the place, and he skipped ahead so quickly that I struggled to keep up on my leaden legs. After around five minutes or so, he disappeared completely into the fog. I stopped and looked around me, shining my phone to see if I could pick him out.

"Hey!" I called again. "Where are you?"

I heard giggles to my right. I flashed the torch in that direction. Nothing.

The hairs on my neck were standing on end and my heart was beating faster. "Please, come out," I urged. "I'm injured and need to get out of here."

The sound of leaves crunching underfoot and twigs snapping led me to some grass bordering the edge of the path. My torch picked out a gravestone and I crouched down to read the inscription.

Marcus Chedworth
Our little star
We will watch you as
You play in the sky
Jan 2012 – Sept 2020

A faint breeze tickled my ear. Someone was standing next to me. I turned my head and saw the boy, but this time he looked different. He was much thinner; his face was hollow and his head was bald. His jeans and football shirt were gone, replaced by a hospital gown. An IV drip hung from his arm.

"Please, stay and play with me," he whispered and held out his hand.

I stumbled backwards and fell on to the damp grass.

"I'm so lonely," he whispered. "The other children are buried further down in the cemetery. I'm on my own here. No one else likes playing."

"Sorry," I stammered. "I can't help you. I'm not dead."

He looked at my head. "You will be soon."

Shit!

"It's all right," he said. "It doesn't hurt."

I scrambled to my feet and ran, trying to ignore the pain in my head.

I couldn't run as fast as I wished with my injury, so I stumbled over the jumbled gravestones trying to leave. My whole body felt heavy and I just wanted to curl up against a tree and go to sleep. A couple of times I stopped, ready to give into the dizziness, but thoughts of Mum and Immy and Tom kept my momentum going.

I turned a corner and ran smack into someone and we both tumbled over on to the path.

I screamed. They yelled.

A bright beam shone into my eyes and I tried to shield them from the glare.

"Lindy – thank goodness! I thought I'd never find you."

51. SPYING AND LYING

"Tom!"

I was so relieved to see him that I threw my arms around him and sobbed into his shoulder. He patted me on the back, making soothing sounds, until I had calmed down and was ready to let go.

"You don't know how glad I am to see you," I said.

Half-brother.

"I think I do; I feel the same. I've been looking for you for hours. What are doing here?"

He'd never believe my ghost story, so I opted for a simpler explanation.

"I came to find the grave of one of my ancestors. I got interested in all of this after . . . you know. I read one of them was buried in the cemetery."

He nodded but didn't look completely convinced.

"Is that blood on your face?" he asked, shining his torch on to my face and looking for the source.

"Yes. I tripped over my rucksack and banged my head against a gravestone as I fell."

"It looks bad."

"I lost consciousness. That's why I've been here all this time – I only just came round when it was dark and then I couldn't find my way back to the entrance."

"Where's your rucksack?"

"I don't know. I was so disorientated when I came round, I started walking and only realised too late that I'd left it behind."

He nodded. "Well, I'm glad we bumped into each other; I'd almost given up hope."

"I'm grateful you didn't." Then it hit me. "Hold on – how did you know I was here? Were you following me again?"

He paused and looked away.

"Immy called me last night after you two had that argument," he said. "She told me she didn't want to speak to me after what I'd done but she didn't know who else to turn to. She told me you were planning on coming here and was worried you'd get into trouble, so I said I'd follow you again. Sorry – I know it sounds creepy."

"It's OK," I reassured him. "Were you following me from the start? I never saw you."

"I was trying to keep out of sight."

"But if you'd followed me, as you said, why has it taken so long to find me here? You'd have been with me all the time, wouldn't you? I've been here for hours and we only found each other by accident."

"I followed you from your house to Paddington but then I lost you in the crowd. I assumed you'd caught the Tube but I didn't know which line, so you must have been well ahead of me. I knew you were heading for Highgate, but I lost time figuring out the route on my phone. I arrived just before the cemetery was meant to shut. The woman at the entrance wouldn't let me in – she said it was too late – so I waited until she was distracted and slipped in. I've been wandering around trying to find you ever since."

"Wait a minute! I never told Immy which cemetery I was going to. I said I was travelling to London to track down a relative buried here but I never gave the name, so how did you know that?"

He looked shifty, refusing to meet my eyes. "Tom?" I repeated.

"Lindy, I really don't know how to say this without freaking you out."

"Just tell me."

"I've been tracking your phone for a week or so now—"

"*What?*"

"Immy and I were so worried about what you were doing, and you wouldn't listen to us. We just wanted to make sure you were safe—"

"By *spying* on me?"

"No! Look, it's just a really simple app you can download to track someone else's phone. I managed to install it on yours when you went to the toilet in the café, the day we went to St Sepulchre's."

"You're worse than my mother!" I yelled.

"Lindy – we wouldn't normally do something like that. You've been acting so strangely "

"And what about you, Tom? Stalking me all this time and pretending that you didn't know me when all along you knew exactly who I was. That's not right! I feel violated."

I stormed off along the path, no clue where I was going. I could hear Tom hurrying after me.

"I agree that what I did seems wrong," he said, "but I wanted you to like me. I thought that if you did then, when I told you who

I really was, you'd want to be friends still. If I'd told you at the beginning, then you might never have spoken to me again."

"You've made it much worse now, don't you see?" I countered. "You lied by omission to start with, and now you tell me you've been following me on a phone tracker. How much creepier can you get?"

"If I hadn't, I wouldn't be here with you now, would I?" he argued.

"Well, you haven't done much good, have you? You've only just found me! Unless that was you who let me out of the mausoleum—"

"What are you talking about? What mausoleum? The last place the app tracked you at was Karl Marx's monument. I lost reception, so I hadn't a clue which path you'd taken or even whether you'd already left or not."

I stopped again. I was standing here – with probable concussion – for the first time aware that I was staring at my half-sibling. He had come for me, he had found me, and he was totally unaware of the unspoken thing between us, revealed by an apparition he couldn't see or hear or believe in. I couldn't say the words. Now was not the time.

"Can you remember which way we need to go to get to the entrance?" I changed the subject.

"I think the way you were heading when we bumped into each other might be the right direction," Tom said. "And since I don't have a clue one way or the other, why don't we just go for it?"

52.
A NEW MEDIUM

We walked for a while without talking. I kept vacillating between feeling angry then grateful for Tom's interference and, on top of that, the pain in my head was so bad that I kept thinking that I would pass out. At one point, I had to stop and bend over to throw up, which should have been embarrassing but I was beyond caring at that point. I felt I had lost most, if not all, of my self-respect, so it really didn't matter.

Around me, translucent figures rose from the ground. Some beckoned, others whispered, filling my head with disparate voices, wanting help, friendship, revenge, forgiveness. I thought that this would all be over now – that by reuniting Esme and Charles, I could get rid of my paranormal abilities. It seemed, instead, that I had strengthened my connection to the afterlife – I was seeing and hearing the dead everywhere I turned. Tom was oblivious – exhaustion was the only expression on his face.

Eventually, we arrived at Karl Marx's monument; Tom and I both sighed with relief. We knew the way from here. Our phones vibrated to life again as they picked up reception, but I felt strangely reluctant to look at mine. I didn't want to stay in this place but, for a while, it was a relief not having to explain my reality. Sitting with the dead is more peaceful than sitting with the living. Now, I knew I faced a barrage of desperate texts and voice messages from my mother – I didn't even know how to answer her questions. How could I explain what I'd been doing here? No one would believe me. I suppose I'd have to just spin out the brief lie I'd given Tom, the one I knew he wouldn't have believed, about me coming to look for my ancestor's tomb.

Was I going to tell him about us?

Eventually, we arrived at the entrance and looked up at the main gates which were, of course, locked.

"What now?" I asked Tom, shaking from both the cold and exhaustion. The fog, thicker than ever, had begun to soak my clothes on to my body.

"Well, we can try the handle to see if it turns," Tom suggested, with a lack of enthusiasm that made it clear he didn't believe it would work.

It didn't.

"I think our only option is to break something and set off the burglar alarms, so someone comes and lets us out."

"Why not?" I agreed. "I'm already in so much trouble, I might as well add vandalism and trespassing to the list."

Tom looked around and found a rogue brick on the ground, which he picked up and hurled into the window of the entrance hut. An alarm started screaming and I nearly joked that it was loud enough to wake the dead, but the murmuring of their voices behind us made the comment die on my lips.

Tom and I sat on the ground and waited for someone to arrive. I was shivering so much that he put his arms around me and pulled me close, rubbing my arms to generate some warmth.

My brother . . .

"Lindy," he said, a cautious tone in his voice. "What exactly *were* you doing here today?"

"There's not much point in telling you, Tom," I said. "At best, you won't believe me, and at worst, you'll think that I'm crazier than you already do."

"I don't think you're crazy."

"Well, do you believe that I can talk to the dead?"

The pause before his reply told me everything.

"I honestly don't know. I'm not saying I don't believe you, but the whole idea is so bizarre to me it's hard to accept it unquestioningly."

"But when Immy and I first met you, you said that you'd done a lot of research about all this. Why have you suddenly changed your mind?"

"I haven't changed my mind. Over the past few years, I've read some articles about psychics and other people who can apparently talk to the dead – you know, through séances, spiritual meetings and automatic writing. Most of the evidence points to so-called experts being skilled in reading their clients through body language, clever questions and cold reading. It's an art, but I am not sure if it's a science."

"So, do you think that I'm like all these people?" I asked. "Do you think I'm making all this up?"

"No," he said slowly. "I think you believe what you are seeing and hearing – you're not doing it for any financial gain, are you? So it's not like you're conning anyone."

"Except myself," I replied glumly. "So, if I'm not like any of these charlatans, what am I? Insane?"

"I've been reading more into this since we met, Lindy – trying to get a hold on what you're going through. I do believe you're seeing and hearing people . . . but they might not necessarily be there. You might be having waking dreams – which are kind of like hallucinations. You see and hear things in real life that look genuine, but aren't. They're subtle, so it's really easy to believe that they're real. It doesn't mean you're insane," he added. "It's just your brain giving you very realistic visions."

There was no point in arguing. My mind felt too muddled to hold a decent conversation.

"So . . ." he continued. "Do you want to tell me why you came here?"

"Does it matter, if it was all made up?" I asked.

He shrugged. "I must admit that I'm intrigued. What were you looking for?"

"Like I said before, I was here to find my ancestor's grave."

"And did you find it?"

I hesitated. An easy way to put an end to this conversation and move on was to say that I hadn't. But then it would feed his theory that I was making all this up – unintentionally – but still . . .

I was saved from this dilemma by the arrival of flashing lights. Two dark figures with flashlights hurried towards the entrance hut and, moments later, the door leading into the cemetery crashed open and a couple of men stood in the doorway. They shone their torches around but the dense fog made it difficult for them.

"I can hardly see in front of me," said the shorter of the two men. "How are we going to find anyone here tonight?"

"We're not," said the taller one. "Might as well call it in as petty vandalism."

"We're over here – on your right," Tom called, standing up and waving his arms.

The shorter man directed his flashlight in our direction, blinding us.

"What the hell are you two doing in here?" he demanded. "How'd you get in?"

I shielded my eyes from the light. "I was visiting a family grave earlier but fell and hit my head. When I came around, the cemetery had closed."

"Yeah, right," dismissed the taller man. "And, of course, you weren't drinking at the time, were you? Bloody teens," he continued. "Always going into graveyards to get drunk."

"She's telling the truth," said Tom. "We lost each other inside the graveyard and, with this fog, it took me ages to find her. I brought her up here. Since we couldn't get out, we had to break the window to get help."

"She doesn't look good," Shorty said, nodding down at me before looking at Tom, suspicion plastered all over his face. "Did she really hit her head or did something else happen?"

"She did hit it – really badly," Tom insisted. "It bled a lot. She might have concussion."

"He's telling the truth," I promised.

Shorty didn't look convinced. He crouched next to me and asked, "Can I see?"

I nodded and lifted my hair up. He flashed his torch and whistled. "That's a massive egg you've got there."

"Better call for an ambulance, then," Tall Guy said and pulled out his phone. Shorty leant closer and I could smell coffee and cigarettes on his breath. "Are you sure that this was an accident?" he whispered. "That boy there didn't push you or hit you, did he? He didn't do anything else to you, did he? You know—"

"No, it was definitely an accident," I insisted. "If it wasn't for him, I'd still be wandering around this cemetery, hoping that someone would find me. It wouldn't be an exaggeration to say he probably saved my life."

Shorty and Tom helped me walk into the ticket office so we could wait for the ambulance in the warm. Tom took my phone and called my mum to let her know I was safe – I couldn't bear to face the conversation the way I was feeling. I could hear her fear-ridden voice talking faster and louder than was humanly possible – Tom had to hold the phone away from his ear to avoid being deafened. She was already on the train to Paddington; Immy had caved in and called her to say where I was, worried about me and Tom after not hearing from either of us in hours. To his credit, Tom remained calm and reassuring, before passing the phone over to Shorty, who wanted to speak to her.

"Your daughter's fine but she had a nasty fall and injured her head, so we're getting an ambulance out here to check her out. She may have to go to hospital. We'll call you back as soon as we have any more information."

He paused and then looked at me. "She wants to speak to you. You can do that, love, can't you?"

I nodded and took the phone. "Hi, Mum."

"Lindy! I've been so worried! They said that you're injured—"

"I'm fine," I replied, but I don't think she heard me. She kept gabbling and I wondered what the other passengers overhearing her side of the conversation on the train were thinking.

The ambulance pulled up and Shorty indicated that I should pass the phone back to him. "We have to hang up now – the ambulance is here. We'll call again as soon as we have news."

He hung up without waiting for a reply, which was probably the best thing to do. I doubted she was listening anyway.

The paramedics checked me over briefly in the office before saying I needed to go to hospital – I might need stitches and it was clear they were concerned after finding out I'd lost consciousness after the fall. They helped me up and supported me under my arms as we made our way out of the ticket office but just as I was about to climb into the vehicle, I saw a movement out of the corner of my eye. I turned my head as a hazy figure appeared by the cemetery gates.

It was a man, holding his arms out towards me, a pleading look on his face.

The last time I'd seen him was in my kitchen on the morning of his death.

"Dad?"

My world turned black.

53.
LAND OF THE LIVING

I was in an overheated hospital ward. There were foreign smells and noises – beeps, clattering, hushed voices. When I opened my eyes, the lights were too bright and I snapped them shut again, longing for the darkness of Highgate.

Where had Dad gone? Was he another waking dream?

Two people were talking – one of them was my mother, the other, presumably, a doctor. My attention peaked when I heard my name.

"Lindy's out of danger now with the concussion, but we're still worried about her mental state."

"I understand, but I think that if she were back in her own home—"

"She might wander off again, Mrs Pennyworth. And next time, things might be worse . . . a lot worse. She's too much of a risk to herself. Just look at the number of times you've had to call out the emergency services in the last few days alone."

"I'll keep an eye on her, I promise."

I felt a mixture of relief that she still loved me and wanted me home after everything that had happened and guilt for putting her through all this.

"I know you would try your best, Mrs Pennyworth, but your best might not be good enough for Lindy right now. Her history of self-harm has increased alarmingly. The Trichotillomania was a warning sign, but inhaling the WD-40, suffering smoke inhalation from running into a burning shed, scalding herself in the shower and now concussion after running away from home – all these show an extremely troubled state of mind and an escalation in her self-harming tendencies. To be honest, she should have been referred much sooner. I don't understand why she wasn't."

"I promise I'll keep her safe."

I'd never heard my mother beg before. I felt awful.

"I understand and admire your commitment to your daughter. However, when young people are affected by psychoses, they can be very hard to manage, especially when you're . . . uh, on your own, and after a very traumatic life experience for Lindy. The passing of her father appears to have triggered something, and Lindy seems to be acting out her compulsions. Troubled minds often do this – it's not abnormal, considering everything she's been through, but we must make sure she learns to process her grief in a healthy way. Consider this a helpful warning for us all that we need to intervene now."

"All right," Mum agreed, and I hated how small she sounded, like a little girl meekly doing as she was told and knowing that she'd messed up big time. Except I was her mess. I was the one who'd put her there.

I kept my eyes shut; I wasn't ready for the land of the living yet. I allowed darkness to envelop me once again, safe in the lulling embrace of my unconscious mind.

54.
INVERTED REALITIES

Dr Anderson smiles as I walk into the room. She always looks pleased to see me, which is nice, but I'm sure she does this with all her patients. How does she remain so kind and welcoming when she spends all day, every day, listening to teenagers who are so emotionally disturbed that they have to be kept in a special unit until they are deemed fit for release into society again?

The day after my trip to A&E, I was transferred to a special adolescent mental health unit in Oxford. They told me that I'd hurt myself one too many times. No one listened to my version of events – that the only thing I'd deliberately done was pull out my hair and that everything else was either an accident or a paranormal intervention. Why would I burn myself purposefully in the shower? Or run into a burning shed? I was upset about Dad, yes, but I wasn't suicidal.

They wouldn't believe me.

So Dr Anderson and I meet several times a week to talk about everything I've been through. We've talked about how I felt after

Dad died and why I started pulling my hair out. Dr Anderson doesn't react in horror or shock – she treats my behaviour as understandable, even normal – for which I am truly grateful and it is a kindness I will never be able to repay.

She was fascinated about the story with Esme and asked me, at first, just to relay to her what had happened. I told her about finding the picture frame, with the gap where the photo should have been, and how Esme had told me that I needed to find the two parts of the photo to break the curse on our family. She asked if she could see the picture frame but I had to disappoint her by telling her that I'd left it in Charles's mausoleum in Highgate Cemetery. Remembering the grave-finding service, I told Dr Anderson that if we could ask them where the Pennyworth tomb was, they could retrieve the frame. She promised she would make some enquiries.

That was a fortnight ago. Perhaps today she'd have some news.

"How are you feeling at the moment, Lindy?" Dr Anderson asks.

"All right. A little flat, perhaps."

"Do you mean that you don't feel so emotional?"

"Well, I'm not a tyre, if that's what you're thinking."

She laughs. "Good one. Sorry – I just wanted to see if your moods have stabilised from the new combination of medications."

"Yes. But it feels so weird. It feels like I have *no* emotions. Nothing seems to make me upset or angry or happy or anything."

"That can be a difficult side effect for people who have been suffering from extreme feelings. It's hard to adjust to feeling calm when you're so used to being anxious."

I wouldn't call feeling like a zombie calm, but I don't want to split hairs.

Pun intended.

"I want to talk to you about Esme and her family. How, and more importantly, why, they became involved in your life."

I nod – it's not like I have much of a choice about what we talk about.

"So," she says, crossing her legs, "have you ever read any books set in Victorian times? Or seen film or television adaptations?"

"Sure. I saw *David Copperfield* on television a few weeks ago, I think. Or was it a month or two? I can't remember – time doesn't have as much meaning in here."

"I understand," she nods her head slowly, making notes. "Anything else?"

"We read *Great Expectations* at school for our 19th century literature text."

"I love Charles Dickens. He wrote such poignant stories about the conditions of his time and society's attitudes. Would you agree?"

Is this a literature class?

"I guess. I find him a little wordy, to be honest. The stories are good, but it takes him so long to get to the point."

She laughs. "I can't argue with that."

"What's this got to do with Esme?"

"Dickens's characters are larger than life – he really makes us see them, doesn't he? I just wondered . . . is it possible that you remembered some of them from watching films or reading books and gave them new identities?"

I frown. "Why would I do that? I didn't love the stories *that* much."

"Sometimes, when we're really upset with what life throws at us, we invent other people and situations to cope with our stress. It helps us create distance between what we're feeling and our

302

current reality if we can focus on something different. Like a sort of coping mechanism."

"Are you saying that I invented Esme, Charles, Freeda and Linwood? That they were my imaginary friends?"

"Not exactly. I'm wondering if, by creating this whole curse scenario, you were able to stop dwelling so much on your grief over your father."

Anger bubbles inside of me.

"That's a pretty bizarre story to invent, isn't it? A father who uses his only daughter to conduct a medical experiment and kills her accidentally?"

"You didn't know that at first, though, did you? Esme came to you and asked for your help in breaking a curse that prevented her from speaking to her father in the afterlife, at the same time you were searching for a way to speak to your father beyond the grave. That's a pretty striking similarity."

"Yes, but she said that the reason I couldn't speak to my father was because the curse affects every father and daughter separated by death in the Pennyworth family. We had a common problem, that's all."

"The same problem."

"What are you suggesting?"

She waits a moment before answering, as if she's weighing up whether to reveal her thoughts to me or not.

"That you and Esme are the *same* person."

I feel sick.

"So, I'm schizophrenic?"

"No! Not at all. Lindy – you must understand – what you've been through is traumatic and when the mind can't cope with that level of distress, it creates distractions."

I remain silent for a moment, then realise that she can't be right.

"But when I found out the truth about where Dad was going on the morning he died, I didn't want to pursue finding him," I announce, triumphantly. "But Esme still wanted me to help her. That's the only reason I continued. I would have stopped otherwise, but I felt responsible."

"Why? You'd known her less than a fortnight."

"I felt like I was abandoning her by giving up. She's my family."

Tears prickle in my eyes, despite my earlier declaration that I was feeling emotionally detached. *Damn.*

"Did you feel like you were abandoning her or yourself?" Dr Anderson asks, pushing a box of tissues towards me.

When I fail to reply, she carries on in her quietest, kindest tone.

"Just after you had broken the curse, you say the truth about Charles was revealed – that he sacrificed his daughter, albeit inadvertently, for the chance to make medical history. The parallel with you and your father's situation is striking. When your father decided to leave you and your mother, he was, in effect, sacrificing the relationship he had with you for his own gains. Although, as you admitted, at least your father didn't accidentally kill you. You found some goodness to his character – a redeeming feature."

"I wouldn't go as far as that."

"All right. Tell me how Esme dealt with her father's betrayal. Did she forgive him?"

"I don't know. They disappeared before I could find out."

"That in itself is pretty significant, don't you think, Lindy?"

"Why?"

"You're still undecided as to whether you can forgive your dad for what he was going to do to you and your mother. But at least you were thinking of forgiveness and that's the first step on the path to letting go."

Thank goodness I haven't told her about Tom. What would she make of that?

THE DELUSION ILLUSION

The next day, I'm joining Dr Anderson for another session. She gives me her usual warm smile as I enter her room, but this time I don't return it. I can't feel happy when I know she's going to use this session to further pull apart my version of events, thereby suggesting that I'm an unstable girl inventing wild stories to disassociate myself with my own mental state.

Not that she'd put it that way. She'd be much kinder, but what was the point when it all means the same anyway?

"Good morning, Lindy. I know yesterday's session was hard, and I'm sorry to put you through all that. Unfortunately, today is not going to be any easier."

"Can't wait."

Her smile widens. "You have a wonderful sense of humour, you know. Very dry."

"Mum calls it sarcasm."

She shakes her head, as if to commiserate with me about how annoying mums are, before picking up from where she left off.

306

"Today I want to start by talking about the grave hunting. It was quite a mammoth undertaking."

I wait in tense silence, my fingertips itching to comb through my scalp. I hide my hands under my thighs. She has an agenda, so I'm not going to make it any easier for her.

"I'm going to ask lots of questions today and it might feel like a bit of a cross-examination, but I'm just trying to get my head around what happened to you. Is that all right?"

I shrug. "Does it make any difference if it isn't?"

"Well, they're questions I need to ask you, but I don't want you to feel like I am interrogating you."

"Don't worry. I know you have to ask them."

So you can prove that it's all in my head.

"All right – as long as we're clear. First, I want to confirm how it was that you received these clues – sorry, riddles. What exactly happened?"

"Esme usually visited me beforehand; talked to me. But then she'd disappear before she'd had the chance to give me the riddle."

"So when did they come to you?"

"Normally when I was asleep. I'd wake up and the riddle would be there."

"Where?"

I really don't want to go into this – I know how it looks and I know that she knows the answer. Is she trying to provoke me? Why?

"Lindy?" she persists gently.

"On the wall," I mutter. My face feels hot.

"Written on the wall?"

"Have you talked to my mother?"

307

"Yes."

"Then I expect she's explained it to you."

"But I need to hear it from you."

My temper flares. "Why?"

"Why are you feeling angry, Lindy?"

"Because it feels like you're goading me. You obviously know all the answers yet you're putting me through this. Why bother? It's boring for you and embarrassing for me."

She shakes her head. "It's not boring for me, Lindy. I need to hear in your own words what you experienced. Why are you embarrassed?"

"Because I know that you're going to use all this to prove how unstable I am. I know that writing on the wall makes me look insane – though Tom said it might have been automatic writing; that I was used by a spirit as a conduit. But you obviously don't believe in all that, so just tell me that I wrote on the walls because I was hallucinating or whatever and we can move on."

"I'm not here to prove anything. I am here to help you and that's all I want to do." She leans forward in her chair and gives me an earnest look. "You're my patient and you've had a really bad time lately. I do believe what you tell me is real to you, and that's what matters. Not what I, or anybody else, think. OK?"

"Whatever," I mumble, holding back the tears.

We sit in silence for a couple of minutes – Dr Anderson is looking at me with concern and I'm looking anywhere but at her. I enjoyed our sessions until now. Now she's making me feel like everyone else does.

When it's obvious I am not going to speak, she takes up the gauntlet again.

"Let's start with you finding Esme's grave. Did you actually find a headstone?"

"No. I told you before – she was buried in a mass cholera pit."

"So how did you find it?"

"Esme gave me a riddle and from that, I knew it was at St Sepulchre's cemetery, but it was still too obscure for me to find the exact location. Then I fainted or something; when I woke up, I found that I'd drawn the shape of a tree on my hand and I knew she had to be buried near that. While looking in the graveyard, I suddenly smelt violets – they were Esme's favourite flowers – so I followed the scent, and when they got really strong, I knew I'd found the right place."

"But how did you know the exact place to dig?"

"There was a smooth stone that looked like a marker on the soil."

"What made it look different to any other stone you could have found?"

I shrug. "It just looked . . . different, out of place. When I turned it around, the year was etched into it. And when I dug, I found the bottle with half of the photo inside."

"Did you show the bottle or the photo to anyone?"

"No. I was alone. I tried to later, when Tom and Immy came over, but when I gave them the rolled-up cotton the photo was in, all they saw was a piece of blank paper."

Dr Anderson's expression remains neutral. "But that in itself is strange, isn't it? How can a photo change into a blank piece of paper?"

"Esme explained the reason why others couldn't see the photo was because I was supposed to be doing all of this by myself. No one else could know about it," I reply, cringing inwardly at how this all sounds. "It was part of the curse," I add, as if that would make it any better.

"All right, let's move on to Freeda's grave," Dr Anderson says. "I presume you received another riddle, worked it out and then went to the graveyard to look for it. Did the scent of violets help you again?"

"Yes. I knew I was looking for a holly tree, which didn't narrow it down as much as I needed it to. But when I was in the right sort of area, I smelt the violets again and found Freeda's cross."

She nods. "That all sounds plausible, but how did you know the cross belonged to Freeda? Did it have her name on it?"

"No – it was a wooden cross, so it hadn't aged well. I dug around it and found the bottle."

"Mm hmm." She looks down and shuffles through some papers. "I did a bit of internet research myself on Freeda Madill. I found her name and the spiritual church you mentioned. She was a real person, and she is buried in Holywell Cemetery."

I smile for the first time during the session, the sense of relief almost overwhelming.

"But what I want to clarify is when you first became aware of Freeda Madill. Was it before or after Esme first came to you?"

"Before."

My defences rise again. What is she getting at?

"So, you knew all about her before you knew anything about Esme and your family curse?"

"Yes. Well, I didn't know all about her. When I looked for the details of a psychic to help me, I found the spiritualist church and decided to give it a try. I think that attending the session helped . . . open my psychic channels or whatever you call it," I reply. "I hadn't really succeeded in speaking to the dead before that."

She considers this for a moment.

"I talked with your friend, Immy, and she told me what had happened at the session – that the psychic became agitated and started saying strange things to you – a girl's name beginning with the letter E, for example."

"Exactly. She was right!"

"But psychics aren't always the most . . . reliable people," Dr Anderson says. "They don't always know the truth and, when they don't, they'll make it up."

I narrow my eyes. "I don't understand what you're saying."

"Psychics have been known to invent stories – they have to give their audience something. She just as easily could have given you the letter R and you could have been visited by a girl called Ruth."

"But she didn't. She gave me an E and I was visited by Esme."

"What I am trying to say is, perhaps the psychic planted the idea in your mind that a girl whose name began with E was trying to get in touch. It just seems too much of a coincidence that Esme came to you after the session. If she'd appeared beforehand, then perhaps it would have been more . . ." she struggles to the right word, but has to settle on the truth . . . "believable."

I refuse to answer her. What can I say, when she finds a reason to doubt me at every opportunity?

"Let's move on to Highgate," she continues. "How did you know to go there?"

"What's the point? You're just going to try to prove me wrong again!"

"I'm not doing this to be unkind, Lindy. I am trying to understand how you arrived at each point in your story and to suggest alternative interpretations. The world you've been engaged in recently is quite remarkable."

"Is remarkable a euphemism for crazy?"

"Absolutely not."

I don't want to give in, but I know if I don't, we'll never move forward and I'll never get out of this place. She can say what she wants. I know what's real.

"Esme was punished by Linwood for helping me find the burial sites, so she couldn't give me the riddle. Freeda did instead – and not on the wall, either," I add pointedly.

"OK. So, you travelled to Highgate to look for Charles Pennyworth's grave. What happened when you got there?"

"I asked the woman at the entrance if she had heard of Charles or knew where his grave was but she didn't. So I decided to try my best and hope that Freeda or someone would help me."

"And did they?"

"Not for a while. I had to walk to what must have been the most remote part of the cemetery before a cat dashed out of the bushes. It looked like it wanted me to follow it, so I did, and it led me to the right place."

"Interesting. Freeda used an animal – like a familiar – to guide you?"

"Yes."

"Did you smell violets as well?"

"Yes. It was almost overpowering."

"And you say that this place was a mausoleum?"

"Yes. It had a door and everything – like a little house for the dead. Have you been able to find it? Have they found my rucksack or the picture frame?"

I'm leaning forward in excitement now. Finally, I have a chance to prove to everyone that I haven't imagined all this. The picture frame will clear my name!

Dr Anderson hesitates. "The thing is . . ."

Why won't she look at me?

"I asked Highgate to find Charles Pennyworth's grave – told them it was urgent. They were very obliging," she adds, as if to agree with me on how wonderful the cemetery is. "They got back to me yesterday with some . . . news."

"Yes?" I can hardly breathe.

"There is no Charles Pennyworth buried there."

It's like she's thrown cold water over me.

"He . . . he has to be," I insist. "I saw the inscription on the mausoleum with his and his wife's names. Charles and Georgina. Esme was mentioned, too."

"There are no mausoleums dedicated to the Pennyworths in Highgate and no graves, either. The name doesn't exist in any of their records."

She is looking at me with kind concern, like she wants to believe me but, of course, with this latest information, she can't.

"I asked them to double-check, Lindy. Honestly – I wanted this to be true for you. But they were adamant."

"I don't understand."

Her words ring in my ears, and a buzzing takes over that thrums in my head. She is lying, she has to be lying, because what is the alternative . . . My brain can't process the information.

"Charles Pennyworth – or the one you referred to – never existed—"

"But the newspaper article—"

"I spent ages searching for him on the internet, researching cholera articles – I even got in touch with the Records Office in Oxford to see if they had any information on a specialist cholera doctor in Oxford called Charles Pennyworth. They found nothing."

"But he's my ancestor!" Anger and disbelief pulse through my every synapse, threatening to burst out.

She shakes her head sadly. "I asked your mother to look into that. She asked your grandparents. There was never anyone called Charles Pennyworth in your family. Don't you think you would have heard about him before now if there had been?"

My whole body has started to shake and I'm rocking backwards and forwards.

Dr Anderson comes over to me and envelops me in a hug. "I'm so, so sorry, Lindy."

I push her away. And vomit.

56.
R.I.P.

I'm going home.

It's been a long process, but now I can finally see that there never were any ghosts. Esme, Charles, Freeda, Linwood – they were all figments of my imagination. I invented all of them as part of my psychosis.

When Dr Anderson first mentioned that word, I freaked out – I was worried that this meant I was deranged, on the verge of becoming a mass murderer or something. But she was patient with me and explained that psychosis, in my case, was an illness that had come about because I'd been presented with a massively stressful event and I didn't know how to cope with that. Additionally, I never had a chance to say goodbye or tell him I loved him – all I remembered were the hateful words I'd yelled at him the last time we were together. The guilt of that, and feeling somehow responsible for his death, threw me over an emotional edge and meant my mind invented ways to block the grief out once my hair pulling wasn't helping as much.

Seeing and hearing ghosts – or hallucinations – was all part of it, as was my insistence that Esme, Freeda and Charles were real. They were clearly a delusion. Dr Anderson showed me that the very nature of the story that I'd invented for myself proved just how much my grief was driving my moods and behaviour. I mean, I was helping reunite a daughter with her father! You can't get more symbolic than that, can you?

It was all so obvious, it was almost embarrassing.

Now that I have accepted this, I've been able to move on and grieve properly for Dad. I feel sad, sometimes overwhelmingly so, but I also feel angry for what he was planning to do to Mum and me. Dr Anderson reassured me that these feelings are normal, I should accept them rather than fight them. Once I do that, hopefully I can move forwards.

And what about Tom?

There's no way he can be my half-brother. None of the ghosts existed, so the whole story behind that was false too. As an only child, I sometimes wished I had an older brother and I must have thrown that possibility into the rest of my delusion. I am glad I never mentioned him to Dr Anderson – I could work that one out for myself.

Six weeks of my life have been spent in this unit. All in all, it's not been too bad. I've made some friends, and I definitely feel like less of a freak. We're all screwed up one way or another and we're all open about it, so we don't have to pretend to be fine when we aren't. Since we all have different issues, no one tries to say, "I know exactly what that feels like," because – seriously – how can you understand what it's like to be severely depressed or traumatised or whatever, unless you've actually been through it?

It's probably too much or too soon to say that I'm "cured", but I no longer desire to speak to the dead.

Thankfully, I no longer see or hear them, either.

The burns on my arms are healing well but the scars will never completely disappear. I'll always have to be careful now in the sun and can't let my skin get too hot in the bath or shower. The nurses here sometimes check me over – they say they're looking for signs of infection, but I know that they're really making sure that I'm not up to my old tricks.

Dr Anderson's sessions have allowed me to focus on getting my Trichotillomania under control, too. With a lot of practice, I've been able to resist the urge to pull most of the time. My bald patches have new growth sticking up like little sprouts of grass, so I still continue to wear a beanie to cover it for now – but the few centimetres I see make me hopeful for the future.

Mum and I are going away soon for a couple of weeks of winter sun. Dr Anderson thinks it would be a good idea and I'm desperate to go somewhere that doesn't remind me of everything that's happened. Mum's taken the house off the market and I have mixed feelings about that. I love where we live, just not the memories it beckons.

Mum's had my bedroom redecorated. The writing on the wall has gone. Another embarrassing memory wiped away.

Immy and Tom have asked to see me in here, but I've said no. I don't want anyone from the outside world to get a look at this place. My experience here stays here. They wanted to throw me a "Welcome Home" party today – even suggested it to Mum – but I declined. I don't really have the energy yet to fully reintegrate with normality. "One step at a time", Dr Anderson says, and I agree.

The quiet life suits me. I wouldn't say I'm enjoying it, exactly, but it's a relief to be spared all the drama of the past few months. I've settled into a groove of boring routine that feels comforting and relatively free from grief.

Finally, I know what it's like to rest in peace.

EPILOGUE

Caroline Pennyworth sorts through all the paperwork that has accumulated on her desk over the last six weeks since she's been dealing with the stress of Lindy being in the residential unit. She has a couple of hours before she has to collect her daughter for the final time – for good this time – and cannot wait to have her back in the house. It has been too quiet, too lonely, and she has had far too much time to dwell on the horrors that have hit her family. Her husband's infidelity and death. Lindy's rapid unravelling as she struggled to deal with what she believed was her fault. The possibility that Lindy was not only self-harming but turning to serious acts such as arson because her traumatised mind couldn't deal with the death of her father.

The fact that Lindy had to be institutionalised and medicated had terrified Caroline, and she'd fought tooth and nail to stop it. Only the threat of social services or possible legal action made her cave in, but she woke up drenched in the sweat of guilty nightmares each and every day. Having Lindy back was the only thing she wanted in the world and she would do everything in her power to ensure that her daughter returned to her bubbly self.

Caroline turns on her computer and is about to check her emails when she hears a strange knocking sound coming from a corner of the room. It's a faint knock-knock at first, but gets louder and louder the longer it continues. Caroline feels a frisson of fear – are there rats under the floorboards? She doesn't want to deal with rodents again and refuses to take a closer look. Instead, she runs downstairs, grabs Bifur – the more vicious of the placid cats – and carries him into the attic. "Go and sort that out for me – that's a brave boy," she says, pointing the cat in the direction of the tapping.

Bifur is having none of it. His fur stands on end and he emits a sound that is somewhere between a growl and a howl before he streaks past her and down the stairs.

"Bloody cat! What's the point of having you if you're even more scared than I am?"

Yet she is unnerved by his reaction. She could understand him being too lazy to go after the rodent, but to be that frightened of it was unsettling.

The noise is getting louder.

Knock-knock.

A rush of cold air sweeps past her. She looks around but sees nothing, just the shadows of passing clouds coming through the skylight. Just then, a ray of sunlight streaks through the window, casting a line of light towards the corner of the room where the noise is coming from. Caroline spies a few loose floorboards.

When did that happen? She knows she hasn't been at her most observant lately, but she would have noticed these – they're massively out of line with the others.

Then her heart nearly stops.

She walks forward as the noise sounds again, almost like a heartbeat, terrified of what she'll find below.

She crouches down and looks inside, steeling herself for a mouse to jump out, but instead sees something wrapped in what looks like velvet. Frowning, she lifts it out of its hiding place and unwraps it, revealing an old picture frame. Something about it is familiar . . . and then she remembers Lindy talking about a Victorian picture frame – the frame that was at the root of all her earlier obsessions. She'd stopped talking about it a while ago, much to everyone's relief: it meant that her psychosis was improving.

What does this mean?

Caroline carries the frame to her desk and points the light from the lamp on it. Inside, surrounded by an intricate pattern of grasses and butterflies, is an old photograph of a family. The people look familiar, but Caroline can't remember where she's seen them before.

She feels a curious pull towards the young girl seated in front of her parents. Whereas their eyes look dull, uninteresting, hers are bright, alive, and seem to be staring at her accusingly.

Her mind races back to the portrait Lindy drew of a Victorian family that she'd wanted to show Dr Anderson as proof that she'd been communicating with that ghost girl . . . Esme, wasn't it? Like Dr Anderson, Caroline had dismissed it as a figment of Lindy's fractured mind.

Something strange starts happening before her eyes. The faces on the people blur, as if someone is rubbing them off, leaving oval blanks surrounded by hair. Caroline holds the photo closer, then gasps as eyes, noses and mouths reappear, as if being sketched by an invisible hand.

She knows these faces: Lindy, Ben and herself. They're wearing the same Victorian clothes, like the other family, but it's definitely them in the photo.

Caroline drops the frame in shock. This can't be happening. She backs away, as a familiar whisper carries from the frame to her ears – a voice that she never thought she'd hear again.

"Help me, Caroline . . . Help me speak to Lindy."

ACKNOWLEDGEMENTS

Ever since I can remember, I have been obsessed with graveyards. Until the age of twelve, I grew up in rural Canada and whenever I visited my grandparents in England on holiday I made my long-suffering family stop at every graveyard in every old church we passed so I could read the headstones. My family humoured my strange obsession, although they found it slightly worrying and morbid.

This fascination with the dead has continued into adulthood and I now drag my own family around graveyards. Therefore, I offer huge thanks (and apologies) to my family: my Mum (who now, in a bizarre twist of fate, lives next to a graveyard!), Carl and Holly – for their patience with my peculiar obsession and encouragement with this novel.

However, without this obsession, this novel might not have been written. It grew out of a 15,000-word novella that was my creative dissertation for my Masters in Children's Literature from the University of Roehampton and I owe the existence of this

Brent Library Service

Customer ID: *******0433

Items that you have borrowed

Title: The haunting of Lindy Pennyworth
ID: 91120000482132
Due: 11 April 2023

Total items: 1
Account balance: £0.00
Borrowed: 1
Overdue: 0
Hold requests: 2
Ready for collection: 0
20/03/2023 20:14

story to that course and to my supervisor, Dr Lisa Sainsbury's, encouragement to develop it into a full-length novel.

As any writer will confirm, the words don't appear by magic (if only they could!). What you've read here is the result of countless changes, rewrites and edits. I would like to thank my amazing editorial team – Sunshine Tucker, Katie Dandridge and Megan Pressler – for their endless support and confidence in this novel and for keeping my spirits (pardon the pun) up when I was flagging. Thank you also to Debbie Jane Williams, Hazel Holmes and the UCLan team for taking a chance on this book – I am eternally grateful. Thanks also to proofreader Kathy Webb for her sharp eyes and attention to detail, and to my dear friend, beta reader and fellow eccentric, Angela Kecojevic, for the laughs and brainstorming sessions. I can't wait to read your next book, Angela!

I'm sure you have admired the stunning artwork throughout this novel, provided by Camilla Montemaggi. I could not have wished for a more sensitive visual imagining of this book; if ever an artist was psychic, it's Camilla!

Finally, during the many years that it took for this book to be published, I lost my own father in sudden and unexpected circumstances. As anyone who has lost a loved one knows, there are always things you wish you could tell them. My father knew I was writing this book, and was always a keen supporter of my writing, but he died before it was accepted for publication. I hope that, wherever his soul resides, he knows the outcome. I finally did it, Dad!

IF YOU LIKED THIS,
YOU'LL LOVE . . .

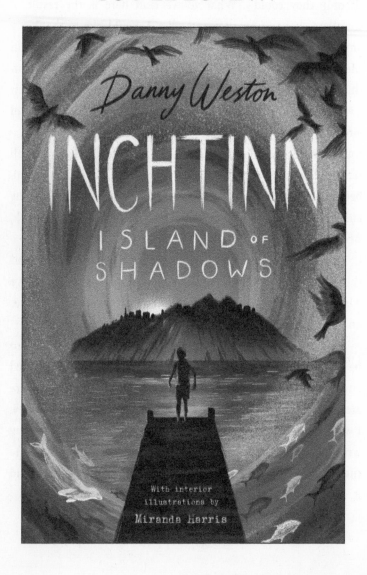

A. J. HARTLEY
COLD BATH STREET
Not even the dead are safe . . .
With interior illustrations by Janet Pickering

HAVE YOU EVER WONDERED HOW BOOKS ARE MADE?

UCLan Publishing is an award winning independent publisher specialising in Children's and Young Adult books. Based at The University of Central Lancashire, this Preston based publisher teaches MA Publishing students how to become industry professionals using the content and resources from its business; students are included at every stage of the publishing process and credited for the work that they contribute.

The business doesn't just help publishing students though. UCLan Publishing has supported the employability and real-life work skills for the university's Illustration, Acting, Translation, Animation, Photography, Film & TV students and many more. This is the beauty of books and stories; they fuel many other creative industries! The MA Publishing students are able to get involved from day one with the business and they acquire a behind the scenes experience of what it is like to work for a such a reputable independent.

The MA course was awarded a Times Higher Award (2018) for Innovation in the Arts and the business, UCLan Publishing, was awarded Best Newcomer at the Independent Publishing Guild (2019) for the ethos of teaching publishing using a commercial publishing house. As the business continues to grow, so to does the student experience upon entering this dynamic Masters course.

www.uclanpublishing.com
www.uclanpublishing.com/courses/
uclanpublishing@uclan.ac.uk